The
Irish
Lake
House

BOOKS BY COLLEEN COLEMAN

Don't Stop Me Now
I'm Still Standing
One Way or Another
For Once in My Life

Colleen Coleman

The
Irish
Lake
House

bookouture

Published by Bookouture in 2023

An imprint of Storyfire Ltd.
Carmelite House
50 Victoria Embankment
London EC4Y 0DZ

www.bookouture.com

ISBN: 978-1-78681-914-7
eBook ISBN: 978-1-78681-913-0

To my daughters, Elizabeth and Sadie, all my love forever x

*

In a forest glade, where the sun shone bright,
Mr Hedgehog and Red Fox chatted with delight.

'Change is the key, my foxy friend,
Don't fight the old, let the new trends blend.'

'Oh, Hedgehog, what do you mean?
Embrace the change, like a dance routine?'

'Exactly, Red Fox! It's a chance to grow
Like a rushing river with a brand-new flow.

Let's leave behind what no longer fits
And build something better, with exciting bits.'

Together they nodded, with new hope in
        their eyes
Ready for adventure, under ever-changing skies.

— *Forest Fables, Matilda Wilder*

CHAPTER 1

THE MESSAGE

The early-morning sun filters through my studio window, dappling the stained wood surface of my desk. I sigh and blink away the glare on my computer screen, squinting at the newly finished illustration of a fox cub peeking out from behind a tree. Another day, another dollar.

If only. My bank account is running on fumes.

My work mail pings. Lenka. *The Big Boss.*

I steel myself and open it, bracing for the usual barrage of criticism sure to come.

Lenka: The cub's eyes are too small and close-set. Makes him look dim-witted and deranged. Fix it. Also, the tree trunk is crooked. I shouldn't have to point these things out.

Me: Will revise. Thanks for the feedback.

Lenka: Don't thank. Just do. Six weeks to deadline.

I grit my teeth and take a deep breath, trying to calm my

frayed nerves. Lenka may be a brilliant children's publishing executive, but she lacks an ounce of tact. Or patience. Which you'd kind of expect from someone working day in and day out with dragons and fairies and dancing piglets. And after months of working for her, you'd think I'd be used to her acerbic tone and frustration with my 'shortcomings'. But her constant criticism still stings.

Bright side is I'm getting better, toughening up. I don't need half a bottle of Rescue Remedy before a Zoom anymore, and Ash says I'm grinding my teeth at night a lot less, so I'll take that as steady progress and excellent professional development, thank you very much.

And Hedgerow Press is *the* establishment when it comes to children's literature, so I'm grateful for the chance to work with her at all.

And no matter how hard it feels sometimes, I'm sticking with it to prove myself as a professional illustrator, to break into the business and build a name for myself – and, ideally, secure an in-house position that'll set me up for life so I can escape this rollercoaster of freelancing with its hit-and-miss success. Most of my time is spent chasing up leads with speculative work and proposals and then chasing down clients for payment and testimonials. It's exhausting.

I thought giving up the nine to five at the call centre would free me up to focus on what I'm really passionate about: art – it's what I'm supposed to be good at – but instead, I work longer, lonelier and with less pay than I knew was legal.

I've always been passionate about illustration, about crafting whimsical worlds and lovable characters on the page. But here's the Thing. (Why does there always have to be a *Thing*?) Working this way is not working out. It's draining all the joy from my life, leaving me burned out, blocked up and questioning my ability. As in, do I have any ability at all?

And questioning my future. As in, do I have a future at all?

It's a bitter pill to swallow – especially as I did all this to myself. All fingers point back to me. Hands up, white flag, full disclosure. I cocked up. Icarus syndrome. I thought I could do it, aimed for the sky, flew too high, panicked and am now mid-crash and burn. This part here is the pre-splat teaser.

Turns out the creative career I dreamed of is turning into a slow-burning nightmare. Worst part is, I invested everything I had in this career leap and jumped in with two feet, desperate to prove that I could do it – all me, nobody else, so this failure sits squarely with yours truly.

I hatched the idea on my thirtieth birthday, loaded with Milestone Birthday Panic, Seize The Day Spirit and Pornstar Martinis. The bit I can blame my bestie Kayla for: pushing me to 'Go For It', to 'Dream Big'. After all, she runs her own hugely successful business and made it look so easy, so doable, so worthwhile.

But it wasn't *all* down to Kayla or the Pornstar Martinis; realising that my mother had never seen her thirtieth birthday was a big wake-up call. I felt a huge whoosh of making the most of time, not taking anything for granted, needing to really make the most of life and every opportunity that came my way. Anyone who has experienced life-altering changes in an instant knows how close it brings you to understanding that nothing is guaranteed.

Fast-forward two years. If I knew then what I know now, I'd say: Gung-ho? Gung-NO. I'd have a little word with myself along the lines of: *C'mon, Daisy, you know that little safe life you think is so boring, the one you could do with your eyes closed and paid you every month? Stay there. Hang on to that baby. Because you know what's really boring? Poverty, never feeling good enough and pretending to your boyfriend that everything is amazing.*

So, the lingering question is when do I draw a line in the

scorched earth of my life and admit defeat? Get tucking that tail between my legs and go back to the call centre.

My phone buzzes – a text from my boyfriend Ash. '*We still on for flat hunting this evening at 6 p.m.? Found a great new listing in our price range.*'

'*Amazing!*' I type, letting a row of cork-popping emojis do the heavy lifting. I hate myself but can't stop. Ash is allergic to inconvenience, failure and cats. We have a tacit 'Don't ask, don't tell' policy in our relationship that covers stressy stuff, period cramps and how much time Ash spends in the bathroom. Speaking of stressy stuff, the next six weeks will be either:

a. More Lenka and employment-related stress.

Or:

b. No Lenka and unemployment-related stress.

'*This could be the one!*' Ash texts.

It could be, but... no point offloading to Ash when I don't even know what's going to happen yet with my current job status. I'll make it work. I'll figure something out.

'*Send me the location and I'll see you there x,*' I type.

Ash means so well. All he wants is to get on in life, get his checklist ticked off – decent house, decent relationship, decent job, amazing car – and I so want to match his drive, his go-get-it mindset. So, when he suggested that we take the next step and rent a little place for us both so we could move in together, I thought it was a fantastic idea. A no-brainer! Of course I want to wake up beside my gorgeous boyfriend every day. Of course I want to get even closer, to share more, to spend more time together; a place just for us, a chance at being a proper couple rather than living separately, across town and with clashing schedules... but this flat hunt has taken over our lives. Every spare moment, every conversation. Yawn and yikes.

He can't understand why I'm trying to be cautious. Probably because I haven't really told him how much everything feels up in the air at the moment. I just don't know if I have the bandwidth for another upheaval – especially as all the big changes I've made workwise haven't exactly lived up to expectations. How can I explain that to the man who wants everything, and wants it bigger, faster and better than anyone else? Especially his brother. As an only child, I had no idea how fierce sibling rivalry could be. Downright Darwinian. And it's made Ash unstoppable – he's never failed at anything he's set his mind to. Whatever his brother Dan does, Ash takes it to the next level – such big dreams, unshakeable confidence, always striving for new heights and thinking one step ahead.

And I admire that; of course I do.

But right now, I'm completely overwhelmed.

And completely underwhelmed.

I just can't seem to strike the right amount of 'whelm'.

I need things to settle. Just a little bit, for a little while. How I daydream of peace and harmony, an empty inbox and a full fridge.

Flat hunting, more debt, unqualified risk, bagging and dragging up my whole life again and carting it across London to a new cramped corner of the city – not so much.

With a heavy sigh, I zoom in on the fox cub's eyes and enlarge them, brightening the amber hue to make them more endearing and expressive. Can't lie, he's still super cute – but now looks less deranged, more dreamy. I then adjust the contours of the tree, but has she ever actually seen a tree? Real-life trunks tend to be crooked? But, hey – I smooth out the trunk and add more foliage up top to balance the composition. Sorry, tree, no more dancing in the wind for you.

Satisfied I've addressed Lenka's 'concerns', I send the revisions and steel myself for the next round of corrections.

Almost immediately, she's back to me. I can picture her literally staring at the screen, waiting to pounce as she taps out 'constructive feedback' while cursing my existence under her breath.

Lenka: Time for face-to-face chat. My office 4.30 p.m.

Oh noooooooooo.

I swallow hard, a knot forming in my stomach. A spontaneous, in-person, one-to-one meeting to discuss an undisclosed subject can only mean one thing.

I'm being let go.

Oh dear. Not the TGIF feeling I was hoping for.

My mouth goes dry as I reread her short message again and again.

Lenka: Time for face-to-face chat. My office 4.30 p.m.

I try different voices, play with possibilities of it sounding cheery and upbeat. But there's no smiley emoji or exclamation mark or row of kisses. 'Chat' isn't a good sign. Means it'll be a quick and easy termination because she doesn't care – never has, never will. Who are you already? Close the door on your way out. Thank you. Next.

I can feel it. The beginning of the end.

Lenka is hellish to work for, but losing this job *will* plunge me into a financial black hole. The cost of becoming a freelance illustrator has already been dizzyingly high: tuition fees, specialised courses, expensive design software. Not to mention the hours, the sweat, the own-brand biscuit-based diet I've adopted just to keep the wheels turning. This is not the 'be your own boss' life I'd manifested.

I let out a frustrated sigh.

I scammed myself completely, letting myself believe I could make this work. Got completely suckered into the idea that I could do this. The constant stream of 'Live Your Dream' propaganda – thanks, evil internet algorithm overlords – you made me do this. All those inspirational quotes, real-life speakers with great hair and glowing skin making 'Anyone Can Do It!' pitches for freedom and fulfilment, escape, autonomy and *joy*! The hourly posts of light and airy home offices, all pastel colours and snuggly pets and pretty vision boards got me good.

Jump and the net will appear!

Update: I jumped. As yet, no net.

She said she could, so she did!

Update: Hmm. Just because she could doesn't mean she should.

What if I fall? But what if you fly?

Update: Only fifty per cent success probability – not great odds in hindsight.

I thought I'd be like a boss babe, all systems seamlessly in place, hottest illustrator in the biz, relaxed lunch meetings in wine bars, I'd set my own hours between yoga, smelling the roses and wandering galleries for inspiration. And I thought that, as a result, I would just automatically spin gold! Everyone would love everything I did. I'd be happy, secure and respected, and my life would be complete.

Happy input, happy output.

Cue Lenka and her honking big dose of realism.

I rub my hands down my cheeks and cringe at myself, opening the jar of Nutella nestled between my knees and scooping with a teaspoon. Full disclosure: I only opened this family-size jar yesterday yet there's only a quarter left and this little spoon is the only piece of silver to my name. This is where my notions of grandeur have got me – fakin' it till I can't take it.

Real talk: It's Friday, 8 a.m. Breakfast is served. Hair is

greasy. Flat is small. Lenka is mad. Dream is dissolving. I already need a nap and then a shovel to start digging myself out of this hole I've painstakingly dug for myself. But for now, at least it's my hole. And it's the only hole I've got.

It'd really help if I could schedule my panic attack before I leave home.

CHAPTER 2

THE GAME

I hug my portfolio close, my fists turning cold and clammy, as I wait in the lobby of Lenka's exclusive city-centre office; sun-lit, spacious and unashamedly Instagramable. My stomach flips with nerves as the time ticks by. I've been sitting here for forty-five minutes now. It's pure torture – how long will she keep me waiting like this?

I think I'm actually, officially done now. I'm ready to give up, to call time on this bonkers venture and go back to the call centre, back to reciting a standard customer-service script within regular hours and with a new appreciation for the mundane. At least in that predictable, beeping, grey-shaded world everything made sense; I know who I am and where I fit in. And where I don't.

And I definitely don't fit in here, in this uber-chic, uber-modern office block. Or even in the professional world of illustration. I'm punching above my weight here. I'm not sure if I even qualify for imposter syndrome. I've poured everything into this latest commission, moving from paper to screen, sketching and drawing and painting and then erasing, scrapping and starting all over again.

But it's a special one.

Forest Fables by Matilda Wilder. The most special one I could ever dream of working on; the highly anticipated release of the year, the updated edition of an already beloved picture-book classic; a wonderful fairy-tale world of furry friends and life lessons back on bookshelves for all to enjoy. And, truthfully, if it wasn't so close to my heart, I feel like I'd walk away right now. Give up freelancing. Give up art and new starts and everything I ever thought I wanted.

But I love *Forest Fables*. So, I'm here, showing up for God knows what.

I gulp and take in my surroundings, noting the walls of the lobby. Three framed photographs draw my attention, each adorned with a different memory. One is of Lenka posing proudly in her formal gown, arms outstretched to receive the medal she was awarded for her contributions to children's literature from the King. Another shows her beaming as she accepts a trophy for winning an international book fair prize. The third is an award for being an inspirational figure in global publishing.

She knows her stuff: so, if I get fired today, at least I've been rejected by the very best. A beacon of genius. A world-renowned expert hates my work. Go me.

Lenka's PA looks up from his desk and smiles reassuringly at me, revealing a mouthful of pearly-white teeth. I'm pretty sure he hasn't got a jar of Nutella jammed between his thighs. I highly doubt he chows down on any monochrome muck that comes from jars or cans or tins; his dewy skin glows with health, his green eyes sparkle. Whatever designer diet he's following is evidently working for him. Vegan? Pescatarian? Flexitarian? Lacto-ovo-vegetarian? I can only guess what's in his fridge, but I'm certain that there'll be no sign of my beloved value-buy hazelnut-cocoa concoction.

'Daisy, Lenka will be with you shortly.'

'Thank you,' I say, forcing a smile while trying to remain calm.

'I apologise for the wait. I'm not sure what she's doing in there either. Can I offer you something to drink? Water? Coffee?'

Wow. I pause, taken aback by the genuine warmth radiating from behind the reception desk. The last time I was here, a different receptionist looked right through me – frosty and dismissive, their stony expression had made me feel invisible, as though I didn't exist. But this guy is altogether different. Maybe I was too hasty in my judgement of Lenka's staff? I hereby retract any impure thoughts I had about his fridge.

I decline with a nod, noticing the familiar accent in his voice.

'You're from Ireland, right?' I ask him.

He smiles and nods, his kind eyes twinkling.

'Yes, I moved over here a million years ago, but you never lose the accent, do you?'

'No, not at all,' I agree. 'My mother was originally from Ireland and her accent never faded even after living in London for years.'

'Which part of Ireland is she from?' he asks curiously.

I hesitate. 'Innisfree. It's just a small village, from what I understand.'

'Have you never been there?' he asks with raised eyebrows.

I shake my head. 'Not yet, but one day, hopefully. I've always dreamed of seeing it for myself. Have you been?'

'Indeed, I have! Ah, the Wild Atlantic Way – on the western coast. That's a great little spot! My grandparents used to take me there. Market fair every year. There was music playing on every corner and people dancing in the streets – good times! Is she from the town or from the countryside?'

I hesitate again. This is always tricky; I don't have many details. I never got to find out much about her before she passed away, so I'm in the dark on her exact origin or whereabouts. 'I'm not sure,' I reply.

He smiles and extends his hand. 'Name's Rory. Nice to meet you, Daisy. Sure you wouldn't like a cold drink? You look like you could use one.'

I nod in response and start fanning myself with both hands, feeling a wave of heat rise within me. My suit seems to be growing smaller by the moment, my body feels too large, my windpipe too narrow, the air too thick to breathe. I'm suffocating. The Panic begins to set in like an uninvited, unwelcome guest. My mind races with thoughts of my impending doom – this doomed meeting with Lenka, the inevitability of losing this job, then possibly Ash and our plans of moving in and our future together... why would he stay with me if I have nothing? And what else can I do? And what if things get even worse?

The horrifying possibility of losing absolutely everything flashes through my mind, like the instant I lost my mother, then all the other monumental losses that followed, the start of it all. I know too well how easy it is to set the dominoes of destruction in motion – one little nudge and it all comes crashing down. No matter what I do or say now, there's no way out. I'm trapped, out of options, cornered. There's no way around it – I can't save this situation.

Rory gives me a glass of cold water, and I quickly swallow it down. He squeezes my hand and whispers soft reassurances. I keep my eyes shut, counting backwards from 300 as I try to slow my breathing. I remind myself that I'm not really dying, just freaking out. That freaking out is natural. I accept and love myself even though I'm freaking out... In the depths of my chest, I can feel a ripple of calm spread throughout my body – a reminder that it's going to be okay.

Rory looks at me with kind eyes and says in his gentle voice, 'It's all right, Daisy – just take a deep breath and relax. Everything is okay.'

I take his words and let them sink into my mind like a soothing balm. *Everything is okay. I accept and love myself even though I'm freaking out – it's part of being human.* We all have things we need to face, no matter how intimidating they seem in the moment. I focus on the coolness of the glass in my hand and thank Rory for helping me find some peace of mind before my meeting with Lenka.

But I think it's now time to get real. I may as well come clean. I clearly don't have the strength for another tongue-lashing. Why even bother going in?

'Truth is, Rory, I'm scared stiff. I think it's best I just forget all this. Press pause here. I mean what's the point? It's already a foregone conclusion that she hates everything I do – I can't even understand why I thought coming here would make a differ-ence. I guess I went into fight-or-flight mode, but now I've taken a breath, I see there's no hope. She's made up her mind. Done deal.'

I stand up to leave. 'Sorry, I shouldn't have come in. I should've never taken this project in the first place; I apologise for wasting everyone's time. Just tell Lenka that I've fallen into a coma, joined a cult, that I'm donating all my organs... so no need to follow up, delete me from the database – whatever you think will work best. Thank you again for your help. It was nice to meet you, Rory.'

'Whoa, whoa... hey, hold up a sec!' He stands up and reaches out. 'You have come so far already, Daisy! There's lots going on behind the scenes – it's not as clear-cut as it seems. I promise you can do this! I've seen your work; your drawings are beautiful.'

I glance up at him sceptically. 'Not according to Lenka,'

'Lenka doesn't have the only opinion that counts, no matter how much she'd like you to think so. And plenty of people really respect your work. I'm telling ya, I know these things – I overhear conversations all over the place! I'm bcc'd into everything.' He taps on his computer for emphasis.

He waves me towards him and quickly looks around to make sure the door is closed and we're alone. 'Right, time to spill the tea – Lenka and Matilda Wilder had a *blazing* row yesterday – it was *amazing*, and horrendous obviously, but it was a *huge* fight and now they're not on speaking terms. The battle lines have been drawn. Matilda Wilder is Lenka's number-one nemesis now.'

'Really? But why?'

'I know, right? But she's frustrated Lenka by still being alive, you know – how dare Matilda still be around, breathing and chipping in ideas for her own books at ninety-five? That's Lenka's view. Usually with classical adaptations, the author has been dead for centuries, so Lenka has full creative control and can do what she wants – take it in a more commercial direction and modernise it for current audiences. But Matilda Wilder is alive and kicking and she isn't having it! She came storming in here yesterday and told Lenka to pipe down. *Forest Fables* needs to stay true to its roots – be reimagined yes but remain faithful to the original work.'

'Wow. That explains why Lenka's been extra ratty lately.'

'Exactly. Lenka is not used to being told what to do.

'So, take a step back. Know you already have the talent of an artist; now you just need to learn the business psychology side of things, how to handle the good, the bad and the ugly – because they all live amongst us, hiding in plain sight.' He eyes the room. 'You're doing great, so hang on tight. It would be nice to have someone normal here who I can enjoy lunch or a few drinks with.'

I gaze up at him, feeling a little bit of hope. 'Really?'

'Absolutely,' he replies firmly.

'I'm honestly terrified of what I'll find when I open that

door – shark pool, electric chair, skull and bones of former illustrators.'

Rory bursts out laughing. 'Don't give her any more ideas! She suggested to Matilda that they should turn the book into a "survival of the fittest" kind of game, like Noah's Ark meets *Lord of the Flies*. They would introduce a flood and all our beloved furries would have to fight each other for survival. Needless to say, Matilda wasn't too keen on the idea. Can you imagine? Nightnighty, little children, sweet nightmares about animal cannibalism! Lenka doesn't connect with *Forest Fables* and it shows. Let's try to preserve a little world that kids might still want to wake up to.'

He offers me another glass of water, which I gulp back.

'You've done amazingly well in your online critiques over the past three months – you're at the top of the leader board, Daisy. Most people have left by week four.'

'This feels like *The Hunger Games*!'

'Dead on,' Rory says, nudging me in the elbow. 'She even has a Mockingjay tattoo on her left butt cheek – something I can't unsee.'

I really don't want to think about how he saw that or why, but I'm grateful for the plan and strategy he's offered me. Rory's glimmers of optimism, that my job won't be a total failure and the story can still be salvaged, is enough to give me hope. It's like a drowning man reaching out for a life raft.

'Okay, how should I do this? I need all the tips you can give me, Rory.'

'I learned a lot about how to deal with her while watching hostage-negotiation documentaries online. Lots of great tactics – super-helpful, world-class stuff. She loves to see how far she can push until she gets resistance. But don't worry, I know all her tricks now. She doesn't realise I've figured them out, cracked her little code of control – and the moment you see them for yourself, it turns into so much fun.'

'Okay...'

'So, round one: play her at her own game – she'll be smiling, sweet-talking to try to confuse you, so respond in kind. Be nice and show empathy, understand where she's coming from. She's expecting an argument, so don't give her one and watch as she recalibrates and adjusts her tactics accordingly. Don't get defensive or she'll make quick work of you. Tell her that you understand what she's saying and that she's right – this will calm her down and give you the advantage. Putting you in control.' Rory pauses for a breath before continuing.

'Okay. I can do that.'

'Round two: FBI mirror technique. Mirror her tone, her body language, repeat her words back to her. She really responds to this one and can't help herself. It's a hoot to watch.'

I bite the inside of my lip. I appreciate Rory's help, but I think this is just too conspicuous. Like, she coughs, I cough? She crosses her legs, I cross my legs? I should probably tell Rory that YouTube isn't how they train the real FBI.

'Won't that be obvious? Won't she figure it out?'

Rory howls with laughter. 'No way! No offence, but Lenka doesn't think you're anywhere near smart enough to try something like this. She underestimates *everyone*. To her, we're all just little people. Pea brains. So, no, she won't have any idea what you're doing, and she won't suspect a thing. She'll be totally absorbed in hearing herself talk to a captive audience of one.'

I gulp back another glass of water.

'Wonderful! All right. For the last round: if you've done everything correctly and it's working as planned, subtly drop in a way you can be of assistance to her – whether that's boosting her profile, sparing her from embarrassment or doing something she can't do – let her come to the conclusion on her own. She'll become your biggest ally in no time; you've made her remember that she's a genius.' He snaps his fingers in the air. 'And *that's* how to turn this around.'

'Do you honestly believe I can make this work?' I ask, my voice tight with anxiety. My stomach churns, and I press my hands against it firmly, trying to calm the sense of dread.

Rory nods at me confidently.

I glance between Lenka's door and him, gauging the potential for failure against possible success. Taking a deep breath, I finally meet his eyes. 'Okay – let's give it a shot.'

He smiles warmly as he presses both hands against his chest. 'Team Wilder all the way. Daisy, you can do this.'

Maybe I *can* do this? Might I be able to actually pull it off?

After all, I've got this far. I've worked so hard. I've got so much at stake with this project, I can't just let it slip through my fingers. My heart begins to beat a little faster; my hands start to tingle as I feel the courage and determination well up inside me. Suddenly, I'm filled with this surge of passion that's just begging to be released. I take a deep breath and slowly exhale, feeling like it's my moment to prove myself and show everyone what I'm made of.

Rory's phone blares loudly before he quickly lifts the receiver.

'She's ready for you now.'

Ding-ding. Round one.

CHAPTER 3

THE MEETING

As I enter the room, Lenka's head lifts. Her steely-grey gaze is on turbo-power mode, scanning me up and down. I meet her eyes with my own as she stands arms crossed, chin raised, ready for battle.

But as I draw closer, entering into her Chanel No. 5 aura, something feels odd and disorientating. A single unexpected detail... Harsh stance, mean eyes and then a super-sweet *smile*; it's almost human-like, surprisingly wide. Uncharacteristically collegiate. Disarmingly gentle.

Rory is on to something. I can sense that Lenka is also playing a game of sorts – her sudden change in demeanour is unsettling but also intriguing. Maybe those YouTube videos were worth a watch after all!

Lenka motions for me to take a seat on a brightly coloured, polka-dot mushroom stool beside her desk. Low down beside her desk, so she looks down at me, queen to courtier. She's not sitting on a throne, but she might as well be, while I'm basically sat on the floor.

Play her at her own game. Tactics, Daisy, employ those You-Tube crisis negotiation strategies. They're all you've got.

I smile up at her.

She smiles back down – Ruby Woo red lips stretched to the max, showing teeth.

Let the games begin.

I return with a smile wider again; I try to flash a little of my gum-cleavage because that's how much I care. We're in a smile-off. And I'm not going to lose.

Her smile widens *again* – even more teeth, possibly more than the standard set? Is this the latest aesthetic enhancement of the uber-achievers? Is this the latest trend among the rich and famous?

I raise my smile game once more, holding nothing back. I pull the biggest, broadest, cheek-squeezing, face-cracking, jaw-breaking grin of all time – I'm gurning for survival, like your first school photograph when the teacher says you won't get your snack or playtime or ever see your friends again unless the photographer gets his shot. I can feel the heat rising between us as we continue to hold each other's gaze, waiting for the other to break.

But I don't break. I don't even falter. For now, yet I can't help wonder how much more she's got? How much more I've got? When will it end?

With a sudden burst of energy, I unleash my ultimate weapon: a small giggle that catches her off guard. She blinks rapidly, her smile faltering just a bit. I can tell she's trying to regain her composure, but it's too late.

Lenka relents. 'Daisy, Daisy, Daisy... finally, we meet again.'

Oh my God – I think I've passed round one. I think I made it. I still feel... okay. Intact. Alive. Now, according to my new mentor and guru, Rory, it's time to play nice.

'It's so great to be here, to see you! What an honour to be invited in like this! I know you're exceptionally busy, so I know it's so kind of you to see me at such short notice.'

She retreats her smile and softens her pose. 'You're

welcome, Daisy. *Exceptionally busy* – that I am. I'm glad you understand. And I do appreciate you coming in to the office for this meeting, especially at such short notice. That's impressive, Daisy – it shows professionalism and I like that.'

Was that a compliment? Rory needs his own YouTube channel. Subscribe me for life.

I take a deep breath and steel my nerves. Here I go.

'I brought my portfolio so it would be easier to show you some of the concepts behind *Forest Fables* rather than try to explain them,' I tell her.

Lenka's gaze narrows; she dips her chin and peers at me over the rim of her glasses.

I do it too. Even though I don't wear glasses, so I just mime along prop-less. Mirroring her every move, like secretly playing Simon Says with the most terrifying woman in the industry. Bar Matilda Wilder, by the sound of it.

Lenka leans back in her seat, her features softening. She exhales.

And so do I. Oscar-worthy stuff by me. God, acting like someone else is so much easier than being yourself! Now I totally get why Lenka opts for pomp and pretence – it takes so much less out of you emotionally. I'm learning lots here and no doubt, this is working – she may think I'm as dim-witted and deranged as our little fox cub, but she's disarmed for sure. She's not screaming or firing insults, she's taking stock, reorientating. This playbook is like a paint-by-numbers kit... genius.

'You've brought your actual portfolio. Interesting. Let's look at it then.' Her accent is a mix of crisp English and lilting Czech. 'It's not often I see hard-copy work these days.' She extends a hand in expectation.

With trembling fingers, I pass her the portfolio. My heart hammers against my ribs as she flips through the illustrations, one by one, a myriad of emotions flickering across her face. She lands on a page, tuts, then mutters under her breath, shaking her head.

'I mean, why is the hedgehog still wearing a waistcoat, Daisy? It's bad enough I must point this out once, but twice? Nobody has time for this coddling, for all this guidance and direction you seem to need – I am not your mother!'

Ouch.

My stomach rolls as I struggle to reply, but I gather myself. I've managed not to break so far, and in fact I would say I've even chipped away at the ice queen a little, so I take a breath and explain.

'With respect, Lenka, Mr Hedgehog wears a waistcoat to cover his prickly spikes. That's his emotional signature, his schtick – he's hiding who he really is, afraid, ashamed, confused; without a waistcoat, he wouldn't make any sense, and then the whole story wouldn't make any sense.'

She clicks her tongue and blinks quickly.

I open my mouth again, but she shakes her head in warning. Okay, I'm sensing that she's not in the mood to hear about the in-depth imagery, the symbolism, the hidden meanings and archetypal themes. I went off-piste there. Tried to improvise and promptly got shut down. Lesson learned – I'm sticking strictly to Rory's instructions from now on. No deviations.

Lenka stands from her seat and strides to the floor-to-ceiling window overlooking the Thames, turning from me, clasping her hands behind her back.

Uh-oh. Have I messed it up?

Lenka turns from the window, eyeing me sharply. Her imposing stance looms over me as I sit on the small stool, making her seem larger than life. Her eyes rake over my figure before settling back on my face. Her lips press together firmly, and then she speaks in an authoritative yet composed voice.

'*Emotional signature*,' she says slowly. She strides around the room, her presence barely contained within its walls. She stops directly in front of me, her arms crossed as if daring me to look away before speaking once more.

'That makes some sense, at least. I can't be expected to understand the inner psychological workings of every little fantasy creature I come across.' She taps a long red fingernail against her cheek. 'You seem to have a good grasp on the subtext – and the author, Ms Wilder, did insist on that, so in that case... I say, adequate.'

This faint praise is the most I've received in months. I cling to it. 'Thank you.'

Lenka stands, the skyline of London against her frame, playing with the string of pearls around her neck, twisting each small white bead between her fingers.

I'm supposed to be FBI mirroring right now... Only thing is I'm not wearing a necklace. So I just kinda bluff it. I'm fully onboard with Rory's strategy at this point. I keep Lenka's eye contact the whole time as I claw at my neck, at nothing and for no reason, but she doesn't seem to notice. She then raises her hand to loop a strand of her glossy white-blonde hair around her ear. I do the same.

She catches my eye and blinks quickly a few times.

Oh God. Is she on to me? I don't know, but I've got to play the game. I blink right back.

And then she smiles at me – a real, genuine, warm smile, no fake gurning this time. 'You know, Daisy, I think I like you. Sometimes you can get the wrong idea of someone when we work remotely.'

She walks over to my portfolio and lightly places a hand on Mr Hedgehog.

'The work looks quite different here in my lap than on my laptop.' She laughs at her own joke, flicking a wrist in the air.

Of course, my laughter chimes in with hers, wrist-flicking in perfect sync. Rory was right. This is quite fun.

Lenka keeps laughing and claps her hands together. 'You

know, Daisy, I surprise myself – always. It's one of the things I love about being me. I never know when inspiration will strike! When I'll be moved by my inner muse to take a totally radical and exciting new direction! I never thought I'd say this, but I think we may be quite similar, you and me... I think we can make something work here.'

Holy smoke.

This is voodooooooooo.

Lenka takes a big breath. 'It's reassuring to me that you know the stories so well, that you appreciate how iconic these characters are, how precious these books are to so many. Generations of readers have grown up with and love these stories, and now it's up to us to make sure they continue to capture the hearts of new readers. Somehow...'

Lenka pauses, her gaze fixed upon me. 'Matilda Wilder was a founding author of Hedgerow Press, so I'm contractually obligated to ensure her works are published in the editions she has requested. No getting out of it – believe me, I've tried.'

I continue to mirror everything: winks, blinks, nose twitches, finger steeples. I never thought I'd say this but I'm in Lenka's company and I'm having a pretty good time. Weird.

'I'm going to reconsider you, Daisy.'

That's when I snap back to full attention.

'Yes, that's right.' She nods, her smile widening even further. 'It's a tremendous honour for us here at Hedgerow Press to reimagine such beautiful work and keep Matilda Wilder happy, keep her vision alive. We're so privileged to be part of this mission of bringing these timeless tales to life again. I gave you the nod for this job – picked your portfolio out of every new illustrator in the business – for our biggest project yet.' She shrugs, throwing her hands up in the air. 'What can I say? I go with my gut... usually, I'm right. It's got me where I am today.'

I feel a weight lifting from my chest and my breathing

steady. I can feel the heat of hope rise through me; perhaps it's going to be okay.

Lenka walks back to her chair, then leans forward on her elbows and takes off her glasses to study me closer. 'As you know, to captivate a whole new generation of readers, we need illustrations that are fresh, vibrant and exciting.'

I feel a chill run down my spine.

Lenka fixes me with a steely gaze and says in an even tone, 'Convince me how these dusty old tales are going to compete in this market – against video games and streaming services and endless options for entertainment.'

Uh-oh. Curveball. Rory didn't equip me with any 'Pitch for Your Life' techniques.

'If you are so confident that your ideas can change things – prove it.'

But we are Team Wilder. It's now or never.

So carefully, and with confidence, I explain why the work should be taken seriously; why it could have a lasting impact on the industry; how it could revolutionise the way we think about classic storytelling.

My voice trails away as I finish, and the air feels heavy with anticipation.

Lenka is silent, her gaze intense and unyielding. The only sound in the room is the ticking of a clock.

'You really believe this?' she asks finally.

Her words hang in the air between us like a shimmering promise.

'Yes,' I reply without hesitation. 'I believe that if we give people something new to think about, a different way of looking at things – then anything is possible.'

Lenka stares at me for a few moments before speaking. Her eyes pierce me, and my breath catches in my throat. I can feel the sweat forming on my palms as her lips part to speak. My heart thumps like a drum inside my chest, and I wait with bated breath for her words.

'Fine. You want to resurrect the dead? You believe that you can pull off the impossible, make miracles? Do whatever you have to do, but don't come back in here with anything less than mind-blowing brilliance. We need to see your creativity unleashed. Daisy, blow our freaking minds. I should be moved to tears – give me a spiritual experience of some kind; make me feel like I've left this world and entered Fable Forest heaven. Understood?'

'Understood,' I tell her as I gather my portfolio and stand from the mushroom stool, head held high.

Team Wilder lives to fight another day.

And who knows... I might meet this impossible brief and set the world alight in the process.

Or it'll blow up in my face. And completely wreck my career, reputation and all my prospects.

An all-or-nothing-type situation.

Not my favourite type of situation, not by a long shot.

There's a knock at the door, and Rory peeks his head around. 'Lenka, your ride is here and your suitcase has already been loaded into the car. The driver said there's a lot of traffic so we should get going ASAP.'

Lenka grabs her purse and claps her hands together. 'Wonderful – never too early for Champagne en route to the Paris Book Fair.'

Rory glances over. 'Sorry to rush off; you can see yourself out?'

I give him a quick nod and a thumbs up in acknowledgement. Lenka is already wearing her sunglasses and making her way out of the door, not even stopping for a goodbye. Oh well, I guess I can't expect everything. She's already moved on, so it's time for me to do the same.

And then they're gone.

And I know I should follow them straight out that door and join the rest of the workweek exodus. But there's just this one thing I need to do before I go.

I approach Lenka's bookshelf and take hold of the antique edition of *Forest Fables* with care, lightly running my fingers over its timeworn cover. I take a deep breath and open it to the very first page. The melody of my mother's voice echoes in the rhythm of the lines, the music of the verse. In my mind's eye, I follow her gentle finger, tracing beneath the words on the creamy paper, voices that appear to drift in the air and characters that seem to move before my eyes. The words on that page captivated me as a child, beckoning me to build a world all my own.

As I glide my finger across the aged page, my mind races with the possibilities. I feel my heart quicken as I read the words, each syllable speaking to me like a lost friend. The hum of the past seems to dance in the air around me, and I let out a shaky breath, remembering how this book saved me when my mother died and I was orphaned and placed in a children's home. It brought me comfort, love, security and hope. Every word was an invitation to explore unknown places, forget what was too real and instead create a world of my own that was so much better than the one I lived in every day. A world where good always overcame evil, where love conquered all and where anything was possible if you just believed.

That's a cute idea, an uplifting notion, an existential life-hack, isn't it?

Whether or not it's true doesn't matter; I *want* to believe it again.

I desperately need to believe it.

I flip through the pages with eagerness, my heart seesawing between hope and anxiety. Whatever awaits me, I have to take the chance. This may not be my fairy-tale ending, but for now, it's enough to simply turn the page.

CHAPTER 4

THE DETOUR

I step out onto the busy street, ideas swirling around inside my head. The sun is beginning to lower in the sky, and the River Thames sparkles in its golden light. Lenka's words are ringing in my ears: 'We need to see your creativity unleashed. Daisy, blow our freaking minds.' I take a deep breath and let it out slowly. The nerves I felt about meeting Lenka are now replaced by a sudden surge of energy and, dare I say, excitement. Wait till I tell Ash... that things are finally on the up. That I'm solvent and successful. Okay, *potentially* solvent and successful.

My brief is clear: to give everyone everything that they want and everything that they don't yet know they want but will love when it arrives. That's it!

Oh, and bake in spiritual experiences and miracles and global commercial appeal.

And deliver it all in six weeks.

I blow out my cheeks at the enormity of it all. I know it's a big ask. But I'm parking all bubble-bursting factoids till later. Way later.

Today, I'm pocketing it as a win. I'm still in the game. One life left. Level up.

I start walking towards home with a new determination in my step. I know that this is my chance to make something truly special – something that could potentially change the entire landscape of art and storytelling forever. I look at the people around me – the way they move and interact – and imagine them as animals in a strange magical land. Each twist and turn in the street suddenly looks like it could lead somewhere extraordinary – somewhere outside our normal understanding of time and space.

The blaring horn of a car breaks my trance, snaps me awake, back to the reality I know so well. I scan the area for anything extraordinary, but all that stares back at me is the same-old inner-city street with its regular attractions: a tanning salon on one corner and a run-down greasy spoon. The smell of exhaust fumes from passing cars taints the air, and the sound of laughter from kids playing in the skatepark is drowned out by traffic noise.

I take a deep breath and try to clear my head of all its jumbled thoughts. I need to focus, to see past this mundane landscape and into another world – a place where anything is possible.

In the distance, I see the dual carriageway clogged with traffic, jammed cyclists and frustrated drivers. Up ahead, road-works are in full swing. It hasn't even been a week since the city's latest anti-road-toll rally ended, and already the protesters' tents and placards are back en masse. A few feet away, a white van spills out a dozen young men and women carrying stop-the-war signs, chanting and marching towards the street corner ahead.

On the left, more protesters are dressed in green camouflage with fluorescent-yellow high-visibility jackets, waving picket signs and chanting something about pollution and the world ending. On the right, a group of topless women shout slogans and brandish banners asking for 'Naked Rights'.

Now that's something I can get behind. This shirt is scratchy, these trousers give me camel-toe and these heels are killing me.

The protesters' cries blend into a jumbled mess, their shouts and rallies all trying to be heard, drowning each other out. No matter which way I turn, there seems to be more protests, road-works and diversions than ever before. As I stand, trying to figure out an alternative route, dozens of people hurry by, their faces drawn and weary under the heavy weight of their bags and responsibilities.

My breath hitches as I glance at my wristwatch. It's seven minutes until I'm due at the flat Ash has booked for us to view. And yet, here I am, miles away. He's so excited about seeing this flat together, but there's no way I can make it in time.

My stomach sinks as I realise the alternative route I know is blocked off too. A huge detour sign flashes towards Peabody Bridge – the opposite way I should be heading. It also leads straight into the middle of my childhood neighbourhood, a direction I avoid at all costs.

With every passing moment, I feel a growing sense of guilt and urgency. I'm going to have to break the news to Ash – this won't go down well. With shaking hands and a heavy heart, I reach for my phone. The impending conversation looms over me like a storm cloud about to burst, but I've got to tell him, so I steel myself as I press the call button.

He immediately answers with: 'Daisy, where are you? I'm in line at the entrance of the building, and it's insane how many people are here! It looks like the line goes all around the corner!'

I take a deep breath. 'Uh... Ash? Please don't be mad. But I'm not going to make it; I'm miles away. The roads have closed, it's mayhem – there's no way to get a cab, and even if I could run the whole way, I'd still be too late. I'm so sorry.'

He groans over the phone. 'You've got to be kidding me! This might be our only chance to get this place – to get *any* place this century the way we're going. There's nothing else close enough that we can afford, and now this one is going to slip through our fingers.'

'I know, I know... I would love to be there with you.'

I'm met with nothing but silence. I can almost picture him in my mind's eye, running his hand through his wavy blonde hair, rolling his eyes and scuffing the ground with his shoe in frustration. I know that a simple apology isn't enough to make this situation better. I have to make it right. We can't afford to lose out on a place just because I can't make it to the viewing.

'Why don't you just head on in, look around and if you think it ticks all the boxes, then go ahead and sign for it – okay? If it feels right to you, we won't let this one get away.'

'Really? You don't want to check it out too?' Ash asks.

'Ideally, yes. But I trust you. It's got to be better than what we're doing now – zigzagging across town, you staying with your folks and me in my poky little flat... it'll be fine, it'll be great.'

My instincts tug one way, my doubts the other. I think of Ash's disappointment if I said no and know the decision is risky. Excitement and dread war within me as I weigh options: Do I take a chance or run away? Lose out or take a leap of faith? The unknown looms ahead, full of possibilities that both thrill and terrify me in equal measure. I take a deep breath and steel myself for what's to come. It's dangerous, but sometimes you have to risk it all to get what you want.

With bogus courage, I exclaim, 'Let's do it!' despite my nails digging into the flesh of my hand. Backing out now is not an option; we've come too far already.

'That's my girl! Now that I'm here, it seems to actually be very close to Kayla's house – so that's got to be a plus, right around the corner from your bestie!'

I gulp. Kayla can't stand where she lives – not just because of the annoying housemates who steal her charger and guzzle her vodka, but she's also not a fan of the area. She calls it a concrete jungle, says the air reeks of burning tyres and she hasn't heard a bird since she moved in there. Still, I guess you have to pay extra for fresh air and birdsong, something neither of us can swing in our budget. Beggars can't be choosers.

In the background, a voice blares out an announcement. Ash replies with conviction, 'That's me! Here! I'm right here! That's the agent,' he tells me. 'He's just called me in. You're sure about this? If it's legit, I'll sign for it now and secure the deal today.'

'Without a doubt! We're on the same team, Ash. Get it done.'

He inhales deeply, his excitement palpable through the receiver. 'I'm going in,' he says. 'Fingers crossed! Talk soon, love you.'

And just like that, he's gone.

I stop at the street corner, eyes darting back and forth between the towering buildings. The Peabody Bridge looms in the distance like a trap I'd rather not get caught in.

Suddenly, a flash of blue catches my eye. A police officer stands on the opposite corner, fingers tapping against his thigh.

I make my way over to him. 'Is there any way I can avoid going over Peabody Bridge?' I ask him, desperately wishing to steer clear of my old neighbourhood – a place filled with memories, both bitter and sweet.

He shakes his head. 'Not unless you want to swim across the river yourself. It's insanity around here today, absolute mayhem. All the lunatics are out and trying to change the world. You're lucky that the bridge is even open. Me? I'd high-tail it outta here before the Friday football crowds arrive – that's when it'll really hit the fan.'

I heave a sigh as I reluctantly decide that Peabody Bridge is going to be my least-worst option.

Joining the throng of people on foot, I can't help but feel

like everyone shares my frustration and disappointment. People grumble their complaints and send rapid-fire text messages as we all trudge together on our unexpected and super-annoying detour.

It seems the universe has its own plans, fate has chosen my path and I have no other choice but to walk this way once more.

Over Peabody Bridge and right by my old house.

Let's *not* do the Time Warp again.

CHAPTER 5

THE HOUSE

As I cross the bridge, a flood of memories overtakes me.

On the other side of the river lies the park where my mother and I had so many joyful times. There were ice creams on hot summer days, playing in the sandpit, bike rides to the bakery and picnics beneath blooming cherry trees. It's hard to believe it's been so long since we were here together.

I continue walking, with a feeling of her presence still lingering around me like a comforting embrace. A gentle breeze rustles the leaves of the trees above me, inspiring reassurance that she is always near. For a moment, I allow myself to be lost in nostalgia before finally I turn the corner and find myself in front of our last happy house together. I stand and take in its crooked form, looking for my mum in the windows, feeling a strange sense of comfort knowing she once filled this space with her presence. Steaming pots of soup warming our small kitchen; laughter as we sang karaoke to cheesy hits late into the night...

But as I step closer, the memories turn sour. The windows are blocked off with thick planks of wood, and the door is hanging off its hinges. Words scrawled in spray paint cover the walls, and the garden is overgrown with weeds that are taller than me. My heart sinks as I'm faced with the reality of what this place has become. It's a far cry from the happy family home I once knew. Gone are the days of love and laughter – replaced by a hollow shell with not a trace of who we once were. This place holds nothing but shades of sadness and emptiness, a sad relic to how much we've lost. And how quickly.

An eviction notice hangs tauntingly up on the wall, reminding me of how we were turfed out onto the streets to fend for ourselves. Everything changed in an instant – my mum working herself to exhaustion just to keep us afloat in our new home, isolated from everyone and everything we knew. I almost expect to see her cycling along the path on her worn-out bike, her guitar strapped to her back and a bag full of supplies in her basket.

If only things had been different.

If only things had stayed the same.

I pause to take a steadying breath before pushing open the old gate that creaks and groans as it swings open. My feet sink into the thick grass of the garden path, each step sending an ache through my chest. I press my fingers to my lips. I can almost feel Mum standing beside me, singing to herself, picking flowers, telling stories, dreaming up promises and plans. Just the two of us, Mum and I, a bag of stale soda bread for the ducks, a biscuit tin of picnic snacks, her buttery honey-roasted ham sandwiches, flasks of tea and home-made scones with black-berry jam. I bend down, feeling the blades of wild grass brush against my hands. I'm taken back to days spent here on a simple tablecloth spread out as a blanket; playing games, weaving daisy crowns and listening to stories.

Remember when we belonged to no one but each other? Nowhere but together?

Our life before flashing sirens and blue lights and shop-bought flowers on the kerbside, the sea of grey faces saying how sorry they were, whispers about children's homes and emergency placements.

My stomach tightens. There are reminders everywhere here. It's tough to separate the bad moments from the good.

After my mum was knocked off her bike and killed, I had to move into a children's home, since I had no other family. My mother was estranged from hers in Ireland, and I didn't know who my father was... it was just another question that went unanswered.

I found my confidante and closest companion, Kayla, at the children's home. She was an anchor in that period of time, always there for me. She still is. We shared a bunk for eight years until we waved goodbye for good to that place. No looking back.

I press the heels of my hands against my eyes, telling myself to keep it together. I can't help it, though; I'm on the brink of tears. Grief is unpredictable; it never fully goes away, no matter how quickly it arrives or how long ago. Just when I think it's dealt with, it's under control, that I've 'got better', am able to move on, heal... it catches me. It clings to me. It crawls over my body and soul, and I'm a wreck all over again. Even after all this time. Over twenty years!

I don't know how. I don't know why... I often feel I'm no further along than the ten-year-old girl I was, still feeling as confused and scared and angry and powerless. I'm still in the same place inside, despite all the changes that have happened in my life. Gathering up my nerve seems like a lost cause right now, yet I realise to even attempt something new I must first overcome my fear. It's a catch-22: you need courage to make the leap, but at the same time, it's hard to find it when you're already scared. That's the impossible conundrum with courage, confidence, commitment; they require themselves.

My steps quicken, my eyes focused on the ground ahead of

me, as if I can somehow outrun the heartache, the despair, the haunting vacancy around me.

But I should know better by now – I've never been able to outrun it; I've never really been able to manage it. All I've learned is that stress and work can help suppress feelings of loneliness and sadness, which is why I threw myself into studying. After grinding away for years, putting in long hours and working late into the night to pass my exams, I finally achieved my art degree. That kept me occupied, stopped my thoughts from straying, helped tire out my brain, so I could sleep through the night. And then Ash came into my life and his high-maintenance needs suit me well. I get to focus my energy on caring for someone else, supporting him, understanding him – ensuring my wandering thoughts are kept at bay.

But today, there is no hiding away any longer from my pining for Mum and all the happiness being near her brought me.

That's why I keep away from this place. I try to push it out of my mind and not let myself get upset. There isn't anything that can be done – the events are in the past, and no matter what, nothing will undo what happened or bring her back. All this I understand – intellectually. Still, the tears swell in my throat right here and now. They're so strong it's impossible for me to pretend that they aren't there.

I imagine Mum here with me: her long auburn hair is wavy and wild around her grinning face; she's showering me with kisses, grasping my hand, caressing my cheek, raising my chin towards the sun. I'm counting the freckles on her nose and the hints of hazel in her green eyes. Out loud, I tell her how much I adore her ever-warm hands. And that I love it when she dabs me with clove water when I cut myself and when she draws me long baths with milk and lavender when I'm scared. Or feeling lost, like right now.

Is it being back here or is there more to it? Could it be the

Forest Fables project that has me feeling uneasy? Or maybe it's fear of failing at work? Or hearing the soft lilt of Rory's accent and him speaking about Innisfree? Or is it letting Ash down? Or the prospect of living in a new flat away from everything I know? Or wondering if I'm even ready for moving in with him? Living together is a major step...

Tears sting my eyes. I wish my Mum was still here. We needed more time. I wish I had asked more questions, that I'd insisted on hearing the answers.

I wish you knew how much I needed you. Need you still. Need you always. Send me a sign, Mum – I could really use one right now.

The breeze picks up, rustling leaves and rattling branches. The sun has long since disappeared behind the horizon, and the world is consumed by twilight. The moon is full and high, and the faintest line of light is visible between the earth and the darkening purple. I quicken my pace as evening draws in and the shadows start to lengthen.

My phone starts to vibrate in my pocket. Ash on an update on the flat situation already? Or Kayla's finally back from her work trip and we can sort a long-overdue catch-up? I pull my phone out, holding it up to examine it. I inhale sharply as I see the number on the screen – it isn't Ash's or Kayla's.

Big Sean's calling.

Now that only happens once in a blue moon.

CHAPTER 6

THE CALL

Big Sean is my only link to Mum's past. When she came to London from Ireland, young, pregnant and alone, he offered her a job in his pub and became like an uncle to me. But after Mum died, it got harder to keep in regular contact. And that's on me. But he understands. He always does.

I used to visit him all the time: a big meal, a few drinks, a round of pool and a gutload of laughs. That was before life got so chaotic, complex and overwhelming.

Though I've moved numerous times across this city, Big Sean has stayed in the exact same place: behind the counter at The Fox and Hound.

Same phone number.

Same mop of curly brown hair, same open-collar white shirt, same huge, soft hands with sovereign rings and faded, old-ink tattoo letters on the knuckles.

Despite the time apart, I know he'll always be around when I need him, with his special way of helping me feel like I'm doing okay, keeping me connected to reality – especially when I'm struggling.

But usually he texts or leaves a message, just to check in.

He's not one for ringing me... in fact, I don't think I've ever got an unexpected call from Big Sean before.

I cover the screen of my phone with my palm just to make sure I'm not imagining things. I look again, look closer... It's definitely Big Sean. Out of the blue like this? Maybe he needs my help? Unlikely – Big Sean doesn't need help from anybody. Still, I need to be sure.

'Hello?' I say, my voice trembling slightly. 'Sean? Is everything okay?'

'Hey there, kiddo,' Big Sean's voice booms. 'Yes, yes – nothing wrong so don't fret, Daisy love. Long time no speak! How've you been?'

I take a deep breath, trying to steady my nerves. Phew! 'Oh, great stuff. Glad all is well. Sorry I've not been in touch. Just busy with work and everything – like everyone, right?'

'Ah, I see. Right you are, right you are.' His deep voice softens. 'Well, I hope you're taking care of yourself.'

There's a moment of silence on the other end, as if he's trying to figure out what to say next.

'Listen, I know this might sound a bit random, but I've got some unusual news for you. Something that I think you'll want to hear.'

'Random' from Sean could mean anything. My heart races as sweat forms on the back of my neck. 'Okay – you said everything's all right, though?'

There's a sharp intake of breath, hesitation in his deep Irish accent. 'I'm sure it is, Daisy, but better safe than sorry, eh?' He gives a heavy sigh. 'There's a fella, a lawyer no less, from Ireland snooping around the pub, asking me and a few of the old-timers about your mother... And asking about you too.'

A lawyer? Why? And after all this time?

'Don't worry, I've told him nothing, but you know yourself, no smoke without fire...'

I straighten up and clear my throat. 'Mistaken identity, maybe? Some kind of mix-up...'

'That may well be the case but...' There's a wheezy cough down the line; Sean's voice lowers to a whisper: 'The thing is, he's a bit different from the usual sort, a cute fox he is... seems to know his stuff; all his facts check out – names, dates, addresses and the like... Daisy, love, I hate to bring this all up for you – you're busy getting on with your life, and that's all we want for you. But he says he's got business he needs to sort out with you...' There's a desperation in his voice. 'I wouldn't call you up like this if I didn't think it was important. Will you come to the pub? He's here right now, having a bite to eat. You never know, it could be good news. He seems decent enough. He has some documents for you...'

My skin prickles. 'Documents like what?'

'Very official ones. O'Connor & Sons Solicitors. He was very tight-lipped, though; you know how lawyers can be. But the fact that he travelled all the way from Ireland in search of you is proof enough.'

I bite down on my lip, not sure what to think or what to say.

'Daisy love, he's come from Innisfree. So, it's best if you met with him. Get to the bottom of it. Whatever it may be.'

I stand frozen to the spot for a moment, the weight of his words sinking in. My mind races with a million questions. A lawyer looking for me? From Innisfree?

'It's best you come and see for yourself,' says Sean. 'Are you nearby? I can send a cab for you if it's easiest?'

I'm not too far away from the pub, so I manage to keep my voice even and tell Big Sean that I'll be there soon, no need for a ride.

'I'll make sure he stays put until you arrive. He has a flight tonight, though, so don't dally. See you soon, kiddo,' says Big Sean before hanging up.

As I hurriedly navigate the darkness along the cobblestone alleyway, illuminated only by the single lamp post, my mind spins with questions: What does an Irish lawyer need to talk to me about? And why now, after all these years?

CHAPTER 7

THE PUB

I thrust open the creaking, weathered door to The Fox and Hound, one of London's most iconic Irish pubs. The punters' eyes dart up from their pints as I enter. A faint fire crackles in a stone hearth, and the atmosphere is saturated with centuries-old wood and freshly poured Guinness, coupled with the scent of fried chips and sausages. The jukebox in the corner blares out an old ballad of love lost and exile, emerald eyes and fields of green, while glasses clink, raucous laughter echoes through the rafters and someone sings along off-tune.

Business as usual at The Fox and Hound. I walk up to the bar, feeling the weight of the day starting to lift off my shoulders as I take in the lively atmosphere around me. The bartender greets me with a warm smile, and I order a pint of Guinness. She nods and slides the glass across the counter to me, the foam cascading down the side. I take a sip, relishing the bitter, smooth flavour. The pub is a bit of a dive, but it's also one of the only places in London where I feel like myself. It's where I used to come when I need to escape the monotony of my daily life and just be myself – no expectations, no judgement.

It takes a few seconds for my eyes to adjust to the dim light.

The dark, low tables and mismatched cushioned stools have seen better days; a string of tiny green bar lights flicker against the deep mahogany walls and stained-glass windows. Mirrors and photo frames reflect light off each other, obscuring the haze of dust hovering in the air. I feel the weight of a lifetime of memories in the air. The low murmur of drunk voices echoes throughout the pub.

'Daisy!' Big Sean exclaims, eyes wide and hands outstretched. 'God, it's great to see you.' He shuffles around the counter, untying his apron as he steps closer to me, his every movement exaggerated by his ample girth.

Big Sean is a giant of a man, with a heart to match. He stands a full head and shoulders above me, his bulging arms barely contained within the sleeves of his greying T-shirt. The light catches in the intricate filigree of his gold chain, accentuating the weathered lines on his freckled skin. His calloused hands rest reassuringly against my shoulders, and he smiles down to me with kind eyes set beneath tufts of his thick, white brows. Ancient tattoos ripple around muscular forearms, hinting at stories untold.

He wraps his arms around me, pinning mine to my sides, my frame completely enveloped in the soft warmth of his embrace. 'Daisy! Let me have a peek at you!' he exclaims. 'You look very important indeed, all dressed up in your fancy attire! Are you keeping well?'

I shift my gaze to my figure-hugging black suit, towering heels and tailored blouse. 'Yes, everything's fine. Just came straight from work – I don't usually wear this kind of gear.'

'Your mother was a hard worker too, wasn't she just?' He brushes his hand lightly against my cheek as his eyes glisten. 'Look at you, Daisy. The same long red hair she had, the same green eyes... even that little smile of hers!' He closes his eyes tightly, trying to keep the tears from flowing freely down his cheeks. Big Sean may look tough on the outside, but he had a special place in his heart for my mother; they were close friends for many years, and he was one of the few people who knew her well.

'Your mother was an incredible woman, Daisy. Strong and brave.' His voice trembles with emotion, and he has to pause again, biting his lips to compose himself before continuing. 'She used all her energy to protect your little family, never once giving up no matter the odds. She could have done anything with her life yet chose to stay here, wanting you to have everything you deserved...'

I take his hand in mine and give it a reassuring squeeze, which brings a faint smile to his face.

After taking a deep breath he starts speaking again. 'Time passes but know this – nobody will ever replace her in our hearts or forget the fine woman she was.'

He pulls me to him, and I lay my head against his shirt where I can hear the thud of his heart. After a beat, he wipes his face with his arm and claps his hands. 'Would you like some bacon and cabbage? Is that still your favourite?'

A wave of fond memories washes over me and I nod, a smile breaking onto my face. 'My long-time favourite! Thanks, Sean, but I can't stay for long. I have to meet my boyfriend for dinner, so I can't this time. But thank you. You always remember the little things.'

Our eyes meet in sudden understanding, the silence between us taking on a heavy urgency.

'Yes, indeed, for my sins... Sometimes I'd rather forget, but, sure, we must play the hand we're dealt...' He forces a big smile. 'Haven't seen you in a long while – are you still busy with the big job?' His voice is soft and full of concern. 'Making sure they know who's in charge?'

'You bet,' I tell him.

He breathes deeply, and his jaw sets firmly as his brow furrows in thought. He's not buying it. 'Well, don't let anyone be thinking they can push you around and get away with it, d'ya hear me?'

You can't lie to Big Sean. That's why he liked my mother so much – she couldn't lie. He trusted her with the whole shebang – running his empire. She oversaw the staff, the stock, accounts, code for the safe... and she kept all his secrets.

And, in return, he guarded all hers. Even from me.

He takes my arm and guides me to a secluded booth in the corner. 'Wait in here a minute – I'll go round up our lawyer friend, James O'Connor. I'm just over there behind the bar if you need me.' He taps his finger to his nose. 'Any trouble and give me the sign, Daisy. Me and the lads will be right over and he won't cause you any further bother.' He straightens, dusts his hands on his trousers and gives me a tight-lipped smile. I feel such comfort that he'll keep a watchful eye over me, and I know beyond doubt that if any trouble comes our way, he'll be able to handle it no problem.

I slide into the snug booth and run my fingers over the flat oak table, the grain deep under my fingertips, the surface smooth and worn by the hands of many. Every touch resonates with the ghosts of those who once sat here. The flicker of the candles makes the air seem alive, as if it's breathing, carrying a hint of sweet earth or dried grass, a sense of belonging that I can't explain and have never understood.

I sit waiting, my mind churning. What could this lawyer want to go over after all this time? The investigation into my mother's death had been closed years ago; concluded as an accident. If she'd been wearing a helmet, or had her bicycle lights on, or hadn't been riding so late at night, she may still be here, they'd said.

My heart aches as I remember standing on the side of the road, staring at the flowers and candles that adorned the spot where she'd been hit by a car. It didn't seem fair that she was gone, that her light had been snuffed out so soon.

Whiskey glasses clank noisily against the counter, the volume intensifying with each passing second. The room is thick with a pent-up tension, a fever pitch. I'm relieved Ash isn't here – he'd hate a chaotic, sticky-floor place like this, preferring sophisticated cocktail bars, with their hushed conversations and low-key, well-lit décor. I'm much more drawn to places like The Fox and Hound, where people are eager to joke over a beer and join in on lively conversations. I feel so much more at ease here – no stilted small talk or intense scrutiny, even when surrounded by strangers.

Suddenly, there's a loud crash from behind me, followed by an eruption of rage and shouting. I whirl around quickly to find two men brawling on top of the pool table in the far corner of the room. Big Sean slams his fist on the counter and rallies some huge-looking skinheads to restore order. But, instead, a tall, dark-haired man leaps from his bar stool and raises both hands over his head. He's dressed in a plain white tee that does nothing to hide his toned physique, plus a well-worn pair of jeans. His face is chiselled and angular, and his vivid blue eyes are framed by jet-black hair. As he steps forward, a hush descends; the room feels like it's suddenly wrapped in a cocoon of silence. His eyes flick briefly to Sean, and in a voice of unquestioned authority, he calmly says, 'I'll take care of it.'

The room stills in an instant; everyone's attention is riveted on him. His gaze slowly sweeps across the room, taking in the scene with a practised ease. Sean nods and clicks his fingers, commanding several of the bulky bodyguards to stand by, ready to pounce if called upon.

The man radiates an air of confidence, moving with a grace that speaks of years of experience in these types of situations, unfazed by chaos. He steps between the scuffling men, tearing them apart with one strong, swift movement. His hands grip each by the shoulder, and he keeps eye contact with them while speaking in a low, steady voice. His words are too hushed for me to hear, but by the wide eyes and lowered gazes of those in the room, I can tell the men get his point.

He turns to Sean, and I pick up his strong Irish accent. 'Let this fella take my cab – it's outside. Call me another one and let him go home and sleep it off.' He gestures to the back door, where a taxi had been called for him. The drunk man who had been shouting moves away in defeat, his body deflated and head hung low. Big Sean then helps the other man to a secluded corner of the room and sets out a hearty helping of stew and piping-hot coffee to help him sober up.

I blow out my cheeks, exhaling a breath I hadn't realised I'd been holding. Fights, brawls, disputes and arguments were all too common here, but today something different happened: there wasn't a knock-out punch thrown or drop of blood spilled, not even as much as a bottle broken. This handsome stranger managed to stop the fight from happening before they'd properly got going.

Maybe The Fox and Hound has changed after all.

The man returns to his stool by the bar, a wall of muscle shrinking back as he passes. The mood lightens instantly – cheerful banter and laughter fills the air again, but this time without any sense of unease. Big Sean claps an open hand on his back, leaning forward to whisper in his ear before pointing to my booth with a jut of his chin.

The man nods sharply, picks up a briefcase and strides in my direction.

'James O'Connor at your service,' he says with a mock bow before pulling up the stool opposite me and setting down his briefcase on the table.

This is James O'Connor? The lawyer? I open my mouth to say something, anything, but my mind stalls as a million queries jam my brain, keeping me from finding the right words. I take in his strong jawline, the stretch of his T-shirt across his chest. He looks like he could be in his early thirties, but there's something in the way he holds himself that makes me think he's older. I squirm in the seat, trying to keep my foot from bouncing on the ground. Every atom of my body feels ready to jump. I bunch my hair behind my ears and hastily rub my clammy palms on my thighs.

'Nice to meet you, Mr O'Connor.' I try to sound confident, but my voice comes out shaky.

'Please, call me James.' He flashes a charming smile, and I can't help but feel a flutter in my stomach.

'All right, James,' I manage to croak out. I clear my throat and try to exude an air of nonchalance, even though my heart is thumping hard in my chest. 'I apologise for being a bit taken aback – Sean mentioned a lawyer wanting to see me, but I had a different idea of what one would look like. Maybe I've just been in the city too long...'

The truth is, whatever I expected – it wasn't James O'Connor. I've never seen anyone like him, one moment splitting up a pub fight, the next ready to talk law and order.

He chuckles softly. 'Are you suggesting I don't look like a lawyer?'

Um, that's putting it mildly; this guy is a world away from the typical stiff and upright lawyers I'm used to. He could be mistaken for a combination of Chris Hemsworth and Colin Farrell! His hair is jet black, while his eyes gleam electric blue. His presence is strong yet his voice smooth and easy. My face heats up in embarrassment. 'Oh, sorry, I'm just completely baffled right now.'

I need to get a grip before I make a complete fool of myself. Today has been A LOT.

'No need to apologise – totally understandable. To be honest, my dad has said the same thing about me. But nowhere near as diplomatically.' He laughs and holds out his hand. He has a wide smile that crinkles the corners of his eyes. His teeth are white and even, framed by a full mouth with pouty lips. He is tall and broad-shouldered, and his handshake is firm and warm. I hold his gaze, my cheeks burning with disbelief. If you had told me this morning that I'd be standing here, face to face, eye to eye, with this completely gorgeous person from my mother's hometown, I'd have never believed it. I'd have brushed it off as nothing more than a far-fetched dream. But here we are, connected in an unexpected way, on this unexpected day and I'm filled with a strange sense of something. Something I can't put my finger on, but it's something I like.

'So, what can I do for you?' I ask, settling back into my seat and feeling a sense of composure now the introductions are done.

'Actually, it's what I can do for you,' he replies, his tone smooth and assured. 'Daisy, you and I are going to have a very interesting conversation. But first, let's get us some more drinks. We're going to need them.'

CHAPTER 8

THE NEWS

'Inheritance? Are you joking?' I blurt out, staring at James O'Connor with wide eyes.

He chuckles and shakes his head, turning serious. 'Would I joke about something as important as this, Daisy?' he asks, raising an eyebrow in amusement.

'Ah, well... maybe? Sorry, I just don't know what to think. It sounds surreal, I suppose. Or like a prank or an elaborate hoax...' I offer weakly, my mind still reeling from the news.

James laughs again, a hearty sound that fills the room and eases some of the tension coiling in my chest. 'Believe me, none of the above. I'm here as your professional legal advisor and representative. Rest assured I'm trained and experienced in all the legal processes involved, and everything you see in front of you is one hundred per cent verifiable' he explains, his blue eyes twinkling. 'This is very real, Daisy. Mick Kennedy left The Lake House to your mother in his will.' He clicks open his brief-case and slides out a file. 'You can read it all for yourself, in black and white. Last will and testament of Mick Kennedy.' He taps on the middle lines of the covering page. 'Says it right here that he's left your mother, Rose Clarke, his entire estate.'

'Uh-huh.' I exhale, trying to wrap my head around the situation as I browse through the documents in front of me. 'But who is Mick Kennedy and why did he leave anything to my mum?'

'Good question. I can answer half of it,' James says with a tilt of his head. 'Mick Kennedy was the owner and occupier of The Lake House Estate, Innisfree, as was his family before him. The estate includes ten acres of woodland, a boatshed, barn and surrounding fields.' He hands me an extensive file with blurred images, a list of possessions and stacks of plastic-pocket notes. 'I'm sorry to say that Mick died tragically ten months ago. Perhaps if he knew he was dying or that his life would be cut short so suddenly, he'd have shed some light on his final wishes, but at only fifty-five years old, I suspect he felt there was plenty of life to be lived yet and plenty of time to enlighten the rest of us about the rationale of his will.'

James gives a slight nod. 'So the short answer is, I don't know why he left it to your mother. Because, sadly, it seems that Mick did not know that your mother had passed away. He must have believed her to be still alive and in a position to accept.' He dips his chin and tries to meet my eyes. 'It's a lot to take in, Daisy – if you need to pause for a moment to go through it all, just say so.'

I shake my head and take a long sip of my whiskey. He does the same.

'No, it's okay – carry on,' I say.

James taps the stuffed Manila envelope on the table before him. 'Right... so Mick passed away and left all that for your mum, but as to why, well, Rose had no familial ties to Mick, not even distantly. We know she came from just outside Innisfree originally, but cut off contact with family and then the rest of the community at eighteen when she moved to London. We thought you might know. Perhaps your mother talked about Mick at some point over the years? Do you know if they had any kind of relationship?'

I shake my head – my mum never talked about her past in Ireland or anyone from it. And I had never heard of Mick Kennedy. But the link to Innisfree is solid. That much I do know.

'I have absolutely no idea. I wish I had, believe me. All I know is that my mother's favourite possession was an old postcard with a picture of Innisfree's rolling hills, a stone house and two swans gliding across a lake. It was the first thing she grabbed whenever we had to move, so I knew that Innisfree meant something special to her, but I could never quite figure out what. And, sadly, that's pretty much all I can tell you.'

I take a hearty gulp of my drink. 'So, what's next? I guess the next in line will get the inheritance and we can wrap this up?'

James narrows his eyes at me. 'What do you mean?'

'Well, my mum can't take the inheritance because she's not here anymore, so there must be a second in line – maybe Mick had siblings or friends or something?'

James leans back into his seat. 'I'm afraid I haven't been clear. I promise you I'm usually a lot more professional, but this instance is a little different, I suppose, as I was very close to Mick. I might even go as far to say he saved my life, more than once...'

He shifts the papers and folders away and creates an empty space on the table. 'Daisy Clarke, as next of kin to Rose Clarke, you become the sole beneficiary of The Lake House in Innisfree, according to Mick Kennedy's last will and testament. In a nutshell, it all belongs to you now. All you have to do is come over to Ireland, sign on the dotted line and the keys are yours.'

I open my mouth to speak, but no words come out. Me? The beneficiary to a complete stranger, in a place I've never even been? Part of me is over the moon – I mean, who wouldn't be excited about inheriting a charming lake house in the Irish countryside? But there's also a gnawing feeling of apprehension clawing at my insides. Did James say 'go' to Ireland... like, physically go there? His face swims in front of me before his voice grows distant.

'It's yours to do as you wish,' he confirms with a nod. 'Sell it and reap the monetary benefit, or maybe, you'll decide not to sell and you can live there yourself – it could provide you with a new place to live and work.'

I laugh at that idea.

James raises an eyebrow. And I immediately feel like a city snob.

'I'm sorry – I meant that it's unlikely because I live and work here, my boyfriend, my friends – everything is here. London's all I know, so it's just unlikely that I'd ever move, to be honest. Never crossed my mind before.'

But maybe that's not such a crazy idea? Just in the short term? I can do my job anywhere, and we're already thinking of moving. I could save on some rent here in London and get a much-needed change of scene – space, quiet, fresh air... This inheritance could be the answer to my prayers: a way to break free from my financial worries and get a chance to work on *Forest Fables* in the beautiful Irish countryside. I take another big gulp of my drink, glad that I ordered a large measure.

A house key, as well as an opportunity to try to reconnect with my mother and her roots. I've always wanted to see where she came from, to get a sense of the place that shaped her into the woman she was.

I remember how often I asked her to tell me all about Innisfree. I'd pester her for stories about her own childhood – what games did she play? What was her school like? Who were her friends? And then, as I got older, bigger questions like why hadn't I ever met my grandparents? Why couldn't we go to Ireland? Who was my father? Why wasn't he in my life?

She'd take my hands in hers and promise that 'one day, when the time is right' she'd tell me the whole story – once I was ready to understand. She never got to tell me, but is it possible I may be able to find out? This could be my only chance to finally uncover truths about myself and where Mum came from.

Big Sean saunters over to us with two fresh pints of Guinness.

'Have you ever come across Mick Kennedy?' I ask him.

He takes a place opposite me, his eyes deep and pensive. He hesitates before speaking, gathering a large breath as if uncertain whether to continue. 'A man by the name of Mick Kennedy came looking for your mother some time ago, when she was expecting you. He had an immense affection for her and left a message that she should come back home. Apparently, he'd heard she was in London and he'd set off to look for her to make sure she was safe.' Big Sean turns away, then carries on in an undertone. 'I ran out back to tell your mother, but she just shook her head, saying it was better to have loved and lost than never loved at all. She asked me to act as if I didn't know her and send him away.' He stops again, trying hard to keep his composure.

The sudden news hits me with a force that steals my breath away; surprise, shock and confusion swirl around in an overwhelming whirlpool inside me. I nervously pick at the beermat. Why has it taken so long for me to find out about this?

I turn back to Big Sean. 'Why did Mum ask you to send Mick Kennedy away? What could she possibly have against him, to not even want to hear what he had to say after travelling all the way here?'

He sighs, scratching his big curly mop of hair. 'Daisy, I don't know the whole story, but I know this: she wanted to live her life, her way. Your mother made up her mind to keep herself hidden away from Mick and everyone else back in Ireland. Knowing your mother, she'd have her reasons, so I left it at that.'

Big Sean looks to James. 'You're from Innisfree?'

'Born and bred,' he answers.

'And what do you believe to be the truth of it all?'

James blows out his cheeks and strokes his chin. 'Well, I'm here with two hats on. Primarily, as a lawyer. And, in my professional capacity, I don't tend to believe that we ever get the truth. Especially anything involving more than one person – too many mitigating factors, too much subjectivity, far too much emotion.' He then looks to me. 'But, equally, I'm here as a friend of Mick's. And, with that in mind, I will absolutely help you in any way I can to find the answers you're looking for, wherever they may lead.'

That's one of my concerns – it's one thing asking questions; it's a whole other thing being prepared for the answers. I could be kicking a hornet's nest here. I consider his words carefully and then take a deep breath before deciding my next move.

'Okay. If the truth is probably out of reach and asking questions might just lead to dredging up the past for no positive reason, should I just sign for the house but leave all the whys and what ifs alone?'

Big Sean grows silent, and for what seems like an eternity, the only sounds filling our corner of the pub are the clinking glasses and murmurs of other patrons. When he speaks again, his voice is low and resolute. 'Well, that's the real question, all right.'

I want to know more, but I'm a little fearful of the answers that may come. James gives me a look, and I can tell he understands what's at risk if I open this potential Pandora's box – especially since my mother chose to hide it away so long.

'The past is hard to grasp. People change and memories fade,' Sean says.

'And then, sometimes people don't change and memories linger forever. Especially in small towns,' James adds, and Sean nods in agreement.

'Daisy, I've known you since you were a little kid running around London with your cheerful little laugh and not a care in the world. If it's answers you need, then now is your chance to get them – but tread carefully. Take it one step at a time.' Big Sean squeezes my hand reassuringly as his words of wisdom sink in. 'No matter what happens, you get to go to Ireland and claim a house that belongs to you.' He nods towards the paperwork. 'That's something worth celebrating.'

Big Sean smiles at James. 'Sounds like Mick Kennedy was a good man. He wanted to see Rose safe and looked after. Even after all this time.'

I hold the cold glass of Guinness in my hand; its dark, smooth liquid swelling to the top of the rim. I look to James and raise my glass in a silent toast. Our eyes met for a moment before taking a deep sip. I agree with every word Sean says. If there is any chance of learning more about my mother, then it is worth a shot.

CHAPTER 9

THE NEXT STEP

'So, what's the next step?' I ask James.

'Come to Ireland as soon as possible. We lost a lot of time looking for Rose and then yourself, so it's important we start the paperwork process right away – going through the documentation, sorting out insurance and other administrative details.'

A wave of eagerness and nervousness washes over me as I nod in agreement. Going to Ireland means getting an inheritance and coming closer to unlocking the secrets of my past that I had abandoned hope of ever knowing. 'How soon is soon?' I ask.

'How about next week?' he suggests. 'I can meet you Monday at my office.'

'As in Monday in, like, seventy-two hours... I can do that?'

'Please do just that!' He laughs. 'In all seriousness, though, I was quite close to Mick, and I feel a certain responsibility to make sure his final wishes are honoured, so the sooner, the better. Innisfree is a community that looks after its own, and you're one of us now. I'll help with whatever you need.'

'Thank you, James, for all of this – for finding me, for helping me so much,' I say, feeling a warmth in my chest at his words. The prospect of joining this tight-knit Irish community feels like a much-needed hug after the lonely months I've spent struggling with my art and finances and worries about what's lurking around the next corner. So why wait? Why not head out there on Monday?

I *can* do it. Lenka is at the book fair and has no problem with me working from home. What difference will it make if I just work from Ireland instead? As long as I have my essentials – my laptop, my art supplies – I can continue working on *Forest Fables*, no matter where I am. Maybe it's the change of scene I need.

I give a slight nod in agreement. 'How long should I plan for?'

'Let's say three weeks, just to be safe. That way, you won't need to make another trip.'

'I'd make it longer – give it a month,' Big Sean suggests with a shake of his head. 'These legal meetings can be unpredictable, and you don't want to feel rushed. You need to go through everything carefully, Daisy, and know exactly what you're getting into before signing on the dotted line. These lawyers are crafty bastards.'

James chuckles. 'If it makes you feel any better, Sean, Mick looked out for me when I was younger, so this isn't strictly business for me – more of a way to pay back an old friend.'

I give a quick nod – a month sounds perfect. I can work on *Forest Fables*, get this straightened out and look into my mum's roots at the same time. 'All right, I can work with that, we're off to a good start!' I say.

James nods. 'Well, as we say in Ireland: *Tús maith leath na hoibre* – a good start is half the work.' He presents his business card with a smile. 'If there's anything you need, Daisy Clarke, don't hesitate to call me.'

Hearing my name on his lips gives me goosebumps, and I

can feel my cheeks burning slightly as a blush spreads across them.

The barman comes over then and claps James on the shoulder with a hearty laugh and says, 'Your lift to the airport is out the back, James. Safe travels. Make sure to say hello to the folks at home for us, yeah? Don't be a stranger.'

James nods and smiles in appreciation. He turns to each of us, shaking our hands one by one. 'Well, it looks like I'm off. It was nice to finally meet you.' He reaches down for his briefcase and then turns to me. 'Collect all your important documents – birth certificates, proof of address and so on – for yourself and your mother. It'll help us process everything quickly.' He smiles sadly before adding, 'I know The Lake House isn't Buckingham Palace, but it was Mick's home and it deserves a chance. My father and myself will help you every step, so don't be daunted or worried. It's a lot all at once, but you're not alone – there's always a way to figure things out together.'

With one last wave, James lifts his old leather briefcase off the floor and makes his way towards the door.

I sit in the dimly lit bar, holding my 'inheritance' in my hands. My hand shakes and my heart races.

Big Sean rises from his chair and slides in beside me, wrapping his strong arm around my shoulder, pulling me close. 'I'd go with you,' he says then taps his chest with a sigh, 'but my old ticker isn't the best – my doctor said I've got to take it easy or else.'

'Oh, Sean,' I say worriedly. 'Is there anything I can do for you?'

'No, not at all – it's on myself that I need to rely. Got to keep away from the booze and cigarettes, and get to bed early. But if you ever find yourself needing any help, you know who to call,' he says, tapping his nose knowingly. 'You don't run a pub like this for forty years without picking up some useful contacts along the way.'

I smile gratefully at him, feeling a wave of warmth wash over me. 'Thank you so much. I really appreciate it.'

He leans in and kisses my temple softly. 'I'll always be here for you, Daisy,' he whispers. 'Don't let pride hold you back from asking for the help that you need. Life isn't easy – we've all had to beg, borrow and steal sometimes to get by. I only wish your mother would've asked for help – if she had, everything may have turned out very differently.'

I cast a final, lingering glance at the envelope. If it weren't for the detour I'd taken, I wouldn't be here right now. Ash and I would have been viewing the flat across town, the call from Big Sean would have gone unanswered, and I definitely would have missed out on meeting James and whatever may come of it.

But here I am, with the opportunity to uncover the truth about my mother, and even inherit enough to help me out a little financially. Taking a bit of the pressure off living pay check to pay check would be a relief. A *major* relief.

I find myself bouncing in my seat with excitement, licking the creamy head of my Guinness from my lip. My imagination is running wild with visions of luscious green hills and open blue skies during the day, and cosy drawing nooks by crackling fireplaces come nightfall. I'm going to Ireland. For real.

For the first time in my life, Monday can't come soon enough.

CHAPTER 10

THE BOX

I slide the rusty key into the chunky old lock, the sound echoing through the hall. As I push my front door open, the familiar musty smell welcomes me in as the hustle and clamour of outside life fades away. The flat in the converted warehouse I call home is old, tired and overpriced, with exposed brickwork and water damage, constant creaking and clanging, but I jumped at it on the first viewing for two reasons.

1. The central location.
2. The super-hot, criminally flirty rental agent who showed me around the flat. And then showed me around the area. And then showed me around the bars and restaurants, and the next thing I knew, his toothbrush had moved in and I was in a proper adult relationship with Ash Saunders.

And I'm fairly settled here now, have added homely touches here and there – a colourful throw blanket draped over the sofa, my favourite paintings lining the walls, a few plants perched on windowsills giving life to a lifeless space.

I let out a deep sigh of relief, my shoulders falling slightly with the release of tension that comes from being in my own one-bed oasis. In one swift movement, I kick off my shoes and slip out of my bra, allowing my poor trapped boobs to breathe freely again. I shake out my hair and gather it into a messy topknot on my head before settling down on the couch.

Alone at last. Peace at last—

Until my phone vibrates beside me – a voice note from Ash.

'Bloody agent completely blew me off – raised the asking price when he saw the line of people waiting outside... Absolute tosser. Waste of time – again. To be honest, place smelled like feet and the Wi-Fi was crap, but still, it would have been a start. I'm on my way over. Already eaten. Get wine.'

I can hear the frustration in his voice. What a day.

I send him a message back.

'Ah, sweetheart, so annoying! Never mind, could be for the best, I've got some news I think will cheer you up... See you later, opening wine now! Dx.'

With a bottle of red in hand, I make my way to the small kitchenette, unscrew the top and pour myself a glass, savouring the rich flavour, feeling the warmth of the alcohol spreading through my body. My thoughts keep returning to the shock news about my unexpected inheritance and the snap decision I'd made to travel to Innisfree. In a mere seventy-two hours, I'll be on a plane alone, destination Ireland. Sean's regret that he couldn't come with me runs through my mind. It would be better if I had someone with me, to not face this challenge solo. This trip may get emotional. Ash can't drop everything at work for a month to join me in Ireland, but Kayla could.

I pick up my phone and dial my best friend's number, but all I get is her voicemail – 'Kayla at Social Media Solutions here; I'm busy doing you-know-what until God-knows-when. So, you know the drill. BEEP.'

Where is she right now? Most likely on the Tube, where her phone doesn't have any reception.

'Kayla, no joke, call me as soon as you get this.' I articulate each syllable carefully into my phone so that she understands every word. 'I've inherited a house from someone I've never heard of... well, Mum inherited it and now it's been passed to me... I'll explain later. Anyway, long story short, I'm going to Ireland to sign it all off ASAP... Come with me. Please.'

I'm hoping Kayla says yes as this inheritance news is a double-edged sword. Yay! I've got a house! And eugh! I've got to face the truth that there are loads of great big gaping plot holes in my story and I don't know who I am, or what makes me 'me'. I don't know where I come from, or who my father is – if he knows whether I even exist. Without any reference points in my life, anything could be true and that's a terrifying thought. I could be anything or anyone; I have no bonds, no context, no quality stamp. And that's scary.

But Kayla understands 'the fear'. I remember only too well when her past caught up with her. After years of nothing, suddenly family started coming out of the woodwork – wanting to meet up, make amends, start anew – and at first, it was great, but soon she realised she'd just opened herself up to pain, hurt and heartache all over again. She thought she'd broken the chain of deceit and desertion – but nope. Her family story wasn't the fairy-tale ending she'd longed for; instead they disappointed her yet again with empty promises, false hope, wild tales and hidden secrets. It took her a long time to come back from it, but we got there. Kayla made a conscious decision not to let their betrayals define her. She picked up the broken pieces of her heart and resolved to build something new out of them. We both understood that life hadn't been especially kind to either of us, but we were determined to rise above it. From there, we forged an unbreakable bond, becoming each other's family. We're stronger together – always have been, always will be. I'm aware that the same thing might be awaiting me in Innisfree, but forewarned is forearmed.

As I think back on my childhood, I want to believe that it was all a fairy tale, but I know the truth is far more complex. My mother had been pregnant and alone in a foreign city, and it was a mystery who my father was and why he was never in the picture, never even mentioned... The care system I found myself in after Mum's death certainly wasn't the loving extended family I'd dreamed of, but nobody else stepped up. I was unclaimed. Big Sean tried his hardest to take me in, but he failed the criteria: single man, pub landlord, a few run-ins with the law.

I tried to make the best of my lot, not dwell on all I'd lost, all I didn't know, but there were questions – there are still so many questions. I can't help but wonder why certain secrets were kept from me. My mother must have had good reason to withhold so much – a perfectly logical and well-intentioned explanation, right? And maybe that's what's at the heart of this. And that's what makes me nervous. Maybe it was all for my own protection? Maybe I wasn't told because the truth is an ugly story full of heartbreak and lies and loss and fear. A sad and sorry story no one could bear to retell.

After all, I saw it with my own eyes – every time someone in the pub inquired about my mother's hometown and acquaintances, she'd cast her eyes downwards and shake her head, change the subject, busy herself with distractions. Was everyone trying to hide something truly awful?

But whoever Mick Kennedy was, he must've thought well of my mother to leave her this inheritance, so that's a positive. It's either an incredibly kind gesture, or he felt like he owed her something – or maybe he's a bit unhinged. Perhaps it's a combination of all three. But this place was willed to my mother and not to me. So I need to accept it in her honour. The problem is: where is her birth certificate? James said I need that and some other documents to prove ownership. This might be easier said than done.

I flick on the light in the back cupboard of my bedroom and gather my courage. If my mother's birth certificate is anywhere, it'll be here – a cardboard box tucked away in a black bag, double-wrapped with duct tape to protect it from years of wear and tear, humidity and moth damage. I crouch down and worm my way beneath the low shelf and reach for it, dragging it into the light. It's smaller than I recall – and heavier. It contains all my mother's 'personal articles' – that's what the social worker called them.

At ten years old, I was too young to sift through them. The social worker told me that there were important items that might come in handy in the future. Things like her wallet, keys and cards she had on her when she was knocked off her bike. Also, anything that was deemed official. I was told to keep them safe and secure, and that's what I've done. This box has followed me everywhere, always tucked away in some dark corner out of view. I've been struck with fear whenever I've considered opening it, an instinctive dread of what might come out if I do. Like Pandora's box, I figured that whatever contents lie within should remain undisturbed. Until now.

I hesitantly pick up the scissors, my fingers shaking as I cut open the packaging. When I peel back the protective wrapping, I see her name scrawled on top in neat handwriting: 'Rose Clarke'. I slowly lift off the lid and find a pile of envelopes, pictures... My eyes close and my mouth tightens to contain the tears that have been building up inside me for years.

This is exactly where I didn't want my mind to go. To be overwhelmed by sorrow. To be filled with recollections of the most incredible and gifted woman I've ever encountered. To sink into the reality that she's really gone forever and nothing can ever bring her back.

I run my thumb over the faded image of my mother and me.

We're standing by the duck pond, our faces illuminated by the sun. She has her arms draped around me, and I can still feel the warmth of her embrace, even after all these years. Our laughter captured forever, frozen in time, unaware of the tragedy that was to come.

Now, as I look at her image, I remember the moments before the accident that changed everything. My mum preparing to go out into the stormy night for her late shift at the Fox. I knew the drill – I don't cook anything or answer the door, and just close my eyes and dream of beautiful adventures.

I heard my mother's gentle footsteps coming down the hall. She entered my room, the soft light of the hallway lamp illuminating her face. She carried a mug of hot chocolate and sat on the edge of my bed, then started to stroke my hair and sing softly, her voice soothing and calming. She tucked me in and placed a heavy blanket over me, the fabric soft and snuggly against my skin. I felt her soft lips press against my cheek one last time before the door clicked shut.

Lying on my side, I felt a deep sense of calmness. With a relaxed sigh, I rolled over and nestled under the covers, expecting that I'd open my eyes to see her in the morning when I awoke.

But when I did open my eyes again, a twirling blue-and-red light lit the room. A police officer stood firmly in the doorway with his hands clasped together in front of him.

'There's been a fatal accident.'

'We did everything we could.'

'Can we contact your father?'

So much to take in, so few words.

At that time, I didn't understand the significance of what hit-and-run meant. No suspects, no witnesses, no hope.

The police officer apologised but told me my mum wouldn't be coming back. I tried to plead with him – nothing worked. There were no calls that could bring her back, no miraculous fix, nowhere for me to go to find her. The police officer shook his head sadly from side to side, and my world felt like it was falling apart as an emptiness started to fill me up.

I sit in stillness, holding her photo to my chest, my thoughts flooded with what could have been, what *should* have been... I can still feel her hand in mine, and the gentle breeze against my face, our laughter ringing out like music. No matter how hard I try, I know it's impossible to relive those memories. It's a longing deep within me that I can never fulfil, yet foolishly I still hope for another way to feel close to her again. There's this crazy, irrational part of me that believes maybe, just maybe, we still have one more chance.

CHAPTER 11

THE TAKE-OFF

'How much do you think it's worth then? What kind of money are we talking here?'

I roll my eyes and stare at him with disbelief. 'Really, Ash? That's your initial reaction?'

He brings his hands to his face and stares upwards. 'Of course! That's all that matters! It means nothing more to you... you've never heard of this guy Mick, you have no connection whatsoever to his house. The past is completely irrelevant. Nothing can ever change it, so what's the point in even thinking about it?'

I take in a deep breath. I don't want to fight. I can tell he's still angry for being shafted at the flat viewing. But this inheritance is good news and it couldn't have come at a better time. I'm keeping it that way.

'It's not worth getting all emotional, Daisy. Just use your head, like you always do, and fill out the forms. It's easy – you can't mess it up, I promise.' He pauses, his eyebrows pulled together as he waits for a response.

I reach out for the wine and take a large swig.

'When you get there, they need to verify your identity as

the sole heir of this property, and once that's done, you get the keys. After that, you list it for sale and whoever bids the highest will get it as is. Goof-proof, eh?'

Goof-proof. I take another long swig. I can't expect Ash to understand. How could he? He is the yin to my yang, the rationality to my emotionality – if that's even a word. We're quite opposite in our approaches; he's more composed while I'm more sentimental. Opposites attract and all that. So, Ash is approaching the situation from a practical point of view, and that's understandable. Especially in his line of work. He deals with property changing hands day in, day out. And I see his point. This doesn't have to be a major ordeal. It's just a legal process – just sign the paperwork and move on with life.

If only. It's not as simple as signing the paperwork and that's it, no matter what anyone tells me. I can't simply move forward with life when the past keeps resurfacing. So many secrets remain unsolved, ones that mum took to her grave with her. Now, with this lawyer and this inheritance, it's like I've been tossed into a labyrinth with no map or compass – only uncertainty.

He takes out his phone and searches for the location of Innisfree. 'Oh dear, this place is the wilderness; remote and rainy. Hardly a tropical paradise.' He raises an eyebrow. 'But if the property itself is in decent condition, we could be looking at six figures with the land. Easily snag a buyer on an online auction so it goes fast – no waiting around for months with viewings, et cetera. Whole sale can be wrapped up with one click. See, told you: goof-proof.'

Ash leans back on the worn leather sofa, staring at himself in the mirror. He stretches his arms over his head and then down to his sides, runs his hands under the waistband of his Armani boxers and unbuttons his shirt. He pats his chest and grins at me to come over. My heart usually melts whenever Ash flashes that confident grin, but today I feel a sharp stab of disappointment. For him, this isn't about adventure and uncovering my heritage at all.

Belonging to a traditional nuclear family has made him oblivious to the fact that I'm still in search of my identity, desperate to look for my true self. Perhaps I'm overthinking it all? Is this Ash's way of showing his support or is he just in it for the money? It would be easier to just keep everything strictly business and get out of there as quick as possible, but is that really what I want? Have I reached the point where I'm looking for something else, something more than a straightforward exchange...?

Ash bows his head, offering me his hand. 'I'm sorry,' he whispers, 'I was only trying to make things easier for you, but I...' His voice cracks and trails off as he sighs heavily. 'It came out all wrong.'

I shake my head, trying to clear my thoughts. It's not fair to blame Ash for not understanding what it's like to grow up without knowing your whole story. My family history is complicated, painful even, but that doesn't mean I should let it define me. I take a deep breath and step forward, accepting his invitation with a smile.

My stomach does a somersault as I take a deep breath and slide in beside him on the couch. His lips touch my bare shoulder, leaving a trail of goosebumps behind. As he wraps his arms around me and holds me tight, I breathe him in, savouring the scent of his skin. He whispers gently in my ear: 'We need this money, baby. It can be our ticket out of here... we can use it to move next level, buy our own place, together, no more shitty landlords, no more hiking rents... buy our own place.'

I pull back and gaze into his deep, dark-brown eyes. 'Buy a place together?' I question him. 'That's a pretty big jump, Ash.'

He softly shakes his head and caresses my cheek with the tip of his finger as he watches my lips. The corner of his mouth curves upwards, revealing that adorable single dimple that makes me swoon. 'We're ready for this. We love each other, I'm doing well at work and your business is thriving. And with the help of Paddy or Mick – whoever it was that'll set us up with the deposit – we can do it. We can buy our own place.'

'But we haven't even rented together yet to see how it works out. We haven't even found a decent flat! Why don't you come and live here for a bit before we think about buying a place?'

He looks at me in surprise, his eyes wide and brows raised in bewilderment. 'I know you like it around here, but for me this area is still quite edgy – you know I hate leaving my car parked out there overnight, there's lots of noise from the street, sirens blaring all night long, there's hardly any storage and the land-lord is... well, never mind.' He pauses, taking a deep breath before continuing. 'Daisy, I love being here with you – but if we're going to be together for the long haul, I need us to have somewhere that feels more... homely. Safe. Somewhere we both feel we belong.'

'Hold on, Ash Saunders, when you got me to sign for this place, you didn't mention any of that stuff. Remember talking about how amazing it was, how diverse and lively it was, how creative and cultural?'

'Ha!' Ash grins, licking his lips, satisfied with himself for a moment. 'Of course I'd say all that – I wanted the commission! Anyway, it suits you arty types, and it brought us together, so it worked out just fine, right?'

'True,' I say and snuggle back into his chest.

'And that was a million years ago; things have changed now... We're moving up in the world. We don't fit here anymore... we need a—'

'I get it – you don't want to move out of your parents' house. I can't compete with a five-bedroom detached house in the leafy suburbs.'

'Correction – I am happy to move into another flat for us to be together, hence the flat hunt. But what I won't do is leave an already great living situation for one of lower quality.'

He takes a sharp inhale through his nose as he grabs the last of the wine and pours it into his glass. He sits on the couch, his shoulders slumped and his elbows resting on his knees. 'I'm living with my parents for our future, Daisy, so we can afford to upgrade our lives – I can work from home and invest what I save on rent in cryptocurrency. That will surely skyrocket soon. Is that such a bad thing?' He rubs his nose with one hand as he speaks, glaring at me with a hard look in his eyes.

I place my hand on his knee and try to look him straight in the eye. 'Ash, I didn't mean it like that. I'm sorry.'

He leans forward and cups my chin with his hand, scanning me with a mix of hope and desperation in his gaze. 'Daisy, didn't we agree this was something we both wanted? To eventually buy our own place? Isn't that what everyone wants? A roof over their head that they can call their own?' His tone is gentler now but still charged with emotion. 'Everyone else is passing us by – all my friends have their feet on the housing ladder, all of them are making huge money and here we are, still struggling to find a decent place to call home.'

He runs his fingers through his hair and pauses for a moment before continuing. 'Do you know how embarrassing it is to be a real estate agent and have no place of your own?' I feel the tension radiating off him. 'I'm seeing these guys, I take them on viewings and they're maybe five years younger than me, and they can afford to buy what they want. I mean, how did that happen? I'm not having it – it's not on.' Ash tries to mask his frustration, but it's obvious from the look on his face.

'I know, but we will get there, Ash. They could have money behind them, a head start.'

Ash shakes his head. 'The other day, this kid – no more than twenty-three – cash buyer. I think to myself – no way... but he completes – in cash! So I ask him – how did you do it?

And you know what he tells me? Cryptocurrency – investment, stocks and shares, buying and selling – in less than six months he goes from nothing to millionaire... that's what I want. That's what I'm going for,' he says determinedly. 'He who dares wins.'

I squeeze his shoulder gently. 'We don't need to rush anything. Let's just take our time, so we can make the right choice for us.'

He pulls away from me and runs his hands through his hair. 'No! We do need to rush!' His tone shifts from frustrated to pleading. 'We need to strike while the iron is hot; we need to stop waiting around and start making things happen – you snooze, you lose. And we are losing, babe.' He glances around my tiny flat with a shake of his head before turning back towards me. 'We need to be decisive. We can't keep waiting around and miss our chance. But if you don't want that, if you'd rather just dither about, then let me know now, Daisy. I'm not here just to pass the time.' He looks at me with a bittersweet expression, awaiting my response.

My gaze lingers on my mother's personal effects – her life and memories now condensed into one small box. I know that if I take this final step with Ash, then I'm taking the first towards something new. If I don't turn away from the past, and from her memory, I can never truly move forward.

A text arrives from Kayla: 'Yes x 10000! INSANE news! Checking flights now.'

I take a moment to recognize how lucky I am that this 'insane' opportunity has been handed to me; a golden ticket to a golden life. My mum would want me to go ahead, to swap this inheritance for a decent roof over our heads here in London. This can be our life now, free from sorrow and anxiousness, filled with love and hope. Ash is right – I can't undo the past even if I want to; all I can do is move on.

'Maybe this inheritance is the key to fixing everything.' For a moment, I let myself believe it and give Ash's hand a reassuring squeeze.

His face softens. 'Exactly. If it can give us a leg-up, then why not take it as an opportunity?' He pulls me closer and kisses my forehead. 'You know I'm just looking out for you, sweetheart. I know things are tricky and it's scary. That's why we need each other. We've got to stick together, because if we don't have each other's backs, no one else will.' He squeezes my hand gently. 'We're going to be okay. You know that, right?'

I give a small nod. 'Of course. You're right, I know you are, it's just—'

He puts a finger on my lips and shakes his head. 'No need for a drawn-out drama, Daisy. Just go to Ireland, get what's yours and come back with the goodies. You can't change the past, so don't waste tears on it. This isn't a long-lost family reunion. The only thing that's important is what's happening right now. All that matters is you and me... Now, let's wrap this up. How much time do you need to do the business?'

'Four weeks. That should cover any potential delays.'

'Not too bad. We'll need to move fast once you're back, though. Dan was talking about a new build coming available; he thinks he can afford it – he can't – but with the inheritance sale we'd have a chance at buying off-plan. Our own place, all mod-cons, no more landlords... our own little piece of paradise. Imagine it, Daisy; a place that's ours where we can make our lives together.' Ash's eyes light up. 'We could get in there and buy before Dan and his girlfriend snake in on the deal. Oh my God, what I would pay to see the look on his smug little face if we ended up with a place like that – puts us light years ahead.' Ash cracks open another bottle and pours us both a glass. He laughs, acting victorious already even though we haven't done anything yet. Or have we?

CHAPTER 12

THE GHOST

I press my nose to the cool window of the airplane. An endless skyline stretches out as far as I can see, and greyscale buildings reach higher and higher into the sky. The plane starts to ascend and soon all that's visible is this vast expanse of concrete and steel. As we soar into the air, I look down at the city below; floating away like tiny specks of glitter.

'We're really doing this! We're like Thelma and Louise!' Kayla exclaims.

'Let's not try to be like Thelma and Louise, Kayla... unless you want to wind up in a car off a cliff with a trail of devastation behind us. This is a business trip. Strictly business.'

She grins widely before pressing her hands together in delight. 'Not a chance. I'm going to drink Guinness, dance under the moonlight, swim in the sea and do all the leprechaun-type stuff.'

Kayla is always ready to take centre stage, always dressed to impress. Her dark brown skin and giant curls accentuate her natural beauty, but she also has an amazing style – tattoos on both arms, wild eyeshadow, piercings. She stands out in a vintage pink leather jacket that matches her bold lipstick perfectly, and a pair of black studded boots that lace up to her knees. As always, Kayla is the life of the party, commanding attention wherever she goes. Strong and confident, her head held high and her dark brown eyes sparkling with mischief.

I've always envied her courage and ability to be unapologetically herself, but I've also always been afraid of the judgement that comes with not fitting in. As Kayla winks at me, I feel a sense of relief settle in me. She may be unconventional, but she's also fiercely loyal and accepting of others. I'm more the shy type, preferring to stay behind the scenes, peeking out from under my red hair and happiest in ripped jeans, paintbrush in hand.

'Hey, girl, get ready to have some fun. We're here for a good time, not a long time.' Kayla grins at me and I can't help but laugh. I wouldn't want anyone else by my side right now, even though Kayla is sure to keep her promises about guzzling Guinnesses and moonlight dancing. I guess I have no choice but to join in the fun.

I nudge her in the ribs, teasing her. 'Kayla, this is our first trip abroad together! Check us out – all grown up! And this really is a very grown-up trip – serious lawyer-stuff is top of the agenda and of utmost priority...'

'Oh yeah, sure. You think you're some kind of high-and-mighty heiress already? Well, let me tell you something: even if you find the pot of gold at the end of the rainbow and become Queen of Innisfree, you will always be Daisy Clarke who drools in her sleep, can't catch a ball to save her life, makes terrible coffee and has a PhD in people-pleasing. Shall I engrave that on your crown, Your Majesty?'

'Knew it was a good idea to bring you along, keep me grounded... at 30,000 feet.'

We coast along with fluffy clouds surrounding us, my heart pounding with excitement. I feel as if I'm suspended from reality, not knowing what lies ahead or beneath anymore. The engines roar loudly as I sink into my seat; there's no turning back now.

Clutching Kayla's hand tightly, I consider if I've packed all the documents James O'Connor requested. I run through my mental checklist to ensure I have originals of birth certificates, death certificates, IDs, autopsies and police reports. Everything is safely stowed away in the hold, packed carefully in my hard-cover suitcase, double-wrapped alongside all my art essentials so they arrive in one piece. So far, everything is going exactly to plan. Green lights all the way.

Kayla turns towards me, lands her wide brown eyes on mine and engulfs me in her large, soft arms, pulling me close. 'Daisy! It's going to be just like old times, sharing a room... remember when I first arrived at the children's home? And you were the only one who'd share with me because I snored so loud?'

'Yes, I don't really think I'll ever forget your snoring, Kayla. Saying that, it was good training because now I can sleep through anything! Freight trains, fire alarms, screaming sirens.'

'This is going to be so fun.' Kayla giggles.

'Fun! Are you sure about that?'

'When have I ever not been sure?' She winks at me, her tongue poking out from between her lips.

'Hmm. Anyway, I might not be able to catch a ball and I may drool, but I'll have you know I make amazing coffee. I think you might have stunted taste buds... they're blocked or faulty... or maybe you just have no taste.'

Kayla waggles her finger and smiles. 'When it comes to men, at least, I have terrible taste, the worst...'

'What's happened?' I ask. Her love life is something she's been avoiding discussing for a while.

She rolls her eyes before responding. 'It's just another dead end, Daisy. It seems like every man I meet is either taken or not looking for anything serious,' Kayla says with a shrug. 'I'm tired of the games, the swiping left and right, and the endless dates that lead to nowhere.'

I nod sympathetically, understanding her frustration all too well from my own single days. 'I totally get it,' I say with a sigh. 'It's hard out there.'

Kayla shrugs. 'I've tried everything. I just can't make it work, you know? It's like I'm cursed or something. Destined to be on my own forever.'

I shake my head. 'You're not cursed. You just haven't found the right one yet. And you've got me so you'll never be alone, ever, okay?'

Kayla smiles at me gratefully. 'Thanks, Daisy. You always know how to make me feel better.'

She opens up more about her current relationship woes – or lack of them. 'So, there was this guy, from the gym... I know, right?' She shakes her head. 'And things were going so great. Until he disappeared. Like, *poof*! Gone.' She rolls her eyes in disbelief. 'Ghosted.' She grabs her phone and begins scrolling through her contacts, showing me all the lovely messages early on, but then her repeated attempts to reach out to him without a single reply. 'It's so disheartening,' she says with a heavy sigh, 'being just abandoned like that, no word, no warning... after building up what seemed to be a real connection.'

We sit together, neither of us saying a word. By the pinched look on Kayla's face, I know exactly what she's thinking, how she's feeling. Thoughts of heartache and loneliness fill us both, but neither one of us is willing to express it. We're both well aware that finding love in this day and age could never be easy, but for us, it can feel harder than ever, hyper-aware of the fragility of love and security; the hurt of being left behind and the fear of abandonment still haunts us both. Our pasts weigh heavy on our hearts, threatening to tear away any hope of a happily ever after. I hate that Kayla is going through this. I can't help wondering why love can be so fickle, so fleeting and if, in some way, we are to blame for feeling so alone? Are we too broken to love or be loved properly?

'How hard is it to find somebody just normal, just real?' she says quietly, her voice heavy with emotion.

I don't know what to say, so I just put my arm around her. She leans into me, and I appreciate the tenderness of the moment before she exhales.

'It's so crazy,' she says. She flutters her eyelashes and bites her bottom lip; her eyes widen and her brows furrow with frustration. 'I mean, I thought it was something special – he was hot, we had chemistry, you know? But now it feels like it was all just an illusion. I don't know what happened or what I did wrong.'

My heart aches for her as I see the deep sadness in her eyes. 'How about we track him down then? Be super-sleuths like when we were kids? I'm more than happy to put on my mac and sunglasses and stalk him out – where does he work? Where does he live? He can't just vanish into thin air, right?'

Kayla shakes her head. 'No, no, no. I'm not chasing down anyone who doesn't want to be found.' She pauses for a moment before continuing. 'It's better to just leave it alone. I'm not forcing anything – I just trust that if it's meant to be, it'll happen naturally.'

I nod, understanding the logic behind her words. 'Yeah, you're right. Maybe it's better to just let things be and move on. What's his name? Just in case I know him,' I ask.

'I'm not telling you,' she replies. 'It's embarrassing.'

'Come on, Kayla.' I tilt my head and roll my eyes. 'I'm not twelve years old. This is grown-up stuff! Tell me.'

She takes a deep breath and turns to face me squarely, looking me straight in the eye, almost challenging me. 'Romeo...'

I can't help but laugh. I hold the back of my hand to my mouth, biting down on both lips.

She smirks at me. 'I know, right? Ghosted by damn Romeo!'

And together we exclaim, 'Romeo, Romeo, wherefore art thou...?'

She looks at me with a small smile. 'Married or arrested or on the run...' she says with a quiet laugh, then she shakes her head and runs her hands through her hair. 'I guess I should be thankful that I got away lightly, finding out what he's really about sooner rather than later. I mean, I would rather be by myself than tied up with some lowlife coward... in fact, I'm much happier on my own, much happier being single. I'm going to put all the strength and energy into things that deliver – my business and my friends.'

It's then that I'm hit by a sudden wave of admiration for her strength and courage. Despite the pain she's endured, she's still able to make light of her misfortune and pick herself up again.

I give her a gentle hug, my heart brimming with love for this strong woman in front of me. 'You deserve so much.'

Kayla nods. 'Exactly. Life is too short to waste it on what ifs and maybes.' She nudges me gently. 'You're so lucky to have found "The One" you know...'

'You think Ash is The One.'

'Well of course... Don't you?'

I nod slowly, unsure of what to say. 'Yeah, I mean, I'm sure he's The One – if there is such a thing as The One.'

Kayla gives me a curious look. 'You don't believe in The One?'

I shrug, feeling a little unsure. 'I don't know. I want to believe that there's someone out there who's perfect for me, but at the same time, it seems a little unrealistic.'

My lack of experience with the idea of true love taints my view; I was raised without the Disney notion of romance and marriage that many others have growing up – with my mother and I being each other's biggest loves – and it's left me a little doubtful of these larger-than-life romantic ideals. In a way, I want to believe that there is someone perfect for everyone out there. But on the other hand, from what I've seen, only a rare few seem to be able to make it work, so why would I? But I don't think this is what Kayla needs to hear right now, so I bite my tongue. Nevertheless, I find myself hoping that the data is mistaken and one day we'll get to all experience something out of this world. Double fingers crossed, eh?

'What do you think?' I ask her, changing the focus away from myself.

Kayla chuckles. 'I think there's more than one person out there who could be right for us. It's just a matter of finding the one who fits into our lives the best. Relationships take work and effort. It's not always going to be sunshine and rainbows.'

I grin, feeling a little more optimistic. 'Yeah, I like the sound of that. It takes some of the pressure off.'

'Did your mum ever meet anyone? Like have a boyfriend or anything when you were growing up?' Kayla asks me.

'No, never – she was just all about work and home and me, really – never a date or anything like that.' I pause for a moment before continuing. 'I don't think she ever had time to even think of relationships or dating, but deep down, I always got the impression she didn't want to be with anyone... maybe she'd had her heart broken in the past or just felt it wasn't worth the stress.'

Kayla nods, her eyelashes fluttering as she clicks her tongue. 'Oh, I get that.'

'Big Sean told me that Mick, the Irish guy who left her this property, came looking for her once at the pub and she completely snubbed him. He said she hid out, pretended she wasn't even there.'

'Sounds like your mum ghosted Mick,' Kayla concludes with a grimace.

'Yes. It does a bit.'

I ponder the connection between my mother and Mick, as well as why she'd avoided relationships in the past. Was it merely because of me? Or him? Someone else maybe? Or was there no definite cause at all?

I stretch out my arm and wave to the flight attendant with the drinks cart. Maybe not all ghosts are players or small Victorian children.

CHAPTER 13

THE BAGS

The baggage carousel is going round and round, but our suitcases are nowhere to be seen. The flight was on time, so where is our luggage? I start to feel a bit panicky. I need my toothbrush! I need my clothes! I need my charger and my straighteners and my make-up and my PJs and my trainers. And Kayla is certainly not dressed for the west of Ireland in those towering stilettos and that mini pink jacket. She's going to need whatever she's packed to make it through this trip.

'No more bags?' I ask the airline rep hovering nearby.

'Nope. Sorry. It happens a lot, not just to you. You're not that special!' He grins at me, and I give a feeble smile in return.

Reality begins to kick in as my gaze shifts from Kayla to the spacious bag belt. This is really happening. We have nothing but the clothes on our backs. But way worse than that, every document I'd carefully gathered for James, as well as my irreplaceable art supplies, is tucked away in that suitcase that's now missing. Without it I'm screwed – I have nothing – nothing to sign with, nothing to work with, nothing at all. Everything of legal value is somewhere else... Goof-proof, indeed.

Kayla trots off to the loo while I head over to the lost luggage desk. The woman behind the counter takes down my details and assures me that they'll do their best to find my suitcase. She gives me a dizzying stack of forms to fill out and a reference number.

I race back to the carousel, eyes darting around desperately as if I could will my missing luggage into view. I leaf through a seemingly endless pile of paperwork, each line more confusing and complicated than the last. Each tiny word blurs together until I'm in a panicked stupor. But what choice do I have but to follow the instructions and hope for the best? It's out of my control so I reach for a pen and try to make sense of it all. My handwriting becomes erratic and my breathing quickens as I grapple with understanding what the documents are asking me to do, but if I don't get that suitcase back soon, both James O'Connor's and my trip will have been pointless, an utter waste of everyone's precious time.

I return to the desk and drop off my filled-out paperwork. Kayla's completely distracted by a new friend she just met in the restroom complimenting her make-up, so she doesn't seem fazed at all if our bags ever show up or not...

The woman behind the counter takes it from me and sighs. 'Ah.'

'Ah?'

'Aha.'

'*Aha?*'

I pray aha isn't some sort of Gaelic for uh-oh.

'Well, it seems your luggage never left London.'

I can't believe it. Our suitcases are still in London! How on earth are we going to get them?

'Okay, at least they know where they are. That's something,' says Kayla.

The woman behind the counter gives me a great big smile. 'Sure, that's brilliant news!' she says.

I stare at her in disbelief. 'How is this good news?' I ask incredulously.

'Well, it means it's not lost! It means we know where it is! Usually the luggage just vanishes, without a trace, like a veritable Baggage Bermuda Triangle – how's that for a tongue-twister, eh! I wouldn't chance that one after a few whiskies.'

I'm not sure whether to laugh or cry.

'Sometimes, they turn up, months later... Mexico, India... we even had one case turn up in New Zealand, can you believe it? But it's very rare.' It sounds like this is all just a great big game to everyone, except me.

'So, what do I do now?' I ask.

'Well, we'll put a trace on your luggage and let you know as soon as it arrives.'

'And how long will that take?'

'Oh, anywhere from a few days to six weeks – it varies, but don't you worry, as soon as it arrives, we'll give you a call. Oh, yes, bet your bottom dollar, we will be straight on the blower to deliver the wonderful news...' She's beaming at me now, as if this is the best thing she's heard all day.

Well, at least my luggage isn't lost forever, and I might even get it back one day. But six weeks? I'm going to have to buy some new clothes...

'And, in the meantime, here's a toiletries kit to tide you over.' The woman behind the counter offers us two small cotton pouches, presenting them as if they're made of solid gold. We thank her for her thoughtfulness and generosity.

Inside are a few essentials – though the toothbrush is barely larger than my pinky and the deodorant already smells of teen armpits. But beggars can't be choosers – or any kind of judge!

I take a deep breath, reminding myself that this was what I wanted, an adventure. I nod and try to smile. 'Okay, thank you.'

The woman looks up from her computer and gives me a

sympathetic smile. 'We'll try our best to get both your bags to you as soon as possible.'

I thank her and leave the desk, feeling a bit deflated. I let out a deep sigh as I loop my arm with Kayla's, trying to shake off the feeling that this was all pointless. Maybe I should just cut my losses and book a flight back home tomorrow. I knew it was foolish to hold on to hope, but I couldn't help myself. I wanted to believe that there was a chance to salvage this mess and make it all worth it. But now, as I wait, I feel the weight of disappointment bearing down on me, threatening to drag me under.

Kayla nudges me, a small smile on her face. 'We'll get our bags, don't worry. I have a feeling they'll turn up soon.'

I roll my eyes, but I'm secretly grateful for her optimism. It's infectious and helps keep the hope alive.

Kayla looks at me with concern. 'Are you okay?'

I nod and let out a deep sigh. 'Yeah, it's just... I'm feeling a bit helpless without my things. Everything I need for the lawyer is in that bag.'

Kayla nods in understanding. 'I know, but it's not the end of the world.' She places a hand on my shoulder and says in a comforting tone, 'Don't worry, Daisy. We can handle this – if there's anything that living in care taught us it's how to make do.'

Without Kayla, I can't even imagine what my life would be like. My breath catches at the thought of a world without her in it. How could I have gone on living if not for her unwavering kindness and support? Tears prick my eyes as I offer her a small, grateful smile. To think that I'm so lucky to have had her by my side all these years – she's the best friend anyone could ask for. She's *my* best friend.

She's been like an anchor throughout all our rushed packing and leaving, through the highs and lows we faced while growing up together. When she holds my hand tightly in hers, the truth of how much she means to me suddenly becomes crystal clear.

In this moment, I understand just how precious our friendship is.

'Anyone we should call?' she asks.

I have the contact details of James O'Connor tucked into my pocket; I could call to let him know that I'm missing my luggage. But I'm hesitant. How can I settle the will without any documents? I don't want my first conversation in Ireland with James to be about me being at a loss, appearing as though I'm a complete hot mess – no luggage, no plan, no papers. For some reason, I don't want to seem helpless around him. Maybe because of the way he straightened out that fight in the pub or that he came all the way to London to keep a promise to a friend; whatever it is, I feel compelled to make a good impression.

Kayla and I exchange looks.

'Hope you like wearing those clothes, because you'll be in them for a while,' I tease.

She starts giggling. 'It's only for a few days,' she says. 'Might as well use this as an excuse to go shopping when we get there. Now, come on! We have a bus to catch.' Kayla checks the board and beams. 'The bus leaves from outside the airport in ten minutes.'

'If we hurry, we could make it!' I declare. I glance down at Kayla's stiletto boots. They must be at least four inches high. 'It's almost worth it to see you running in those heels.' I laugh.

She takes a deep breath, straightens her back and turns to face me, a sly grin growing across her face. 'You just watch me,' she replies before sprinting down the footpath with astonishing speed and grace.

The sound of tapping heels is soon echoed by our laughter as we reach the exit. Paperwork, paints and fresh pants – who needs 'em when you've got your best gal pal? I'm rolling with my dearest friend and that's worth more than anything to me.

Onward to Innisfree.

CHAPTER 14

THE BUS

The pick-up zone outside the airport is a flurry of activity – engines roaring, gleaming buses rolling in and out of the gates, people shouting and suitcases clattering as they are thrown onto overhead racks. But there's no sign of our bus. We're about to give up when my eye catches a flash of electric orange: an ancient coach with '11' painted on its side. As we approach, the driver bellows from his seat, 'Last chance for Innisfree!'

The coach is old and a bit rickety, but it's charming in its own way. When we step inside, I notice the interior is worn and the windows have a bit of a draught, but it's immaculately clean and welcoming. Passengers grin at us from their seats.

We settle into our row and Kayla turns to me, her voice brimming with excitement. 'What have you brought us to?' she asks before erupting into laughter.

As the bus fills up with people, I can't help but feel a sense of camaraderie. We're all on this journey together. I feel a twinge of nervous excitement. This is it – the start of our new adventure.

The ride is long and bumpy, and we have nothing except our handbags and the clothes we've got on, but Kayla and I gossip and giggle as if we were back in our days of riding the school bus without any real sense of responsibility or worry. It feels good to be carefree for a little while, to let go and escape the weight of adulting.

'Thank you so much for coming, Kayla. If it weren't for you, I think I'd have turned on my heel as soon as I found out we had no bags...'

'How you feeling about it all?'

'Excited... A little out of my depth. But mostly excited, with a splash of terrified.'

'We're here now – together.' She squeezes me into a hug. 'Everything else is just details.'

We soon leave Dublin city behind, crossing the river and passing by the tourists and locals, the tall buildings and bustling pubs. The dreary grey of the pavement shifts to a sea of deep-green countryside and a sky of dazzling blue. The bus's windows frame picturesque scenes of the Irish countryside as we trundle along the narrow road, the sun transforming the lush fields into emerald jewels under its warm, golden light. Gently swaying trees dot the landscape, their leaves whispering melodies that mingle with the hum of the bus's engine. A delicate scent of blooming wildflowers tinges the air, as the salty perfume of the nearby sea wafts through the slightly cracked windowpanes. I stare wistfully at the passing thatched cottages and stone walls draped with colourful bunting. This really is the Emerald Isle – a land of eternal youth and beauty.

We ride through villages bursting with life and culture, quaint pubs and old castles, each one untouched by time or modernity. It's a land filled with mysterious folklore and tales of ancient heroes, all perfectly preserved by stories passed down from generation to generation.

As I look out the window I'm mesmerised by the simple elegance of this place, how it's seemingly been forgotten in a world full of hustle and bustle. It's as if on this small island things are running smoothly; it's like you can hear time ticking away slowly but surely without any sense of urgency or worry. There's a peace here that almost seems sacred, something that will never die no matter how much technology advances or progress takes over our lives.

Kayla too sits in awe at what she sees; her bright eyes reflect what mine must have shown earlier – pure amazement at how beautiful our world can be when we forget about ourselves for just a few moments. We both take it in until finally I tear my gaze away from the window to look at Kayla, who still stares out at everything surrounding us with admiration in her eyes.

'It's so beautiful,' she whispers reverently, her voice barely audible over the sound of the engine beneath us.

I nod in agreement, thankful for having this moment together with Kayla – before things change again once I meet with James O'Connor empty-handed and reality comes barrelling back in like a freight train.

I'm sorry, Mum. I'm sorry I've already messed this up for you... I'm sorry you're not here with me to come home, to see Innisfree for yourself.

Kayla squeezes my hand. 'Daisy... why do you look so sad? Don't worry about the bags.'

I pause before replying. 'No, it's not just the bags. I feel like I've been here before, Kay. These scenes... they're like the bedtime stories my mother used to share with me. Thatched cottages, stone walls, green fields – she described them so lovingly. I can't help but wonder...'

Kayla's gaze softens. 'Wonder what?'

'Why did she leave such a beautiful place for a big city with nothing, all alone? She was never quite at home in the city; she belonged here – among nature. It makes less and less sense, the more I think about it.'

As the seconds tick by, my thoughts become increasingly muddled and confusing. It suddenly dawns on me that my mother had always seemed happiest surrounded by nature, cocooned in the lush greenery of a sprawling park or basking in the serenity of the outer city limits. With every mile we put between ourselves and Dublin, I could almost see her coming to life in these idyllic settings; rosy-cheeked and smiling, taking in the world around her with wonder and joy.

Kayla lets out a gentle sigh, uncertain how to ease my troubled heart. 'There must be a reason. There's always a reason.'

'But why did she keep it so hidden? What was there for her to hide? To keep secret from everyone – from me, for my whole life?'

'Maybe she was freaked out because she was pregnant. Her family threw her out or she thought you'd have a better future in London?' Kayla says.

'That must be it,' I agree in a stifled voice. 'She must have been so scared and she didn't want the shame of being an unmarried pregnant woman. It was different back in the day – small village, I suppose...'

It does makes sense and it could explain why she left Ireland. But why didn't she ever open up, explain it to me, her daughter? Surely I'm the one that needs to know the whole story? I can't shake this feeling that she was holding back something... something bigger, more frightening than what Kayla and I can imagine.

Kayla gives my hand a reassuring squeeze just as a warm sea breeze filters into the bus, caressing our faces like a compassionate embrace from those who seem far beyond reach.

I shift in my seat and try to steer the conversation in a different direction, wanting to avoid talking about my problems. There's no answer to be found on this old bus that's bouncing over broken, potholed roads so there's no point dwelling on things I can't change.

'So,' I say, 'anything else been happening aside from men being jerks?'

Kayla snorts and rolls her eyes, but seems relieved to have something else to think about. 'Work has been great,' she replies. 'Business is booming – everyone wants digital marketing, so I'm busy as can be and I love being my own boss.' She sighs and adds, 'But my house-share situation is grim. My roommates are impossible to get along with and it's so noisy all the time.' She pauses for a moment, looking out the window at the rolling hills and deep-blue sky. 'So, heading off with you like this couldn't come at a better time. I need a change of scene so bad.'

Just as I'm about to reply, the bus suddenly lurches to a stop. A few frustrated grumbles are heard, but they quickly die down when the driver's voice comes over the loudspeaker.

'Sorry, everyone, I just need a quick look at the engine. Please stay in your seats. Shouldn't take long and then we'll be on our way again.'

The bus stops at the roadside, and I can see the beach in front of us. The driver opens the doors to let in some air, and I take a deep breath of the salty sea breeze. I watch in awe as a couple walk hand in hand along the shoreline, chuckling to themselves. The sun casts its glimmering rays onto them and the sky sprawls out into an endless blue ribbon above. The waves roar against the shore in a steady rumble, like the heart-beat of the earth.

Suddenly, the couple stop in their tracks and turn to face each other. The woman gazes up at the man with a look of pure adoration, and he cups her face tenderly. It's as though the whole world fades away, leaving only the two of them in their own little universe. Watching them, something stirs within me. A desire. A longing. I want to feel that kind of passion. That kind of love.

'Looks like she's found The One – lucky her.'

'What are you saying?' Kayla's eyes light up with curiosity mixed with concern.

As I softly breathe out, the thoughts weighing heavy on my

mind finally come to life and manifest into words. If I'm being truthful, those ideas had been in my head for a while. 'Ash. I just feel like we're business partners sometimes, you know? Great business partners, but maybe not so much romantic partners. I don't know if I feel that spark anymore. I don't know if he does either. It feels like we're going through the motions sometimes and suddenly he wants to fast-forward everything – go from living apart to living together to buying together – that's a lot to handle all at once.'

I tell her how he brought up the idea of buying a place together on Friday. I've been considering it, but I've tried to avoid the topic.

'This is a major decision and I need to figure out how I feel.'

I take a deep breath as I look out the window, feeling my thoughts get tangled up in my mind. 'Buying a house together is a huge step in our relationship, and there are so many factors to consider. Is this really what we both want? Are we ready?'

Kayla listens intently, her eyes full of concern. 'Have you talked to him about this?'

I shake my head, feeling a lump form in my throat. 'No, not yet. I don't want to hurt him or make him feel like I'm not committed to our relationship. He wants us to move to the next level.'

I'm torn between feeling excited about the prospect of us taking such a big step forward and scared at the thought of making such a commitment and tying us to each other for years to come. Will it make us closer or push us further apart?

Kayla places a comforting hand on mine. 'Daisy, you can't keep your feelings bottled up inside. You need to talk to him and let him know how you're feeling. It's not fair to either of you to keep pretending that everything is okay when it's not.'

I take a deep breath. 'Who knows, I might be overthinking it. Perhaps it's just a phase and we'll get that spark back. I think we've just had a hectic time lately – and now I'm here, for a month, so it's not the best time to bring up any heavy stuff over the phone, you know?'

Kayla nods understandingly. 'I get that, but at the same time, you owe it to both yourself and him to be honest about how you feel. Maybe you can work through it together.'

We sit in silence for a moment, watching the couple on the beach. Suddenly, the man drops to one knee, pulling out a small box from his pocket. My heart skips a beat as the woman gasps in surprise, tears streaming down her face.

Kayla lets out a squeal of excitement, clapping her hands. 'Oh my God, he's proposing!'

I watch in awe as the woman nods frantically, throwing her arms around the man as he slips a ring onto her finger. The whole bus erupts into cheers and applause as they kiss, and the driver does a little jig in celebration, the moment feeling almost magical.

Seeing the couple so happy and in love, I can't help but feel a pang of jealousy. Will I ever experience that kind of love? The kind that takes your breath away and makes you feel like you're the only two people in the world? I'm not at the same level with Ash yet, but trust and understanding could grow over time and our relationship could become even stronger.

Kayla nudges me. 'What are you thinking about?'

I shake my head, trying to push the negative thoughts aside. 'Nothing, just feeling happy for them. I'd love something like what those two have.'

Kayla's expression softens. 'Nobody's relationship is perfect all the time. We've just caught these two having the best day of their life. But don't forget what you already have. You have a good man who loves you.'

'I know,' I reply, my voice barely above a whisper.

'I'm sure you're just going through a phase. It happens to all of us. Trust me, there's no such thing as the perfect person.

Relationships take work and compromise. You have a good thing going with Ash.'

I take a deep breath and nod in agreement. Maybe Kayla's right. I just need to appreciate what I have and stop thinking about something that may not even exist. I'm not about to throw everything away because of a feeling, a fantasy. But there's no need to rush either, not when there's an obvious solution to how to move forward: Ash and I use the inheritance money to rent a place that will be absolutely perfect, way above our current budget. That way, we can move in together like we planned, while putting off purchasing a house until later. I need to be completely sure I'm right for Ash and both of us want the same things out of life before taking on the commitment of buying a place together.

The bus jolts forward, and the driver announces that there's, 'Nothing to fear, she just needed a bit of love and patience and she's on her way!'

His words seem like they're directed straight at me. A prophecy. An omen. A sign.

As we drive away, the engine now melodically humming, I look out the window one final time and spot the couple strolling along the beach hand in hand.

And I can't help but think that maybe there is nothing to fear.

Maybe all we need is a little love and patience to get going again.

CHAPTER 15

THE NOTEBOOK

The Irish landscape delivers. No filter required. There really are forty shades of green, everywhere!

The winding country road snakes through verdant hills, stretching past thick forests and alongside glistening lakes and rippling rivers. Dappled horses and lazing cows dot the meadows. Scattered among them are quaint cottages with thatched roofs, painted white with bright red doors, all draped in ivy and roses. Kayla is now passed out asleep in the seat by the window, her head resting against the back of the seat and snoring loudly as usual. Even though she'd love to be wide awake to take in all the sights, I don't dare disturb her rest – there'll be plenty of time for viewing beautiful green fields and adorable farm animals when we reach our destination soon enough.

I rise from my seat, rummaging through my handbag for a pen or pencil. Eventually, I find one, but it's blunt and barely usable. I can't believe my art supplies are still somewhere in London. Usually, if my luggage were to go missing, it would just be filled with swimsuits I won't wear and paperbacks I won't read, or party shoes that will give me blisters. But this is different – what I had packed is anything but trivial: my mum's papers and – what I'm longing for right now – all my art supplies. If I had them with me, I would immediately start drawing – here's the sort of inspiration that you can't put a price on. After all, I do need to conjure up a masterpiece, with a creative fusion of modern and traditional styles, in the coming weeks, or Lenka will blacklist me forever.

I sigh out loud and curse myself under my breath. It's so unbearably beautiful! And I can't do anything but stare at it all longingly. The way the trees move in the wind, how cows gather in the meadow, the colours of the horizon and clusters of wild-flowers – all will be gone before I even get a chance to try to capture it.

I feel a gentle tap on my shoulder from behind. I whirl around and see a man wearing a flat cap and with long silver hair, inches away from me. His grey eyes sparkle with bright-ness beneath his white, bushy eyebrows. 'Do you need some-thing to write with?' His voice is deep and raspy, yet it carries an unmistakeable warmth.

'Oh yes, something to draw with actually – pencil, pen, crayon – anything at all. It's just so beautiful out there, and I want to sketch it before it disappears from my mind.' I have some random pieces of paper stuffed in my purse, wrinkled notes and used receipts that I could use as a makeshift sketchpad to jot down some minimal ideas.

He nods as if understanding exactly what I mean. His hands are thin and gnarled like old tree roots, and he has simple gold hoop earrings in both ears. An elegant black silk scarf is tied around his neck casually, adding a touch of sophistication. Then he opens his satchel and pulls out a narrow case of fine-tip pens while saying, 'I'm a newsagent; I never travel without my supplies. Would you like some paper too?'

I nod gratefully. 'Yes please! That's wonderful, thank you.'

A newsagent. The patron saint of all stationary sniffers and gel-pen fans. I spent so much time in Paperchase, they added me to the staff WhatsApp group.

The man hands me a little moleskin notebook, and I turn back to the vista outside, beginning to sketch out all the beauty that passes by – from small village churches to lush green pastures. As I continue to draw, I can feel the man in the flat cap watching me like a proud parent, happy to have helped me out of a jam. I thank him from across the way, expressing my gratitude and relief.

'You're right to seize the day, take the opportunity while it presents itself,' he says with a knowing nod.

I can sense that he has experienced something similar in his life – like he knows the restlessness artists feel when they need to get their ideas out of their head and out into the light.

About an hour later, I feel a second tap on my shoulder from behind and I turn to find a little old lady wearing bright purple lipstick and a jewelled turban, with a big smile on her face. She's sitting next to the newsagent. She pulls out a flask of tea, a stack of plastic cups and opens a tin of thickly buttered tea brack, offering it to a bleary-eyed Kayla and me.

'For the journey, to keep you going. Very pretty artwork there! Lovely! Are you going all the way to Innisfree?'

Kayla turns towards her too. 'Yes, that's right. Do you know it?'

'Ah, yes. That's where we're headed! Home sweet home! Do you know where to get off? We know Innisfree inside out – any directions you need just ask... My name is Jacinta; this here's my brother Fintan.' She nods at the silver-haired newsagent beside her. 'We live in the centre of town. We have our shops, side by side in the square, so we'll spot you – not much gets past us!' She chuckles warmly.

Kayla and I look at each other with excitement in our eyes. 'Yes, that would be great! We're staying at McDonagh's Guest

House...' We introduce ourselves and shake hands with our new friends.

'Ah very good. Marianne McDonagh does a good breakfast, though her husband Gus does a better one! It's only a stone's throw from the bus stop... we'll get ye there, safe and sound, not a bother.' Jacinta then pokes her head through the seats. 'Are ye here on holidays?'

'We're going to make it a holiday,' Kayla assures her, shooting me a warning glance. 'I can't wait to go out, go dancing, explore the area. Any recommendations?'

Fintan replies, 'Ah, plenty. You'll not be stuck. There's music, crafts, food, drink, dance – you'll have a great time.'

'Sounds like fun!' Kayla and I say in unison.

'Sure, we might have a drink together in The Tap House – the more, the merrier,' says Jacinta.

I smile at Kayla as I lick the taste of sweet cinnamon tea brack from my lips.

The remainder of the journey passes in a whirr of conversation, stories from Fintan and Jacinta's childhood, about running their shops, and how the annual market fair sees the town come alive. I'm reminded of Rory and his fond memories as a child. Good times, he'd said. From what I've seen and how I feel already, I don't doubt it, Rory.

We happily take their advice on where to go and what to do while we're here, enjoying learning so much before our arrival in Innisfree.

Jacinta pokes her head forward once more. 'And what's bringing you to Innisfree? I'd have thought two fine young girls such as yourselves would want a big city like Dublin with the nightclubs and what have you.'

'We were invited by James O'Connor – he's from Innisfree,' I tell her.

Jacinta smiles knowingly and shimmies back in her seat.

'James O'Connor, is it? Well, I cannot say I blame you one bit. He's an absolute ride...'

Fintan gives her a playful slap on the hand. 'Jacinta Mooney, God forgive you! Where do you think you're talking?'

Kayla and I exchange grins.

'Sure, amn't I only saying what every woman with half a pulse is thinking? There's no shame in admiring a thing of beauty, Fintan! I've told James O'Connor a thousand times if I told him once, if he was thirty-two years older, we'd be riding' – she giggles – 'into the sunset together. Sure, he was devastated when I told him he was too young for me and he'd never get his chance...'

'Arah, will you stop with yer nonsense, Jacinta! Honestly, you're losing your marbles.'

Jacinta drops an eye to her brother and he curls his lip at her.

Fintan shakes his head, brow furrowed. 'Which James O'Connor are you on about? I can't place him... Sure, my memory isn't what it was.'

'O'Connor's Solicitor's – the office is across from The Tap House?' Jacinta reminds him.

Fintan still shakes his head. 'Is it Jonathan O'Connor, you mean? Small man, serious, always wears a bow tie, has a limp now – arthritis probably no more than myself...' Fintan glances down at his stiff and swollen fingers.

'Aye, that's the father you're thinking of, but right family,' Jacinta says knowingly. 'O'Connor's Solicitors are in Innisfree for generations. One of the best solicitors around. The father is very by the book. James was a bit of a headcase when he was younger, but he's come up in the world. Very handsome, lovely head of black hair on him. He's settled down now, sure that's only natural – there's a little wildness in us all... even you back in the day, Fintan.'

I think on James as being a bit of a wild one. I guess that

makes sense – the way he stepped in to break up the fight at the Fox tells me he's no stranger around trouble. His eyes were intense, his body tense, and he had a certain air about him. He said something that made everyone stop and take a breath, then turn around and walk away. You don't learn that kind of thing at university, only from lived experience.

But Fintan still looks at a loss. 'I can't place this James fella.'

'Surely you remember him...' Jacinta leans closer and speaks into his ear, her voice low and hushed.

Fintan's eyes open wider, as if hearing something shocking, then squint carefully as he takes it in.

As soon as Jacinta pulls away, they both make the sign of the cross and murmur, 'May they rest in peace.'

Fintan nods, a look of admiration on his face. 'Ah, now I know who you're talking about – he doesn't fit the typical solicitor stereotype, which threw me off. He's a decent guy – he shouldn't beat himself up over what happened; it was an awful accident. Tragic. It shook the whole town. And not the first tragedy he's met with either. But he's doing his best and that's all anyone can do. He helped Jacinta and I out with some computer issues – we're both none too savvy when it comes to the modern technology...'

Did I hear that correctly? James shouldn't blame himself for something? What awful accident occurred?

Kayla senses my confusion and quickly jumps in to change the subject and lighten the tone. 'So, The Tap House, is that a pub?'

Jacinta nods excitedly. 'Aye, it is indeed. They're open till midnight most nights, often later than that, live music and the like – you'll find James in there at some point of the week. Very sociable, knows everyone, but sure, he's working every hour God sends, no time for anything except a few pints in the village.'

'Bless me soul, brothers and sisters! Will you listen to our good lady here? Sure, she wants the whole town to know their business! Jacinta's like a Sky News reporter – up to date with the goings-on, whether we like it or not.'

Jacinta feigns innocence and stares wide-eyed at us all before continuing with her story. 'It's true though, they do keep late hours at the office... James is always there late – you can see the lights on from the street. Someone told me they heard he's working on some big mess of a will – when there's a will, there's a headache...'

Kayla looks at Jacinta curiously. 'What do you mean? What messy will?'

Fintan takes a deep breath, clearly amused by his sister's chatter. 'Well, now we're curious, are we not?' He laughs heartily.

Jacinta smirks as she looks back at her brother before responding to Kayla. 'Well, I hear tell that James O'Connor has been out and about trying to find the inheritor of Mick Kennedy's estate.'

In perfect unison, they both bow their heads, make a sign of the cross and whisper, 'May he rest in peace.' And then they both just snap back into the present moment, right back into the chat where we left off. I'm feeling overwhelmed as I attempt to take in the new facts about Mick Kennedy before we even hit Innisfree. My mind is spinning in circles, overloaded with a myriad of questions and thoughts. It feels like a never-ending cycle of information, and although I want to know as much as possible, I'm struggling to keep up.

'Big mystery who Mick left it all to – he had no children, no wife, no family... but he left it to someone.' Jacinta shakes her head in amazement. 'Cases like that don't come around here often, if ever!'

Fintan pats his sister's shoulder reassuringly. 'Now, Jacinta, don't get ahead of yourself – I'm sure he'll figure it all out.' He turns to Kayla with an apologetic smile. 'As much as my sister loves to spread rumours around town, none of them are ever malicious... just idle gossip.' He squints at me, his brows furrowed. 'Have I seen you before? There's something familiar about you.'

Jacinta gapes. 'Are you a famous person? A musician or an actor? What have we seen you in?'

I shake my head firmly. 'Not in the slightest. Nothing since I played a donkey in the school nativity.'

Jacinta snickers, but Fintan keeps on scrutinising me.

'That's not it... Gosh, I can't put my finger on it.'

Jacinta turns to him. 'Could you please stop gawking at the lady like she's a criminal on a wanted poster? It's way past your nap time, Fintan. Let your poor brain take a break and you'll remember.'

Kayla nudges me, as if to prompt me to come clean.

I take a deep breath before speaking. 'Actually... James O'Connor has found the mystery heir. It was my mother.'

Jacinta and Fintan both gasp in astonishment at my revelation.

'Your mother!' Fintan exclaims, shaking his head in disbelief.

I smile reassuringly. 'And that's why we're here – to check it out and go from there.'

Fintan's hands fly to his face. 'Well, on my oath, I see it now... Rose Clarke. As I live and breathe, Rose Clarke is your mother... Am I right?' He fixes his gaze on me with a round-eyed look of astonishment.

I nod, unable to contain my own surprise. 'Yes! Wow, yes. Do I really look that much like her?' Three decades had passed since anyone's last sighting of my mother back in Innisfree, but, as James had warned, the villagers seem to have a long memory – an almost supernatural ability to recall faces and names from the distant past. Could it be this easy for me to uncover pieces of my history? All I need is a few conversations with the right people, asking the right questions – voila!

Jacinta is practically bouncing on the spot now, clutching at her necklace in amazement as if trying to take it all in. 'Well, well, well! Mick left the lot to Rose Clarke... and now her daughter is here to claim it!' She puts a hand up to her forehead in an exaggerated gesture of shock.

Fintan shakes his head. 'I can't believe it.' He looks me up and down with sparkling eyes. 'I knew it – I knew there was something about you.' He grins warmly at me before continuing. 'No wonder you looked familiar! You have your mother's features! The hair, the eyes...'

I smile gratefully at Fintan before replying, 'It's true – although she unfortunately passed away. So that's why James came to see me and asked me to visit.'

'Oh, a beautiful woman, taken too soon,' says Jacinta, her face creasing in concern. She takes my hand in hers, the soft skin of her palm cool against my own. 'I'm so sorry for your loss, Daisy. My sincere condolences.'

Jacinta and Fintan both lower their heads and utter a silent prayer this time around.

'Thank you,' I reply, my voice little more than a whisper.

For a moment, we sit in silence, all lost in our own thoughts.

Fintan nods thoughtfully and looks around the bus. 'Well, it's no surprise that there was a veil of silence over the whole matter,' he says finally before clapping his hands decisively. 'Goes to show, nobody really knows what goes on behind closed doors.' He smiles at me warmly, but Jacinta coughs into her fist, giving him a warning look.

'How did you know my mother?' I ask, curious now.

'She worked for me for a little while. Very hard worker was Rose; she was always willing to put in a shift wherever she was needed,' Fintan says, a faraway look in his eyes.

'She was a lovely girl,' adds Jacinta. 'A free spirit, very beautiful, I was always so jealous of her long wavy hair... she was like a film star.'

I'm not sure how to respond. It feels strange to be talking about my mother with someone who knew her. 'Thank you,' I say.

Jacinta nods. 'Ah, but she had a light inside her – that's what made her so special. It shone out of her eyes, especially when she laughed. I can still see her laughing, throwing her head back, that cascade of hair tumbling down her back... She had many admirers, her choice of men.'

Fintan pauses and shakes his head, wringing both hands. 'So, The Lake House has passed on to you now?'

I nod.

'How did they find you? Nobody knew anything about Rose since the moment she left – decades ago. It was like she vanished into thin air.'

'I'm not sure,' I tell him honestly. 'All I know is that Mick left her his estate and everything else is still a mystery.'

'Hmmm,' Jacinta mutters, her eyebrows coming together in a contemplative fashion. 'So James O'Connor, as executor of the will, tracked you down and brought you here. And what did your mother tell you about why she left Innisfree?'

'Nothing,' I reply, my voice wavering. 'She never said a word.'

'I see,' Fintan responds slowly, his tone shifting.

'Was she happy here?' I ask, needing to know.

'Yes, for a long time,' Jacinta says. 'But this place was too small for the likes of Rose Clarke, so when I heard that she'd upped and left in a midnight flit, I wasn't surprised. She needed something more, something bigger than this town could offer her.'

'Do you know why she left?' I ask, my heart sinking at the thought of why my mum had chosen to leave everything here for a difficult life in a cramped London bedsit, trying to make ends meet from week to week, always worried about eviction and what lay around the next corner. Was it the promise of a better life, or was it something else that pushed her away? I'm already left with even more questions than before I arrived.

'Nobody will ever get to the real truth,' Jacinta says, shrugging. 'Just small talk, idle gossip. You know how it is in a small place.'

I don't actually. But think I'm about to find out.

CHAPTER 16

THE LOCALS

Fintan looks at the sky from the window, storm clouds gathering. 'I hope you girls brought clothes for all weather – can be changeable this time of year – one moment sunshine, the next thunder and lightning.'

We shake our heads. 'Actually, our suitcases never made it from London – all we have is what we're wearing.'

Jacinta gasps, taking in me in my T-shirt and jeans and Kayla in her tiny jacket and heels. 'Well, we can't have that! Listen, call into my shop tomorrow – I have a boutique! It's called Jacinta's, so you can't miss it. Everyone knows me – if you get lost, just ask and they'll point you in the right direction.'

Fintan winks at us. 'Thrift shop – like a bazaar in there, second-hand, you know.'

She knocks him in the ribs. 'You wouldn't know a boutique if it bit you on the nose, Fintan. Anyway, I have all sorts – shoes, coats, dresses, jewellery, bric-a-brac of every description, a bit of everything. I'll make sure you girls are kitted out for whatever the weather brings.'

We grin at each other, relieved that we have someplace to find some clean clothing to get us through till our bags arrive.

Fintan smirks. 'Yes, you'll fit right in after Jacinta has given you a makeover – be sure to call in to me next door at the newsagents; I like a good laugh. Two young ladies from London wearing the latest trends from Jacinta's boutique!'

Jacinta just smiles.

Fintan turns back to us. 'You two will have a grand time in Innisfree for sure... it's been a pleasure talking; now I'm going to get some shut-eye until we reach the next stop.'

Jacinta winks at us as he dozes off.

We pass farmland, streams and small country lanes filled with hedgerows draped with ivy and wildflowers, cows with their calves grazing on the roadside and tiny villages of stone houses and single-storey shops with smoking chimneys. I wonder about the lives behind those doors. The farmers coming home for lunch after their morning of working in the fields, children sitting up at the kitchen table doing their homework, sheepdogs napping in the afternoon sunlight...

I look out the window, my eyes searching for a hint of the past, something that I can recognise, that gives a clue as to who my mother was. I long for the memories I don't have, to connect the dots, colour in the blank spaces. But all I can find are signs of a life that had carried on, without a trace of her. Sadness washes over me as I realise that the times my mother had known are as far away as they are dear to me. I put down the sketchpad Fintan gifted me earlier and close it carefully, allowing my thoughts to drift away as I do so.

'This is like a dream,' Kayla says. 'I feel like we've stepped into a fairy tale.'

'Hope it has a happy ending,' I tell her.

The bus pulls up to the tiny village of Innisfree, and I can't help but be taken aback by its quaint charm. Picturesque buildings line the town square, each one painted in cheery pastel shades and with window boxes overflowing with vibrant blooms. Pubs and restaurants bustle with locals and tourists alike. It's gorgeous.

We help Fintan and Jacinta with their heavy bags.

'Much appreciated,' says Jacinta, her soft gaze focusing on me. 'Your mother was a good woman. I'm glad she now has somewhere in Innisfree to call home. And I may be speaking out of turn here... but talk to Moya Collins if you get the chance; she can be a hard one to pin down, an even harder one to crack open, but Moya and Rose were childhood friends as I remember.' She wraps a scarf around her neck and ties it tight under her chin to ward off the rising winds. 'She lives in a caravan by the lake,' she adds as she sets off.

Fintan grabs me gently by the wrist. 'But be careful, won't you? Of who you talk to and what you say. Some people around here don't like being asked questions about what's gone before.' He casts a sideways glance, leans in and whispers, 'This place has a habit of claiming its own.'

A chill runs up my spine at these words – was it a warning or just old superstition? I look around the unfamiliar town. The truth is, I don't know what to expect here, and now part of me is wondering if I'll get the warm welcome that I've been hoping for.

The sky darkens as clouds, like massive grey beasts, race across the horizon. Soon, big fat raindrops begin to pour down from the heavens like tears from an endless mourning sky. The weight of it settles on Fintan's shoulders like a shroud, and with one last determined nod, he strides towards the square, his black coat billowing out behind him like the wings of a raven in flight.

CHAPTER 17

THE GUEST HOUSE

'Ugh!' I cry out, as Kayla and I pull our jackets up over our heads to protect ourselves from the downpour. Fintan had been right about the sudden change in weather – the sky had gone from blue to black within minutes.

We stumble wildly across the small, narrow alleyways of Innisfree in the direction of the bed and breakfast as rain pelts us from every direction. A lightning bolt suddenly illuminates the sky, followed by a thunderous boom that shakes the ground beneath us. Then, the rain comes pouring down even more fiercely.

'Look.' Kayla's voice echoes down the cobbled street in a chorus of excitement and relief. Her mascara runs down her face in rivulets, but she doesn't seem to care as she thrusts a long, cherry-red fingernail up towards the faded hand-painted sign swinging above a door. 'This must be it,' she yells with a grin that could light up the darkened alley.

We run for shelter in the doorway of the cute little town-house. Ivy clings to its walls, and soft pink shutters and curtains hang from the windowsills. The flower boxes have been filled with a rainbow of petals, and it appears as if garden gnomes are having parties on each sill, bustling around, fishing and laughing.

Kayla's slender fingers curl around my arm, her knuckles white, her gaze darting between me and our unfamiliar surroundings. We have never been to Ireland before and the cobblestone streets, old, weathered buildings and the salty sea air seem alien and surreal. Yet, something within me stirs with familiarity, my soul recognising a place I've been before. A deep sense of peace settles over me. It's the first time I feel calm in weeks.

I press the doorbell and we wait, trying to catch our breath, completely drenched and shivering. 'Wow, this storm came out of nowhere! I swear it felt like summer a few hours ago!' I exclaim as I look out at the street, now drowning in three feet of water. The path, which is lined with flower beds, has turned into a flowing river. A fierce wind whips my hair into my face and I have to blink to see out of the rain.

Lights turn on in the house, and the door swings open, revealing a gorgeous blonde woman wearing a red tea dress and indoor slippers. She smiles at us from ear to ear with her hands clasped and her shoulders slightly bent, radiating warmth and hospitality.

'Please, come in, come in! Make yourselves at home,' she gushes, ushering us inside and closing the door behind us.' She grabs my hand and pulls me in for a friendly embrace, then wraps her arms around Kayla and gives her two quick kisses on the cheeks. The diamond on her left hand glints in the light, reflecting a spectrum of colours as she motions for us to step into the warmth of the lobby.

'Oh, and look at you; you're drenched through! This weather! Changes by the hour. It'd nearly make you believe in all the climate change hoo-ha. Just hang your clothes over there by the heater and I'll get you some hot tea to warm you up.'

She scans our faces in turn, her gaze lingering longer on

mine. 'My name is Marianne McDonagh. It's so lovely to meet you!' Her voice is soft like the ticking of a clock, with an Irish accent.

'Thank you so much, Marianne. We're sorry for being so late and for arriving in wet clothes. Unfortunately, we don't have any dry clothes to change into as our bags never arrived in Dublin!'

'Well, well, you have had quite the journey, but not to worry – you're here now. I'll gather some nice warm clothes for you.' She looks down at Kayla's stiletto boots. 'I can't claim that they'll be high-fashion designer items – but they are clean and comfy and practical, so that's the most important thing!'

After a few minutes, Marianne reappears with an armful of clothes and leads us up to our room.

'The clothes should fit you fine – there's a bathroom just down the hall if you need it. I'll leave you to get changed and settled in. Tea will be ready in the kitchen whenever you come down.'

As Marianne leaves us to our own devices, we walk up the soft, carpeted stairs of the guest house and open the door to our shared bedroom. The room is from another time, with flowery wallpaper and a mountain of crochet cushions on the four-poster bed. There's a vase of fresh wildflowers on the dresser and a basket of fruit next to the bed.

Kayla throws her arms up in joy, jumping onto the bed and laughing as she grabs a handful of colourful pillows. 'Home sweet home!' she exclaims as she turns around in circles.

She rips off her wet clothes and pulls on the antiquated flannel nightdress and bulky woolly cardigan that Marianne has left out. The oversized pink nightdress drapes over her petite frame, and its sleeves fall well past her hands, the fabric billowing out at her sides like a sail in gentle wind. Neither of us can stop laughing – she looks like Grandma Wolf, straight out of

'Little Red Riding Hood'. A hilarious make-under for a girl who always dresses to impress.

She sinks her feet into huge fluffy slippers, making it look as if she's shuffling forward on two tufts of cloud as she walks over to the window and pulls the curtains. The night sky is dark and starless; all that can be heard is the occasional bark of a dog in the distant night air. Everything is so different here from what I'm used to back home – not just in appearance, but in feel too. It's like stepping into a world sealed from the ravages of time.

'Are you coming downstairs to have tea with Marianne?' I ask.

She shakes her head no. 'I'm exhausted. All I want to do is get into bed and snuggle up for a good night's sleep!'

With that, Kayla climbs into bed and shoves her slippers out from beneath the covers. 'I'm going to buy these from Marianne! Nothing so comfortable has ever graced my feet!' Kayla waggles the giant sheepskin fluffballs and gives a little giggle.

I quickly shimmy into my comfortable fleece pyjama set, with a cute cow emblazoned on the front that says 'moo-tiful' and admire the stunning photographs of countryside vistas on the wall and the exquisite bedspread with its embroidered pink flowers. A swell of happiness surges within me as I realise that we have successfully reached Innisfree. We've made it, and that's something to be proud of.

'You've read this, right?' Kayla says, holding up her phone to show me an e-book cover on her Kindle with the title *Into Your Depth*.

'Self-help? I don't do self-help, Kayla. Since when do you do self-help? I thought you only read erotica and baking books.'

Kayla raises her hands defensively. 'I know, I know – but this is different! I'm doing the social-media campaign for a client – she's an influencer and wants to seem deep, so she's paying me to read it and post ideas on her takeaways.'

I shake my head. 'So instead of a body double, you're a brain double.'

Kayla replies, 'That's exactly what I am. What can I say? Everyone wants a piece of this.' She puckers her lips and blows me a sassy kiss. 'Anyway, thought you'd be proud that all of your reading lessons are finally paying off! I never read anything more than a take-away menu before I met you... it's not like I'm about to get a Nobel Prize or anything, but I know I can do it and that feels good... thanks to you.'

'And how's it going? Any big, deep viral #insights yet?'

'Yes, actually, Little Miss Cynical. It's about how we need to change along with change – nothing is as it was, we are not the same. What other option do we have but to adapt? *Into Your Depth* is a guide for our times. Read it and believe me, you'll never look at life in the same way again.'

I take the phone from her and scroll to read the blurb. It's written by Nami Zen, a renowned academic whose TED talks have gone viral. 'Let yourself really feel your feelings.' I can't think of anything worse than having to sit here feeling all my feelings. 'Your triggers are your teachers.' And what if 'teachers' are actually your triggers? As in you get yelled at for no reason or told off publicly because your PE kit isn't exactly linen-fresh because you share a washing machine with forty other parent-less teenagers. I hated school, I couldn't wait to leave, so I don't think Nami Zen's words are going to change my life after all.

I hand the phone back to Kayla. 'Thanks but no thanks.'

'Suit yourself. Nighty night for me, Daisy,' Kayla says with a yawn. 'I'm wrecked and this bed is sooooo comfortable... I'm turning in. I'll see you in the morning, okay?'

'Of course – you sleep. Goodnight.'

She's already curled up under the covers, breathing softly, her eyelids slowly blinking, the swirl of her dark hair against the pillow. I carefully fold the edges of her blanket, making sure it's snug around her. My fingertips brush against her soft skin, memories of our time together at the children's home flooding my mind: chatting into the night, waking each other in time for breakfast in the morning, sneaking in snacks and treats, especially when there were tears, disappointments and DIY ear-piercing disasters. Without her, I would never have made it this far – family may not be something you can choose, but thank goodness for friends like Kayla.

I'm too buzzed by the day's events, especially meeting Jacinta and Fintan – they knew everybody! Including my mother! They're the first people I've ever met that knew her from here in Ireland. They said she was lovely. No scandal attached. And the landscape as we travelled down – exactly as she'd painted the scenes in our bedtime stories. I can't help it, I feel close to her here. I feel like she could be in the next room. Just out of sight, just next door, just popped out; not gone, not forgotten, not erased. And that feels wonderful to me. So wonderful that I don't have the vocabulary I need to express it fully. That's where art comes in for me. Easier to express in shapes and colours and textures – in ways that can't be put into words. Without my art supplies, I have no other option than to attempt to capture as much of the landscape as I can in quick sketch form. My fear is that some of the details will evade me, that I won't get a chance to fully capture what I'm seeing on paper, and that this opportunity might slip away from me. I'm eager to make the most of every opportunity, both for my art and for my research into my mother's past. I don't want to squander any chance or clue that comes my way.

Jacinta has already kindly given me a name, a contact – Moya Collins, who lives in a caravan by the lake. Moya might be the only lead I ever get, so I'll chase her up. I have a month to uncover all I can and then I'm back to London, most probably never to return to Innisfree. I can't see any reason why I would – the house will be sold, and I know Ash will have no interest in coming here – he's much more of a Maldives kind of guy – sea, sand, open bar and being waited on hand and foot. I can't picture him roughing it on the bumpy bus from Dublin and then languishing in the Irish countryside getting excited about old pubs and local history – a little too much peace and quiet and spontaneous bursts of thunderclap for him.

But at the same time, despite my desire to get answers, Fintan's solemn warning reminds me that I have to tread carefully or I'll ruin my chances of learning anything about my mother. Rather than being too direct and intrusive, I need to take a subtler approach. I know that if I'm going to get any useful information, it's best to stay cool and collected. Settle in, spend some time here, getting to know the locals and the place before I start ruffling feathers by asking questions about people and events from decades ago. By paying close attention, some of the secrets surrounding my mother's past could slowly reveal themselves, without me having to disturb too much earth in the process.

I'm wide awake. All the perplexities of Mick Kennedy, Moya Collins and James O'Connor in Innisfree are rolling around in my head; I need to take some time to process all of this information. It's best I don't keep Marianne waiting so I make my way down to the kitchen for a cup of tea.

CHAPTER 18

THE TEA

The kitchen is so warm and inviting, with a fire crackling in the stove and the hot savoury smell of home cooking in the air. Marianne bustles around, placing a large chunk of butter and a jar of home-made blackberry jam on the table before sitting down.

'Help yourself, my love! You must be starved after your journey.'

I settle into a well-worn chair, steam rising from my cup of tea I've just poured from the cast-iron kettle. I inhale deeply the aroma of the rich roasted beef-and-vegetable stew bubbling away on the hob.

Marianne bends over to light a candle in the middle of the table, and as she does so, I admire her Marilyn Monroe-style hair, glossy waves catching the candlelight and looking like spun gold, with only a few strands of grey visible around her temples. She's perhaps in her late forties. About the same age my mum would have been. Maybe they knew each other? Maybe they were in the same class at school?

She tilts her head and smiles, her blue eyes sparkling in the low light. 'Just to let you know,' she tells me, 'I won't be here in the morning. I'm at my craft morning at the town hall – candle-making tomorrow. Hopefully it won't get on my wick!'

She has a contagious laugh and I can't help but smile in response. Marianne seems the perfect host, making me feel right at home.

'Not a problem though; my husband Gus and my daughter Grace will be here to serve you breakfast – if she isn't out too late partying. Between them, they'll make sure everyone's taken care of.'

'Oh, don't worry about it,' I tell her. 'No need for you to go out of your way. Cereal and coffee will do just fine.'

She shakes her head and looks me in the eye. 'No, I don't think so! Not while you're here under my roof! You'll be taken care of like family!'

'That's really kind of you, Marianne,' I reply.

'Well, speaking of family.' She smiles. 'If you see a grumpy-looking man, with a big brown beard, in overalls stomping around the place, that's my brother-in-law, Stephen – he helps us out with some odd jobs around the garden and such. He's mostly in the shed or garage, but he does pop in here throughout the day.' She lowers her voice and enunciates every word as if she wants me to lip-read. 'He's having some marital difficulties right now, and some personal difficulties, and some professional difficulties, so he's staying with us for a while. In and out at all hours... but that's family, eh?'

She wrings her hands in her apron, pours herself a cup of tea and joins me at the table. 'So, tell me, Daisy, what is it you do for a living?'

Marianne's eyes widen in surprise as I tell her about my work as a children's illustrator, her face brightening with recognition at the mention of the *Forest Fables* series.

'Oh my word!' she exclaims. 'They were my children's absolute favourites. Red Fox and Rev Magpie, Old Owl – my goodness me does that take me back! My two loved those stories so much.'

She pauses for a moment and her eyes well up with tears as she reminisces about simpler times with her family. 'I would do anything to have those days back when I had both my children clutched tightly in my arms – everything was simpler then. Such wonderful days! Unlike now. The eldest has already left and the other is just waiting for her chance to fly away. Do you have kids?' she inquires. I shake my head. 'You'll understand once you do; it's a roller coaster of emotions. One moment you'd give your life up for them and the next, you want nothing more than to strangle them.' She chuckles, lightening the mood. 'So, you're here to find your "muse", right? That's what they say.'

'I hope so! I think it's good to get away from all the city noise, and hustle and bustle. Even on the bus journey here, I already felt a little spark of creativity, toying with some new ideas. Coming to Innisfree might just be the right thing at the right time for me.'

'Yes, you're definitely in the right spot!' she says with enthusiasm. 'I think my two kids loved those books so much because they felt like it was set right here – we used to picnic by The Lake House, reading the stories together. If you're looking for inspiration, go there. It feels as though you're walking into the very heart of it.'

My heart jumps at this description. Fate really has led me here. I want to ask Marianne more about The Lake House. I want to know everything; I don't want to risk wasting my chances by treading too carefully and taking things slowly.

I jump in too quickly to tell her about my connection to The Lake House and end up swallowing a massive hot mouthful of tea at the same time. It goes down the wrong way and I start coughing uncontrollably. Marianne fetches me a napkin and gives me an opportunity to recover myself.

As I get my breath back, a large black cat strides in through the kitchen door and hops onto the counter.

'Oh, you little devil, you! Always up to no good!' Marianne scoops him into her arms and scratches him behind the ears. He's obviously the apple of her eye. 'This is my boy, Oscar. Say hello to our new guest, Daisy, and don't be poking around in her business, making a nuisance of yourself!' She laughs as she tries to shoo him away, but he just jumps back up on the counter and curls up into a ball, purring contentedly.

'I think he likes you.' Marianne smiles as she goes back to her tea.

I laugh, feeling completely at ease in this strange place. 'He's lovely. Hello, Oscar.' I reach out and pet him cautiously on the head – so soft and fluffy. He likes that and purrs louder. 'I'm sure I'll see you around.'

'You most certainly will! Oscar Wilde we call him, because he's a rascal – so cheeky. If he tries to come into your room, feel free to send him away again – you've no respect for boundaries, do you, Oscar?'

I tickle him under the neck. 'Well, he is a real cutie and I'd love his company. My boyfriend is allergic, so we can't keep pets. My flat is too small anyway, so it wouldn't be fair. I'll be in my element with a new little furry friend,' I tell her.

Oscar purrs and rubs his head against my hand.

'He was my eldest son's cat – Ciaran. But he left us all for a shiny new job in America – of course, Mum's here to pick up the pieces, left minding the cat. Innisfree may not be Chicago, but it's home.'

'It's charming,' I say to my companion. 'I can see why you love it here.'

'Aye, that's the truth. It's a special place, to be sure. We may not have much, but what we do have is worth more than all the gold in the world. Certain things you can't put a price on – family, health, happiness. That's what matters in life.'

I nod. 'I can't wait to start exploring tomorrow.' I take my chance. 'First stop, The Lake House!' I tell her, hoping I can resurrect the topic.

'Oh, that's a grand plan,' she says with a smile. She then bows her head as if remembering something. 'You'll be sure to enjoy yourself. But it might look a little different as the man who owned it died recently. Everyone knew him; he was a real character, always wearing that silly cowboy hat of his and making everyone laugh. Of course, it's empty now since he passed; a terrible shame to watch it be left to rack and ruin.'

My heartbeat quickens as my mind races with questions, but I force myself to take a deep breath. To slow down. My curiosity is on overdrive, but Fintan's warnings echo in my head. One wrong move could unravel everything.

My voice wavers as I finally ask my question, slowly and carefully. 'What was his name?'

I know what she's going to say, but I don't want to leap in and push too far and lose my chance to learn anything else.

'His name was Michael Kennedy, but everyone here called him Mick.'

'A character, you say?' I ask, smiling.

'Oh, aye. That he was. You'll be hearing stories about him for years to come, I'm sure. He was a bit of a rogue, but we loved him all the same. Well, most of the time – other times I could have wrung his neck, but it takes all sorts.'

Marianne's eyes mist over with sadness and she takes a sip of her tea before continuing.

'He was always one for a bit of fun, Mick was. He loved a good prank, and he was always up for a laugh. But he had a heart of gold, and he would do anything for anybody. He will be missed. Anyway,' she says, shaking herself out of her reverie, 'that's enough from me. I'm sure you didn't come here to listen to me prattle on about the dearly departed.'

'I don't mind at all,' I say truthfully. 'It's nice to get to know the locals. He sounds like he knew how to have a good time.'

Marianne lets out a soft, tinkling laugh, and the corners of her mouth lift into a warm smile. Her eyes twinkle with amusement as she says, 'Oh yes. He sure did, but he always ended up going too far. Just like Red Fox in *Forest Fables*! About this time last year, I went by his house – a beautiful spot on a fine day – to pick some wildflowers and, lo and behold, who should I see but Mick himself, skinny-dipping in the lake! In broad daylight! Buck naked! Not a stitch on him. Let's just say, the water level wasn't as high as I'd have liked that day.'

I can't help but laugh. 'Really! That must have been quite a sight!'

Marianne nods in agreement and takes another sip of her tea. 'It certainly was.' She chuckles softly, shaking her head fondly at the memory of Mick's antics. 'As bare as the day he was born – standing up stark naked as happy as Larry, like it was the most natural thing in the world! Not a bother on him. I called out to him – "Mick, you've lost your marbles! What will the neighbours think?" But he just laughed, waved and said, "They're used to it, Marianne! And don't bother looking for my marbles – I know exactly where they are." I shook my head at him, though I couldn't help but laugh. And then he beckoned me over – "Don't be shy, Marianne," he said. "There's just about room for two." I told him I wasn't getting in the water with him. His only modesty was his silly cowboy hat and big red beard! He laughed and said, "Suit yourself, Marianne. But remember: To live is the rarest thing in the world. Most people exist, that's all!" And then he went back to splashing about in the lake like a big kid. Anyway,' she says with a sigh, 'that was Mick – wild and free as only he could be.' She shakes her head and blesses herself. 'And God have mercy on him, three weeks later he was dead. In the water no less... wanted to test out a boat James

O'Connor had helped him build – of course, it sank like a stone...'

'I'm so sorry for your loss,' I say with a heavy heart, finally understanding what Fintan had been trying to tell me about James and the tragedy. I'm in shock that Mick lost his life due to this 'awful accident'. Connecting the pieces makes me feel queasy. I hadn't expected it would be this bad, that such an accident directly caused his untimely death. James was clearly involved somehow, but I don't want to delve in too deeply. I don't want to delve at all. I recall how intrusive people were when my mother died; demanding grisly details and gory specifics as if those mattered more than her heart-shattering loss. The weight of the matter is palpable, and the little kitchen feels smaller, suffocating even.

'Yes, well. He was lucky the whole lifeboat rescue team weren't drowned along with him,' Marianne sighs. 'As for James O'Connor, he should just stick to his own business and leave everything else be – stop bringing trouble and tragedy.'

'Was James in the boat also when it capsized?' I ask.

Marianne shakes her head. 'No, James was probably sleeping off pints of ale! He might have saved Mick if he had been with him!'

'So he wasn't even there?' I ask, bewildered by James's connection to Mick's death.

She snorts, her opinion of the situation extremely clear.

'Make no mistake, James is the one to blame for this catastrophe: a good lawyer should know all about liability, and he was helping Mick build this stupid boat, and then Mick set off with it before it was sea-worthy – and we all know what came after that.'

We sit in silence, each lost in our own thoughts. The atmosphere is fraught with an uncomfortable quietness as I try to make sense of all this. I sip my tea slowly. It sounds to me like it wasn't his fault at all, sounds like Mick had taken the boat out on his own, of his own free will. But clearly some people feel James was responsible. Perhaps even James feels responsible. Is that the reason he went to such ends to seek me out in London? Is he trying to atone for something?

'James was a friend of Ciaran. They were born the same year. And from such a good, respectable family, not to mention James' poor mother... Bad luck follows him around like a curse.'

Suddenly, Oscar screeches and lashes out, taking a swipe at Marianne's wrist.

'Oh, another feisty fella here,' she says. 'Two-faced as they come! One moment we're best friends, the next sworn enemies – you never know what to expect from this one!'

I can't help but laugh, and the tension in the room dissipates a little.

'Anyway,' she continues, 'what I'm trying to say is that we must live and let live. No one knows what tomorrow will bring so you must take the bull by the horns and make things happen. Do what you can, when you can.' Marianne's eyes mist over, and she takes a sip of her tea. 'He was a good man, the likes of which we'll not see again.'

For a moment, she seems to recognise something in me, looking on every feature as if she's trying to remember something. Her eyes peer more closely at me, as if she knows me from another time. But then her expression changes and her eyebrows narrow with confusion. She shakes her head quickly, as if trying to erase that thought from her mind, and I feel a ripple of anxiety trickle through my body.

Am I imagining things or is it possible that Marianne also thought she'd seen Rose Clarke's ghost? Every fibre of me wants to ask everyone I meet in this town what they know about my mother, who she really was, what they think happened that made her leave... but I'll watch my step. Not everyone wants the past stirred up, a stranger asking questions about years before.

A bright beam of light pierces through the kitchen window,

leaving behind a searing white line in the night. The crunching of gravel and the rumbling of an engine follows as a car pulls up.

'That's my daughter Grace,' Marianne says to me as she turns away. 'She'll be home from one of her gigs. She sings and plays the guitar all around town – if you hear singing in the shower, it's not a banshee, just her. She's the adventurous sort – loves everything creative, wants to travel the world and throw away her future – bright as a button in school and has been accepted into university to study primary-school teaching. A safe, secure job that comes with summers off and a nice retirement plan – but no one can get through to her about it. Anyway, I better get her some dinner – she'll be starved.'

'Oh my, I hadn't noticed the hour... it's so late!' I say, glancing at the clock on the wall. 'I should let you get back to it.'

'Yes,' Marianne says. 'Grace wouldn't want to hear me going on about old times.' She looks me in the eyes sadly. 'She's heard my tales a thousand times. Well, most of them...'

CHAPTER 19

THE BREAKFAST

'Good morning, miss!' Gus McDonagh, the fill-in chef for this morning, glances at his watch. 'Eight hours straight – you can put that on TripAdvisor!' he exclaims. 'Where's your friend?'

'She's still sleeping,' I reply. 'I've tried to wake her up, but she's so deeply wrapped up in the duvet that it's impossible.'

'Ah, just like Grace.' Gus chuckles. 'She's still flat out in bed and snoring like a sailor – I don't want to wake her. If my wife asks about it, just tell her that Grace helped with the breakfast and we'll keep it a secret, okay? Marianne says I'm too soft, but I don't think that's always a bad thing.' He gives me a smile and throws some bacon out of the kitchen window for Oscar.

I take a moment to stand at the back doorway, breathing in the sweet freshness of the morning air as I get my first glimpse of Innisfree in daylight. The sky is awash with colours ranging from pink to orange, and the sun's rays beam down, making the dew-covered grass glisten. In the distance, I can see rugged cliffs jutting out against the blue-green waters of the Atlantic Ocean. Closer by, clucking chickens dig through thick grass in search of insects, while cows chew contentedly on hay. Everything about this beautiful Irish countryside seems like it's been taken straight off a postcard. A stark contrast to the view from my London flat, where the air is heavy with fumes from the nearby factory and piles of overlooked detritus form mini-mountains in delipidated doorways. I am dwarfed by the rolling hills and lush green fields, but I simultaneously feel liberated. It's as if I'm part of something and infinite – something far beyond myself.

'I can't wait to get out and go exploring,' I remark.

'Fancy a full Irish before you set off?' Gus calls out to me.

My stomach growls in answer, and we gather at the kitchen table for a hearty meal. I tuck into the full Irish breakfast Gus had prepared – delicious eggs, bacon, sausages, black pudding, tomatoes, mushrooms and plenty of toast to soak it all up. 'It'll put hair on my chest!' I joke between bites.

Gus smiles in amusement and watches as I take my time enjoying the meal.

Eventually, the plate is almost clean and I lean back with a satisfied sigh. 'That was delicious! Just what I needed. I'm going to have to hit the gym hard to work it all off.'

'Not much in the way of gyms around here, but plenty of hills and trails if you want to get your heart pumping. So, what's on your plan for today then?' Gus inquires.

'Well, as soon as I manage to get Kayla up, we're making a quick stop at Jacinta Mooney's to pick up some clothes, since our bags never showed up.'

Gus makes a funny face.

'After that, we'll do some sightseeing around here.'

'Sounds like a great plan!' he says.

I startle when I see a small man standing at the back door, his tufted brown beard and worn overalls giving him the look of one of the garden gnomes outside. He kicks off his work boots to reveal socks with holes in them, exposing his heels and toes.

'Good morning, everyone.' He offers a nod to Gus and then

me. 'Do you have any breakfast left, Gus?' He sets down the newspaper he's carrying on the table.

'Plenty, Stephen. Have a seat and I'll get you something right away. This is Daisy, our guest from London.'

Stephen offers me his hand to shake. 'Nice to meet you.' He smiles. 'I'm Stephen McDonagh, and this here is my little brother.' He nods in Gus's direction. 'When did you arrive?'

'Yesterday, just as the storm started. We got soaked.'

Gus sets down a cup of tea beside Stephen, who immediately takes a long sip of it. All the while, he hasn't looked away from me. A mountain of sausages appears on the table in front of him, covered in red sauce.

'Did you come in on the bus from Dublin airport?' Stephen snatches a sausage and takes a hefty bite, his eyes still fixed on me.

I nod, still chewing on some toast.

'You see, I've just been to Fintan Mooney's shop for my newspaper, and I hear that you're here to take possession of the Kennedy estate? Is that right?' His dark eyes bore into mine, the lines of his forehead drawn together in a deep frown.

After swallowing and taking a sip of tea, I answer him. 'News certainly spreads quickly!'

'It really does. So, you're Rose Clarke's daughter?' he asks, the question hanging in the air between us.

I nod slowly, feeling the tension build in the room. 'That's right. Did you know her?'

Stephen stays silent, and I notice his gaze quickly dart away, suddenly avoiding making eye contact with me. He becomes overly focused on his meal, picking apart his sausage with a fork. I wait for Stephen to answer, but he never does.

All I hear is the sound of my own breath.

Gus shakes his head and answers. 'I can't say that I did,' he admits. 'I was away in the States for many years before returning to Innisfree. However, I did know the Kennedys;

they were good people. Old money, of course, but still good people.'

I lean back in my chair and contemplate Gus's words.

'So that solves the mystery of Mick's will,' Gus remarks. 'He left everything to Rose Clarke. And how did they know each other?'

I shrug. 'I don't know – it's all been completely unexpected. James O'Connor came to London saying my mother had inherited a house in Ireland and that the property was now mine to inherit as her closest living relative.'

Gus pauses, head bowed in understanding. 'I'm sorry for your loss,' he says softly. He runs a hand through his silver-streaked hair, an anxious look on his weathered face. 'It sounds like you've got a difficult few weeks ahead. I don't imagine this will be much of a holiday for you. Anything to do with inheritance and property will be messy.' He scratches his chin and nods slowly, showing sympathy.

'Do you think there will be many problems? I mean, I'm the only heir so that should make things more straightforward?'

Gus takes a sip of his tea and thinks for a moment before replying. 'You never know with these things. Jonathan O'Connor will give you some good legal advice. He knows the score on the house, all the personal risk you're now facing...'

'Personal risk I'm facing? I don't follow.'

Stephen nods vigorously in agreement. 'Gus is exactly right. Huge risk now landed on your lap. Get rid ASAP. The last thing you need is a lawsuit for libel or someone getting killed up there. It won't be long until that happens.' His eyes widen as he speaks, and beads of sweat form on his forehead. 'Without any insurance or safety measures, if anything happens, the blood'll be on your hands and the police will be at your door.' He blows out his cheeks. 'I wouldn't sleep a wink while my name was attached to that death trap.'

Blood on my hands? What on earth? Stephen's words have

frightened the bejesus out of me, but it seems he's not finished yet.

I watch and wait as his eyes frantically scan the room, as he hunches forward and says in a lower tone, 'I shouldn't be telling you this, but I got called out to the Kennedy estate last night. Another late-night disturbance. More trouble.'

'Trouble?' I utter, worry starting to set in.

'Yep, troublemakers were raising a ruckus. Whenever trespassers are around, up to no good, the neighbours call me in. We scared them away and made it clear they weren't wanted here.'

'What kind of trouble are they causing?' I ask nervously.

'Drinking, rioting, setting fires, damaging property. Since the old man's death, the place has a reputation for being a party place. Mick's Mansion, they call it. Free – for all. The woods are full of those bums – eco-warriors or whatever they call themselves. Sure, what do you expect when Mick let every waif and stray stay on his land and now people are taking advantage. Look at Moya Collins. She's been there for years and shows no signs of leaving.'

My vision of wildflowers and swimming in the lake has been replaced with images of an old, run-down house surrounded by rowdy partygoers and police tape.

Gus mutters, 'Terrible shame, it used to be such a nice place. Our kiddies loved it there – happy summer days by the lake, picking flowers, not a care in the world.' He shifts his gaze and asks, 'What about the house itself? What condition is it in, Stephen?'

I swallow hard as I wait for his judgement.

Stephen lets out a deep breath and stares at me with weary eyes. 'It ain't lookin' good,' he utters quietly, as if to keep it between the three of us. 'I don't envy you havin' to get that old place back in shape. It's gonna cost a fortune to fix.' He speaks softly, carefully considering his words. 'If you don't mind me askin', what's your plan for it?'

I inhale deeply. 'To sell it. I need the money for a new place in London with my boyfriend,' I confess truthfully.

Stephen nods and grunts in agreement. He steps towards the kitchen entrance, takes a quick glance into the hall and closes the door again. 'Let me give you some advice, Daisy' he begins. 'Get rid of that house swiftly. It brings nothing but misfortune, and it will only bring you grief too.'

'I see,' I say slowly, trying to take in everything that Stephen is saying. It's a lot.

Gus chimes in. 'All is not lost, Daisy. You can put it up for auction and that way you'll have it off your hands in no time – it's all online these days, so you could get bidders in from all over the world – no viewings, no long-winded process, cash buyers only. That's what I'd be looking at if I were you.'

'I'll definitely take your advice into consideration, Gus. Thank you both for your help.'

Which is the complete opposite to how I really feel! What kind of help is this? It only makes me more anxious –if the house is in a complete state of disrepair and looks like it's been taken over by a mob, will anyone want to buy it?

Gus's face tightens as he takes my plate and empty mug. 'Sorry to be the bearer of bad news,' he says quietly.

I offer a weak smile and nod, trying to appear strong. 'No, no it's fine. I appreciate your honesty.' And I do appreciate honesty, even if I'm not always prepared to hear it. Especially when there's so much at stake with this sale.

My phone shrills, and I recognise the number – it's Ash. I excuse myself from the room and slip out the back door to take the call. I give Ash a brief rundown on all the recent events, though not quite in their entirety. I make sure to focus on the good news and assure him that all is going smoothly – which happens to be true. I omit any mention of Stephen; even the mention of his name causes an uneasy feeling in my gut, and I don't want that to carry over to Ash until I've seen the house with my own eyes.

Through the kitchen window, I see the two brothers seated at the table with intent looks on their faces. There seems to be an ongoing conversation between them, even though neither of them speaks a single word.

CHAPTER 20

THE SHOP

The golden sun casts long midday shadows on the cobblestone streets of the quaint Irish village as Kayla and I step into Jacinta's gorgeous vintage boutique, eager to find ourselves some fresh clothes to wear. The mobile on the door tinkles as we enter, the little shop bathed in the warm glow of antique lamps, their shiny brass bases glistening under their soft light. Gorgeous old perfume bottles and elegant jewellery twinkle on the shelves that line the walls, while old-style gowns and tailored suits hang delicately from wrought-iron racks. Fintan had made it sound like a jumble sale, but it's far from it. And I am in love with every last sequined button.

'Welcome! Welcome! It is simply wonderful to see you both,' Jacinta chirps as she steps out from behind the counter, rushing over to greet us with a hug.

As my eyes adjust to the dimly lit room, I can't help but gasp in awe. The walls are draped with fine silks, and shelves of velvet, beaded and lace-embroidered garments of every colour fill the space. I step closer, my fingers running along the luxurious fabric of a dress hanging on a nearby antique wardrobe.

Jacinta watches us excitedly as we browse her wares. The

silver and gold bracelets that adorn her arms clatter musically, and the colourful rings on her hands seem to wink at our reflections in the mirror. With each passing moment, my mouth hangs open a little more and my fingers flex in anticipation. On one hand, I want to buy everything I see. On the other, it all seems so precious and expensive, I want to touch it first, to prove that it's real. Silk and satin, leather and lace, jewels and crystals, velvets and suede.

Each item we choose brings a wave of joy to her face, and when we finish, she looks at us with a mixture of approval and gratitude.

'I can tell you two have excellent taste,' she says warmly. 'It's not often I get customers who appreciate my eclectic stock.'

Kayla's mouth drops. 'You must be joking – this place would be worth a fortune in London! It's got it all – and then some!'

She's not wrong. Jacinta's shop is awash with colour, from the glimmering silver and gold bangles to the pearls studded on necklaces. She has a rainbow of boas, stoles, belts, shoes and bags, so many shapes and colours that it's hard to concentrate on one item for too long. I have never seen such a beautiful place. A gallery of old-world charm.

Once in the changing room, I pull on a dress over my head, the beautiful black silk rippling delicately down my body. I look in amazement at the hand-stitched beadwork that adorns the bodice, as well as the delicate lace along the hemline. The fabric feels like butter against my skin, and I'm suddenly overcome with confidence. The fit is perfect.

Kayla slips into a peachy pink blouse with matching chiffon skirt, while I try on a pair of culotte trousers and a shirt made of fine linen with intricate embroidery along the collar. Jacinta picks out accessories, shoes and even a purse to complete our new looks.

I glance over at Kayla, admiring her newly acquired gold chain belt and buckled Mary Jane shoes. She takes out her phone and we call for a quick selfie. Jacinta finds a feathered hat on the rack, and Kayla and I hug her close. Joyous laughter wells up inside me; it's been far too long since I've felt such lightness, since I've had a good time worth remembering, a moment worth capturing.

Suddenly, my phone vibrates in my pocket. I dig it out, hoping for a message from the airline confirming our luggage has arrived, with all the documents James O'Connor asked me to bring along.

'*ID Passenger Number 3453: We regret to inform you that we are encountering delays in tracking your luggage due to current staffing strikes. We are doing our best to return it to you as soon as possible. We thank you for your patience and understanding and apologise for any inconvenience.*'

I stare in disbelief at the screen, silently hoping I've misread it.

Kayla steps closer, squinting at the screen as she reads the terrible news out loud. 'How can that even happen? It's a direct flight. Honestly.'

Jacinta nods understandingly. 'Ah, my dears, don't worry about clothing – consider this entire store your walk-in wardrobe. Take anything you need for as long as you'd like – it would be my pleasure to have two lovely models wearing these gorgeous dresses around town. These garments weren't made to stay hidden away; they need to be out on display.'

We thank her and I take a seat to keep myself steady. Kayla crouches down beside me and holds my hand, saying, 'Jacinta is right – clothing is sorted. And as for the documents, James can concentrate on other things until they get here.'

I swallow. I know she's right. I'm sure we can get through everything we need to, but there's still one thing that's causing my stomach to churn with dread.

'All my art supplies are in there, Kayla. I'm already skating on thin ice with the boss. She's given me a second chance, but now I don't even have as much as a proper sketchbook.'

I don't know what to tell Lenka; I'm the one who convinced her that I could do this and deliver on all fronts, our ticket to success. What happens to *Forest Fables* if I fail? And me? My career as an illustrator would be over for sure.

I sigh in frustration, feeling overwhelmed. I can't do my job without drawing; I can't draw without my stuff. If I lose my job, I stand to lose everything. I can't afford to put anything in the way of the *Forest Fables* commission, not even this inheritance – not even my mother's story. I'll need to cut this trip short and go home.

Kayla rests her arms around me, attempting to provide some relief, but my heart is still pounding, and my mind is flooding with thoughts of all that's on the line. Feeling utterly defeated, my vision blurs as I blink back tears.

Kayla's voice is soft as she speaks. 'Let's take a step back, okay? We'll find a way through this together. We always have.'

Taking in a deep breath to steady myself, I attempt to refocus my mind on the present.

Jacinta's eyes dance with delight as she lifts a long, jewelled finger. 'Don't worry, girls, I know just what to do – you two stay right there. Don't budge,' she declares, her voice rising as she speeds towards the door.

Kayla and I exchange mystified looks but we stay put, as we are told – not daring to guess what she has in mind.

Within moments, she's back, with Fintan by her side.

'Right, have a look here, Daisy, and tell us what you think.' Fintan hands me a dusty wooden box.

I cautiously open it, my breath catching at the sight of all the art supplies inside. Charcoals, pencils, pastels and paints – the contents of this box are easily worth more and are of much better quality than anything I own.

'Where did you get all this?' I exclaim in disbelief.

'He's always fancied himself as an artist. A great talent in his day, our Fintan,' says Jacinta with a fond smile. 'I got him that set for his birthday one year but you'll see it's pretty much untouched.' She turns to her brother. 'You were going to create your magnum opus with it, right, Fintan?'

He gives a sad smile as he shrugs. 'Indeed, and if I had my time back again, I would have started straight away, without a moment to lose.' He raises his stiff, swollen fingers.

'But I put that particular dream on the backburner, too busy with work and what have you – always something – and then my poor ole hands seized up so I wasn't able. But anyway... at least now it can be put to good use.' Fintan smiles sheepishly as he nods towards the box. 'It's not much, but it might help you get started on what you need to do,' he offers kindly. 'It gives me great relief to see it being put to its purpose. God bless the work, as they say.'

My eyes fill with tears of appreciation as I hug each of them tightly, thanking them for their kindness. Fintan excitedly sorts through the supplies he's brought while handing each item to me individually. His enthusiasm is contagious as I begin to formulate ideas for *Forest Fables*. He shows me how to sharpen pencils with a knife and whispers advice on drawing trees so they look like they're living creatures rather than static objects. Before I know it, we're deep in conversation about our favourite artists and painting techniques, his knowledge far surpassing my own. We spend the rest of the afternoon talking and creating. Not only do I now possess all the necessary tools to complete this project but have also gained a friend and mentor in Fintan. 'Thank you so all much,' I murmur softly, constantly pinching myself to make sure this isn't a dream.

'You look absolutely gorgeous. Dressed up to the nines,' Jacinta exclaims as she tidies up Kayla's collar and gives us both a hug. 'Have a wonderful night and dance the night away!'

'Dancing? Where at?' I ask.

'Why, The Tap House of course. It always has dancing going on just across the road. They have live music every night of the week. You'd better get there early if you want to get a seat.'

Jacinta hands over our bulging shopping bags of clothes that'll get us through the rest of the trip until our luggage appears – *if* our luggage ever appears. 'I always say, we have two hands – one to help ourselves and one to help others,' she says.

Kayla's face lights up. 'I love that, Jacinta! In that spirit, let me do something for you. Why don't I take a few pictures of the merchandise you have here? I'll style it up into a quick gallery and add it to a vintage marketplace app. It won't take long – we can do it now if you like? If I'm right, people will be dying to get their hands on these items in no time at all.'

Jacinta claps her hands in delight. 'Really? Oh, that would be wonderful.'

I pick up Kayla's bag for her. 'I'll drop this stuff off at Marianne's and meet you at The Tap House in an hour.'

Before I leave, she winks at me. I feel so at home here in the village, and with all the villagers; it only makes me wonder all the more why my mother would have ever left.

CHAPTER 21

THE CALL

Tiptoeing across the old wooden floors towards the carpeted stairs of the guest house, I try my best to stay quiet. The early-evening sun casts a warm, golden hue through the leaded glass windows, casting long shadows on the narrow hallway. I pass the once vibrant wallpaper, now gently faded by time, as I reach the turn of the staircase. It may have been grand in another era, but now it's charmingly worn, the scent of lavender potpourris overpowering, creating a suffocating sweetness.

To my left, in the cosy front room, I hear Marianne and another female voice raised, piercing the fragile silence. An underlying tension hangs like fog in the air as I strain not to eavesdrop, but their words filter through anyway. I just want to drop off my bags in my room without disturbing their row.

'Grace, you never pay attention – I'm telling you this for your own good!'

'My own good? No, you're telling me this for *your* own good, Mum! I'm not going to do what everyone else wants from me. It's no surprise Ciaran had to go all the way to America so that he can live his life – there's no chance of that here. If it's not you telling me to go to university, it's Uncle Stephen telling me that I shouldn't be out in the woods at night.'

My heart thumps in my chest as slowly, carefully, I climb the stairs, praying that each step won't reveal me.

'And he's completely right, Grace – you shouldn't be out in the forest after dark. It's dangerous; those drifters are danger-ous! Who knows what they're capable of?'

I hear something crash to the floor.

Grace's pitch gets higher. 'They are not dangerous. They are the most imaginative, gentle, loving people you could ever meet. Uncle Stephen is the one who's dangerous; he's the psychopath – everyone knows it!'

'Don't say that about your uncle,' I hear Marianne warn from the shadows. 'Family is family after all...'

Just as I'm about to reach the top of the staircase, my phone rings out, shattering the silence that I'd so carefully preserved. Panic surges through me, reverberating from head to toe. I quickly press mute.

As if on cue, the front-room door flings open, revealing Marianne and Grace's tear-stained faces.

'I'm so sorry,' I mumble 'I didn't mean to disturb you. I'll just, um, be in my room.'

Marianne's mouth tightens and she nods shortly. The girl standing next to her shifts on her feet, fists clenched at her sides.

I give a small wave and say, 'Hi, I'm Daisy; sorry to interrupt.'

She tilts her head and lets out an exasperated sigh. 'Yeah, hi. I'm Grace. Don't pay us any mind; we were just... "talking",' she says with air quotes around the last word. She's dressed in ripped jeans and an oversized army shirt. Her hair is in a pixie cut with one side shaved, and both her nose and lip are pierced. Heavy eyeliner outlines her eyes. A guitar rests across her back.

Marianne turns to me with a gentle smile. 'Would you like to come in for some tea?'

I hesitate for a second before responding. 'No, thank you – I have to take these upstairs – but that's kind of you to offer.'

She smiles and gives Grace's arm a light touch before heading towards the kitchen. 'Come on then,' she says as they go, talking in low voices, before Grace's voice once more pierces the air like a knife, her words sharp and unyielding. She declares she's heading out for the night and not to expect her back anytime soon.

I scurry away with my bags in tow, feeling guilty for over-hearing more of their argument. As I step into my room, the warmth of the space envelops me like a hug from an old friend. The lace curtains flutter gently in the breeze as I lower myself onto the quilt-covered bed.

My phone vibrates in my hand, and Ash's name flashes across the screen. I slump back, swiping to accept the video-call, and wait to see his face appear. When it does, I quickly sit up, loop my hair behind my ears and force a big, happy, encouraging smile.

'Hey, you,' Ash says. 'How's everything going?'

'Eventful! But I'm really enjoying it – the whole area is gorgeous. Here's the view from my window.' I hold up my phone to capture the rolling hills of the countryside in a single frame.

Ash responds with ums and ahs. 'Looks nice. Empty, but nice.'

'It's great for the *Forest Fables* stuff – feels very fairy tale and that's just what I'm searching for.'

'Well, that's something if it makes Lenka happy too.' A broad smile spreads across Ash's face as he looks directly into the camera lens, his deep brown eyes meeting mine across thousands of miles of land and sea. 'I miss you,' he says, his voice soft and sincere.

'I'm missing you too. Don't worry though, I'll be back soon, once all this inheritance business is finished.'

'Everything going to plan with that?'

'Well, our bags still haven't arrived, so I might need to stay here a bit longer to get everything sorted.'

His eyes widen in disbelief. 'Are you serious?'

'Yes, afraid so. All the paperwork is in my suitcase, so that may hold things up.'

He sighs heavily and starts pacing, his forehead creased in thought. It's obvious something is wrong.

'Are you okay, Ash? Is everything all right...?'

He grumbles before responding. 'Yes, everything is fine. I just want this done and you home. I've had a rough day at work... my parents are driving me crazy. Dan just got promoted – the golden boy strikes again so he's out celebrating. I'm not in the mood...' He pauses, and his voice rises in frustration as he continues, 'My crypto has taken a dip – a big dip.'

'It'll go up, don't worry. There'll always be highs and lows.' I try to highlight the positives. 'Look, I have a meeting with the solicitors tomorrow, but I've been thinking, maybe we shouldn't rush into buying a place together – like, not so soon – we can pause for a second and think about—'

Ash waves his arm in dismissal. 'Think? Daisy, we don't have time to think! We need to act – just make sure these guys don't give you the run-around and they understand that we need the property valued and sold as soon as humanly possible.'

Just as he finishes his sentence, I hear Ash's mum calling him for dinner. This sparks his temper further. 'Listen, I've got to go,' he snaps. 'Call me straight after your meeting tomorrow, okay? It's just one of those days.'

The line goes silent as he hangs up the phone.

'It's just one of those days,' I repeat to myself, realising that I have a relationship that doesn't seem to have another type of day.

CHAPTER 22

THE PUB

I cross the street, drawn towards the lit-up windows of The Tap House bar. The hum of conversation and music fills the air, and a warm, inviting atmosphere hangs over the place. But it's only when we step inside that I truly appreciate its magnificence. The walls are lined with paintings of all sizes and styles, each one radiating its own unique charm. In the centre of the floor moves a throng of people, laughing and swaying to the music blaring from the stage. Everywhere I look, there are smiles on people's faces; it's clear everyone here has come for one thing and one thing only – to have fun.

My eyes immediately find Kayla in the crowd, wearing a peach chiffon outfit that makes her look just like the old Peaches & Cream Barbie I remember seeing under her pillow at night. Head to toe styling by Jacinta means we're both overdressed and pitch perfect at the same time. This place really has something for everyone – there are farmers in big brown boots and gorgeous, glossy women with long locks and strappy minidresses walking through the double doors with intent. No matter what kind of person you are, there's something here for you.

I shout her name from across the room, and she spins around towards me. Her eyes light up and a wide smile spreads across her face as she grabs my arm and pulls me through the crowd, the steady thump of the bass reverberating in our chests. We stop at the edge of the dance floor, and she looks at me with a smile. We join the crowd, entranced by the lively tunes being played by the band in front of us. Flutes, fiddles and banjos fill the air, as the beautiful Grace, with the pixie haircut strums her guitar with wild abandon. As the music swells, Kayla and I dance together in perfect harmony. My feet seem to know just where to go, not that anyone would care if I had two left feet. Kayla's face glows in the soft light. I feel a sense of freedom and joy, as if all my worries melt away and we're floating in a world of our own making.

After a few songs, my heart is pounding and my feet feel like heavy stone, so I drag myself off the packed dance floor, squeezing through the heaving bodies. Sweat drenches my shirt and I can feel it on my forehead. I stumble towards the bar, desperate for a cool drink to help restore some energy.

I give Kayla a wave and witness her attempt at an Irish riverdance. She moves her feet quickly in time with the music, arms held tightly at her sides. Her head is tilted upwards and her shoulders are thrown back as she does her best to mimic the steps. I can see her curls bouncing with each jump, and I'm grateful that she's wearing Mary Janes instead of her usual stilettos; otherwise we would have been spending the night in A&E. The people around us clap along to the music and join in on the fun.

I whirl around to the bar to place my order, only to have a wave of icy beer pour over my chest. The cold liquid washes over me, spilling on the floor. My neck strains as I crane my head upwards and take in the form of James O'Connor standing before me, the trio of beers now just two and a half in his hands.

He looks at me, his lips in an O shape and his eyes wide, as if he can't believe what he's seeing.

My stomach twists as my cheeks heat up with embarrassment. I force myself to look up and speak. 'I... I'm so sorry,' I stammer, wishing the ground would swallow me up.

James sets down the glasses clumsily, sending more beer splashing onto the dark mahogany bar. He extends a white cloth napkin towards me; our fingers brush against each other and I feel a shock of electricity.

I accept the napkin from him, pressing it to my chest, trying to appear nonchalant even though my heart is pounding in my throat.

He runs a hand through his hair. 'I apologise – you're completely soaked, and it was my fault...' His Irish accent is a comforting embrace, its velvety tones ever-so-soft and soothing.

Kayla staggers in behind me, her chest heaving and her face slick with sweat. 'Oh God! I need something to cool me down!' she blurts out, before she notices the beer staining my clothes. Her gaze steadies on me, and her eyes grow wide. 'What happened to you?'

James flashes a sheepish grin and lifts his hands in a small gesture of surrender. 'My apologies, ladies. A round on me. What can I get you?' He gazes at us with a twinkle in his kind sapphire eyes.

I shake my head in disagreement. 'No way! It was my fault. Let me buy you a new one!'

He guffaws. 'Big Sean would have my head if he heard that I let Rose Clarke's daughter buy drinks here in Innisfree.' James lifts a finger to the bartender. 'Make sure these two get what they want,' he says, winking.

Kayla pulls out her hand. 'Thank you! I'm Kayla.'

James takes her hand and they shake. 'I'm James. It's a pleasure to meet you,' he says warmly, his gaze shifting towards me for a moment. 'Enjoy your night. I'll see you tomorrow morning in the office, Daisy – I'm looking forward to it.' He makes his way to a corner booth.

'Me too!' I blurt out, my voice too loud in the busy bar.

Kayla gives me an elbow nudge, and once he's out of earshot, she turns her gaze on me with narrowed eyes. 'Is *that* the lawyer?'

'Yup,' I mutter. 'That's him.'

Kayla starts shaking her head. 'Oh my word! How are you going to be able to keep yourself in check with him?' She giggles and waggles her brows. 'Ash better watch out and start treating you the way you deserve because that man is—'

'Kayla! Enough. You've got your beer goggles on – it's time to go.'

I link my arm in hers and we hurriedly weave our way through the crowd and out into the chilly night. Although the air around me has cooled, my cheeks remain hot to the touch.

CHAPTER 23

THE SOLICITOR

I awkwardly knock on the door of O'Connor & Sons Solicitors and glance down at my hands, empty of any documents. Great start. But I'm making the right choice in coming on my own. I can handle this solo; I'm sure of it.

Kayla is kind enough to take time away from her hectic life to join me here, so I don't want to add any more unnecessary stress to her already full schedule. She had a full day of client meetings when I left her, and from what I could tell, she was scheduled to be tied up until dinner. That girl is a powerhouse. Even with a hangover.

The door creaks as it opens, unveiling an elderly man wearing a dark-green bow tie sitting behind his desk. He lifts his gaze from his work and beams at me. Only now do I catch the resemblance – vivid blue eyes just like James.

'Come in,' he says, extending his hand outwards. 'Jonathan O'Connor – nice to meet you.' He radiates a kind, yet strong energy.

I return the handshake with a smile on my face. His grip is firm, and his skin feels soft and smooth like suede.

'I'm Daisy,' I reply, my voice trembling slightly as I attempt to control my nerves. 'It's nice to meet you. I'm here to sort out some family property matters related to Rose Clarke's inheritance.' I force a small smile, hoping he hasn't noticed the fear that's overtaken me.

He waves his arm towards an empty chair across from him and gestures for me to take a seat. 'Ah yes, my son James has filled me in on the details. He should be here soon.'

The room is small and cramped, in stark contrast to the sprawling Irish countryside outside. His desk is overflowing with mountains of frayed documents. Stacks of legal briefs and yellowing title deeds encroach into every nook and cranny on the worn wooden floor and come within inches of the high ceiling. Old leather-bound tomes line the walls, along with framed Latin certificates of prestigious qualifications from top universities. The smell of old leather, stale coffee and ageing parchment fills the air.

I sit down and take a deep breath. Usually I like to be prepared, but I'm at a loss today since I don't have the paperwork I was asked to bring. It's embarrassing; James travelled all the way to London to find me, only for me to turn up in Innisfree without so much as a proof of address.

'I'll do my best to help sort out the situation with the house,' Jonathan says before fixing me with a piercing gaze. 'It's a bit of a tricky one this... but never mind – we'll get there, I'm sure.' He pauses suddenly, looking up from behind his glasses with a twinkle in his eye. 'So let's not waste any more time – do you want me to tell you the good news or the bad news first?' he asks, his face unreadable.

I clench my jaw and take a deep, steadying breath, acutely aware that whichever path I choose, it probably won't be straightforward. 'Bad news first...' I croak out, my voice barely above a murmur.

He lifts a folder. 'Might as well get the unpleasant stuff out of the way, right?' He adjusts his glasses on the bridge of his nose. 'I'm afraid the property is in a state of disrepair,' he says. 'Not derelict yet, but not exactly an acceptable standard either. Unfortunately, the house insurance policy has lapsed and the company won't renew it as it's vacant and in need of modernisation. You'd have to get the house in a habitable state and get insurance so that you can connect the utilities, water, gas and so forth before you can list it for sale. But all those costs are, luckily, covered by the estate, so you'll not have to worry about more expense.' Jonathan's gaze is intense, and I feel my heart thumping in my chest. 'Presuming you want to sell it, that is? I understand you live in London and have no connection to the house, so I've assumed selling the property is the most likely outcome. Please correct me if I'm mistaken.'

'No, you're not mistaken. I'll have to sell it,' I reply, although now I'm wondering just how simple that's going to be given what Jonathan has just said. And of course, what Stephen had told me earlier about The Lake House being in such a state.

'Selling is my only option as London is where my life is – my boyfriend, my job, everything I've ever known, really. So, I'm not able to stay here, as lovely as Innisfree is.'

And I mean that. I really love it here. A sudden sadness settles in my chest as I realise that this special place, Innisfree, would soon no longer be a part of my life. My time here would soon be over and it would be back to reality with no promise of return.

'I thought as much,' confirms Jonathan. 'Perfectly reasonable under the circumstances.' He smiles reassuringly as he opens the folder, pulling out some documents and laying them in front of me.

My eyes scan the unfamiliar words and phrases for what feels like an eternity before I finally get the gist of their meaning. Jonathan confirms my understanding that the title deeds are outdated and need to be in my name for me to legally claim the house – but it's going to be a lengthy process that involves multiple rounds of paperwork and endless bureaucracy.

I sit in silence as Jonathan goes through every detail of what needs to be done, flicking through legal papers and speaking in technical jargon that only he understands.

'Do you have the required documents James asked you to bring?' he finally asks.

'Err...'

Right then, James appears in the doorway, turning around and pushing the door open with his back while carefully holding a tray of four coffee mugs. He gives his father a nod, setting one mug in front of each of us. He raises an eyebrow at me and silently mouths, 'Where's Kayla?'

I shake my head and mime that she had to work, pretending to type on an invisible keyboard. Jonathan then coughs. James and I both give each other a knowing look, as if we've been caught talking during class.

'Do you have the documents with you, Daisy, at this moment in time?' Jonathan asks again. His voice is all business.

I squirm in my seat, fidgeting and gripping the chair's arms. My palms are moist with sweat as my throat tightens, a lump forming as I anticipate the worst. Time to come clean and fess up. 'At this particular moment in time... no.'

Jonathan's face is a picture of concern.

'The thing is, the airline misplaced my suitcase with all the paperwork in it, but they've assured me that it'll show up. It's not too much of an issue, right?'

His glasses hang on the bridge of his nose, and his mouth is tight. 'It's very much an issue. We can't move forward without verification.'

'I'm so sorry for the inconvenience,' I say in a quiet voice.

Jonathan blows out his cheeks. 'This is quite a setback, indeed.'

James leans in closer to me and asks, 'If I may?'

I nod in response.

'Dad, we take the approach that the documents are merely delayed, en route – not lost. With that in mind, I'm willing to go ahead with the repairs and make sure everything meets the insurance requirements,' James proposes.

Jonathan takes a moment to ponder this, tapping his finger against his lips while gazing upwards.

'With Daisy as sole heir, there's no one to contest – we can assume pro tempore guardianship until the papers get here?' suggests James.

'Okay.' Jonathan offers a nod of agreement. 'Yes, that can work.' He quickly flips through some papers and pulls out a light-green one. After scanning its contents, he hands it to me. 'Here, I'll need you to sign this before we can move forward with the administrative process – without the verification documents, this is as far as we can go today.'

As I finish reading the document, I notice James' eyes fixate on my signature. His brow wrinkles, and he tilts his head as if trying to decipher it.

'I know – my handwriting is terrible,' I say with a sheepish grin. 'Considering I draw for a living, you'd think I'd have better penmanship. My mother said my words always looked like chicken scratches on paper.'

His gaze rises to meet mine, studying me intently. He's about to say something but pauses. The air stretches with tension, leaving me feeling exposed.

Then, he chuckles softly. 'Your handwriting is perfectly legible. It's just... something else.'

'What?' I inquire, curious.

He shakes his head and smiles. 'Never mind.' He hands the document to his father, but I can't help noticing that before doing so, he takes one last look at my signature.

Jonathan signs his name on the page with practised grace, adding his date and seal for archiving.

'Now, I can give you the keys to the house and we can start sprucing it up,' says James.

I find myself looking into his eyes again, until Jonathan claps his hands together to get our attention.

'Yes, you're free to move forward for now. I'm glad that, at least, was resolved today.' He sighs with relief.

James adds, 'Once your paperwork arrives, we can resume the official handover as planned. In the meantime, we can get started researching contractors, gathering supplies and making lists of necessary repairs.'

'Let me just double-check something... it's a quick sale you're after if I understand?' Jonathan asked, his eyes studying mine intently.

I nodded in agreement, not wanting to take any more of his time than necessary. I'd already spent so much time and energy trying to sort out this paperwork mess and don't have any leeway for viewings or waiting for a traditional estate agent to sort out the sale. I need to get working on my illustrations, and I need to get back to Ash.

'Yes, that's right,' I say with a sigh. 'The sooner it's done, the better.'

Jonathan shifts in his chair and leans back, taking a deep breath before continuing. 'Well then, auction it is. Let's get started, shall we?'

Jonathan quickly flips through the pages of a notebook. 'Yes, you'll be able to make the next auction if you act quickly and get the insurance in order – otherwise you'll have to wait another six months.'

I shake my head. 'That's too long; I need the quickest way possible. Is there a lot of work to be done to bring it up to scratch?'

Jonathan and James make the same facial expression, although Jonathan responds with a 'yes', while James answers with a 'no'.

Jonathan turns to me, his expression softening. 'James will give you a clearer picture when he shows you around, but the gist of it is that Mick had put aside enough money to fund any repairs so you shouldn't have to worry about footing the bill if you find a team to put in the work and you don't mind getting your hands dirty with the cleaning and decorating.'

'Don't let the state of the place put you off – it can be fixed up in no time,' James says encouragingly.

Jonathan continues. 'And I have it on good authority that there have been several people who've already shown an interest in it. When it passes inspection, it will make a decent sum once sold.'

He stops briefly, swallowing, and changes his demeanour from lawyer to father. 'Mick was devoted to James; they had a special fondness for one another... an enviable relationship,' he continues in a softer voice than before. 'James knows more about the history of the house and area than I do.' His words fade as his eyes drift to a faraway place, lost in his musings. 'Mick stepped in where I couldn't. I'll be forever indebted. Parenting isn't always smooth sailing; he came just in time, doing the hard things I couldn't bear to do when I was at my lowest, and filled the role of father figure with patience and grace. He was a godsend. With his rough-hewn hands, he helped guide our ship as it sailed through choppy waters. There were times when I wanted to sway from the course, but he held firm, never flinching in difficult moments. His kindness and generosity have earned him a place in our hearts forever. He might not share our bloodline, but Mick is family in every way that matters. As they say, it takes a village.'

James pretends to pick lint off his shirt, and I can see the muscle in his jaw twitching. Meanwhile, Jonathan keeps his eyes trained on the floor. It seems like the three of us have something in common – we've all been taken in by someone at some point.

James rubs his neck and takes a deep breath, then gives a hearty cry of, 'Congratulations, Daisy!'

Jonathan too springs into action, pulling out a rusty set of keys from the drawer next to him.

My heart swells as if it wants to burst out of my ribcage. For the first time since I entered this cramped office, I feel a glimmer of hope. And my excitement nearly skyrockets when James leans in and whispers, 'You want to see it right now?'

'Right now? As in *right now* right now? Can we really do that?'

His blue eyes glint as he continues, 'Why not? You've come all this way. Let's go!'

I smile widely and nod.

James blows out his cheeks as he slowly slides off his tie, undoes the top button of his shirt, then takes off his stiff cufflinks with a sigh of relief. He leaves the room and returns in something far more comfortable: a pair of worn-out jeans, a plain white T-shirt and an old baseball cap. The hat casts a long shadow over his dark hair and bright-blue eyes, making them stand out even more. With 'lawyer James' gone, I can sense his feeling of liberation. He flashes me a winning grin and takes his car keys out of his pocket.

'How you feeling?' he asks as he leads me out of the office.

'Better than ever,' I say firmly, my resolve solidifying with each word. I can almost feel the future opening before me.

CHAPTER 24

THE BOATSHED

The sun casts a warm golden glow on the rugged Irish landscape surrounding us as we drive towards The Lake House, painting the green hills and distant mountains in a delicate brush of light. James, with one hand casually gripping the wheel of his well-loved jeep, gazes ahead with a sense of peace and nostalgia in his eyes. I take in the strong contours of his face, softened by a hint of a smile. I'm entranced by the beauty of the scenery – and the company.

We drive in comfortable silence for a few more moments before James speaks. 'I'm glad you came, Daisy,' he says, his voice slightly hoarse.

I turn to look at him, taken aback by the emotion in his words. 'I wouldn't be here without you; thanks again for all your help,' I reply sincerely. 'From what your dad said, you and Mick had a very close bond. I know how hard it is losing someone you cared about.'

A sadness passes briefly across his face as he nods in response, but it swiftly fades and is replaced with a small smile. 'He was a great man,' he remarks fondly.

We lapse back into silence as James weaves through the

country roads, through valleys and over hills. We pass by
sprawling green fields, cattle grazing lazily in the distance. I love
the smell of the fresh Irish air, and the sound of the birds
chirping in the trees. The peace and quiet is interrupted by the
occasional car or motorcycle racing by, but other than that it's
just us and nature. The scent of woodland and wildflowers fills
my lungs as I gaze out across the rolling hills and lush meadows,
so different to London's smog-filled skyline. An unexpected
sense of connection washes over me here, a calming energy that
sparks my creativity. What stories could these hills tell? I think
as I take in the scenery.

Bright red poppies, their petals reflecting in the sunlight,
dance between blades of grass. A brilliant brand-new hue. Is it
vermillion? Flame? Dark coral? As I stand here watching
nature's colours unfiltered, I'm reminded why coming here,
away from the city, even just for such a short while, was such
a good decision for me. If it wasn't thrust upon me, I'd have
been too scared to take this trip. How long had I wanted to
come to Innisfree but never did? And then, out of nowhere,
James O'Connor shows up and here I am, winding through
country lanes, feeling a sense of belonging like none I've felt
before.

'Can I ask you a question?' I say after a while.

'Sure.'

'Why have you gone to such lengths to do all this for Mick?'
I'm eager to learn more about the man who played such a
crucial role in shaping the person sitting beside me.

He looks across at me, his eyes darken. 'It's complicated...'
he says. He takes a moment, and when he speaks, his voice is
even softer than before. 'Like Dad said, Mick was like a father
figure to me,' he explains. 'He was the one who took me in when
I had no home, no family and no hope. He believed in me when
nobody else did. He showed me that life could be so much more
than what I'd imagined and gave me the strength to make some-

thing of myself.' He pauses briefly and his shoulders slump as if weighed down by memories. 'So, I owe it to him.'

My heart softens at his words; I can't help but admire his strength of character, despite all his pain. I know there's more to the story than he's telling me, but I also know that it's not my place to push him. So I just sit next to him, offering him my support and understanding. Because sometimes, that's all you can do for someone. Just be there for them and wait till they're ready.

Up ahead, a single sheep begins to wander across the road. Then another comes. And then a whole flock joins them. A man in a flat cap is standing in the middle of them, waving a stick around.

James brakes, bringing the jeep to a stop. 'Roadblock,' he mumbles before slumping in his seat. 'Grab a snooze if you'd like; they'll be here for at least twenty minutes – sheep are notoriously slow.'

We sit in silence, then James blows out his cheeks and straightens up, locking his fingers around the back of his head. 'You sure you want to know...?' he says.

'If you're sure you want me to,' I reply.

'Come on then – I'll show you.' James flashes me a sideways grin before shifting gears and leaving the main road for a dirt track. 'We've time for a quick detour.'

We follow the winding track until we reach a clearing surrounded by old-growth trees. James pulls up to an aged wooden gate bearing a sign that reads 'The Boatshed', and we get out of the jeep and cross through the gate, making our way down a narrow path lined with tall pines. We walk down the glen, through the heather and the gorse, to the place where a babbling brook sends its melodic lullabies upstream. The air is fresh and clean, smelling of wildflowers and new grass. This place is unlike any I've ever visited in person, apart from the places that existed only in my mother's stories. I'm starting to

realise how having a vivid imagination is like flipping two sides
of a coin. It's easy to dream up any possibility – both dreams
and nightmares. I find it easier to see things as they could be
rather than how they really are. But here, for the first time, I feel
those two visions are aligned, closer together than they've ever
been before.

James offers me his hand as I try to navigate my way down
the steep grassy drop to The Boatshed, pausing every few steps
so he can point out something or ask me about my life in
London, about my work, about the books and music I like, about
my hopes for the future.

I slip forward slightly. A grassy verge gives way underfoot,
and he catches me, both hands firmly holding me by the side.

'I'm sorry. Clearly I'm not the mountain goat I like to think
I am.'

In an instant, I can feel the weight of his gaze on me. I look
up at him and hold my breath for a moment. Our eyes lock and
the air around us seems to change. My heart races; is he feeling
it too? I want this, whatever it is that's happening here, to be
real. All I can do is hope that his smile is real, and it's not all in
my head. I can't be sure. I step back to regain my stance, and he
fiddles with his watch, blushing.

'Anyway. If you can stick with it, we'll be there in less than a
minute.' He laughs. 'Unless we go into injury time.'

We walk a few more feet until the terrain shifts to flat land,
and suddenly, through the canopy of trees, I can see it all. I gasp
in wonder as we approach – at one side there's a vast lake filled
with crystal-clear water reflecting like glass across its surface; on
the opposite side, a three-story white house with a thatched roof
and two chimneys stands tall. The original windows of the
manor overlook the lake that laps around the estate – all set
against the backdrop of rolling green hills stretching out into
eternity.

James leads me to a little wooden boatshed on the banks of

the lake. Turning over a large stone, he finds a key and unlocks the door. The small space is so cosy and charming, a little workshop with tools hanging on the walls, a large canvas of pencil etchings and scrawled notes. A scratched window, devoid of any curtains, gives a perfect view of the lake and the peaks in the distance. James lights a lantern and sets it on the table. He opens a small chest and takes out a bottle of whiskey and two glasses. He pours us each a glass, and we sit down at the table.

'So... here we are,' he whispers. 'Where it all started and where it all ended...' He takes a sip of his drink and stares out the window, lost in thought. 'Right, so I was a complete tearaway when I was younger – stupid, arrogant, bad-tempered, reckless... you name it.'

'Oh, I'm sure you weren't that bad,' I say, trying to lighten the mood.

'No, I was worse.' He gives me a half-smile. 'I had a mullet.'

'Oh, okay... that is bad.' I laugh.

'Anyway, my dad used to bring me fishing here when I was a lad, and it was the only time I was ever calm. It's like this place has some kind of magical power over me. But as I got older, we fought more and more – I was in trouble at school, in town, out late, up to no good. Of course, he was mortified as he felt he was a respectable pillar of the community.'

'Was it just you and your dad at home?' I ask, wanting to understand his story without being too intrusive.

He nods solemnly, biting his lower lip. 'Yeah, my mum died the day she had me due to sepsis. So, I never knew her. In the hospital, we spent a few hours together until they realised something was seriously wrong. Each year, on my birthday, my dad would tell me that when he woke up on this same day however many years ago, he was a happily married man with a beautiful wife but ended the day as a single father.'

James pauses and takes another sip of his whiskey, his eyes looking miles away. My heart aches for him; my mum had been taken away from me too soon but at least I knew her, remembered her, shared special times with her. But James' situation is different, losing his mother and then never really knowing his father's love either, it must be a unique kind of pain. Jonathan's words cause a swell of anger inside me; how could he talk like that? How could he be so callous? I move closer to him, gently placing a hand on his arm. I can feel his sorrow as if it were my own. He looks at me, and I offer a small smile.

'By the time I hit fourteen, things weren't going well at home. So, I decided to leave, and I came down here and just slept rough, basically... And then Mick smoked me out one evening. I thought he'd send me packing, but he didn't. He understood me, he listened to me, he bollocked me in a way that didn't make me feel worthless. I started helping him out and then ended up staying with him. We became mates; he said I was the son he never had... nor wanted.' He laughs and shakes his head.

I can sense how much he looked up to his older friend, for being there for him when no one else was. 'No wonder Mick was so important to you. Sounds like he was a big support.'

He gives a definitive nod. 'Mick was the one who put me on the right track, saved me from hanging out in bars and pool halls with a bad crowd. Without him, my life could have gone in a very different direction. He helped mend the relationship between my father and me. And then I grew up a bit and it was my turn to look out for Mick, so when he told me he wanted to build a boat...' James sighs and pinches his nose between his fingers, squeezing his eyes shut. 'I couldn't turn him down: he'd taught me so much about woodworking that I could follow his instructions with ease. He only needed a strong hand and a younger set of eyes for some of the more manual labour. The design, the material selection – all of that was up to him. I was just here to do the grunt work and spend time with a great friend.'

His voice trails off and he looks at me, his blue eyes piercing in the lantern light.

'I thought the silly beggar would wait until we'd finished it... but he didn't... And one night, when the moon was full and the tide was out, he decided to take it out, a little test run... just to see how it went.' James pauses and looks out the window, his face solemn. 'But it didn't go well. The boat capsized and Mick drowned.'

I reach out to touch his hand but stop, my fingertips half an inch away from his skin, before quickly drawing back and tucking them into my lap. I can't imagine how difficult this must be for him, reliving those painful memories. He stares out the window, his eyes fixed on some distant point.

His lips are in a hard line and he shakes his head. 'And I blame myself,' he murmurs. 'I should never have let him talk me into helping him in the first place.' He turns to face me, his expression filled with anguish and guilt. 'It was a disaster waiting to happen. If I'd talked him out of it or given him a dose of common sense, he'd still be alive. He'd be here this very day – I know it. I know it too well.'

'It wasn't your fault!' I say desperately. 'You couldn't have known what would happen.'

'I should have known,' he says quietly. 'I should have stopped him.'

After losing the only person who ever really understood him and now carrying this burden of guilt, it's no surprise he's clung to this spot, never wanting to forget Mick's memory.

'I'm sorry,' I whisper.

'So am I.' He nods, a slight smile playing across his face as he begins to recall the adventures they had together, from sneaking out in the middle of the night to go fishing, to swimming in the lake in freezing temperatures.

As he talks, his face lights up and I can see that being here helps him feel just a little bit less alone in the world.

He eventually pauses, looking around as if awaking from a dream. 'We should probably go now,' he says softly. 'Enough hearing about my sob stories.'

As we turn to leave, I glance back and something on the shelf catches my attention. It's a postcard of Innisfree, encased in a heavy wooden box frame – a perfect copy of the one my mum owned. The one that had pride of place everywhere we moved to, the only item she truly seemed to cling to.

'One minute.' I reach up and take it down. 'Do you know why Mick would have this?' I ask.

James shrugs. 'No clue.'

I hold it in my hands and wipe the dust from the glass.

'Framing a postcard – I mean, that's the kind of daft thing he'd do,' James says as he looks at it more closely. 'It's Mick's handiwork though.' He runs his fingers along its edges in admiration before turning to me with a nod.

'Would it be okay if I took this with me?' I ask.

'No need to ask my permission, Daisy. It's all yours.' He opens his arms wide and gazes around. 'I mean that. It really is all yours.'

CHAPTER 25

THE NEIGHBOUR

We pull into the gravel driveway, and I step out of the jeep, taking in the postcard-perfect scene before me. The house, a lovely mix of rustic charm and old-world elegance, has unquestionably seen better days. But somehow, those imperfections only add to its beauty. The sapphire-blue lake gleams in the distance, surrounded by the lush, green hills of the Irish countryside.

'So here it is,' James says.

'Just look at this place,' I remark. 'It's absolutely breathtaking.'

James nods in agreement, eyes wide as he takes in the lake's glassy surface, the blue-streaked sky and wisps of white clouds. 'It's beautiful, isn't it?'

I breathe in the fresh air, rippling through wildflowers and rustling the lake's surface. We observe the meadow, dotted with white-fleeced sheep grazing peacefully in the sun. I point to a group of cows lazily shifting in the grass. 'Nice neighbours!' I laugh.

James extends his arm to me, and together we walk along the rugged trail, admiring the expanse of sky above us. Out of nowhere, a fox appears from its hiding place, its yellow-gold eyes gleaming with a wild glint. It lets out an almost human-like laugh before darting away and disappearing back into the shrubs. A dark figure stands alone atop the hill, her face obscured by long tendrils of black hair whipping around it.

James waves his arm in recognition and calls out, 'Moya!'

But instead of coming to meet us, she shrinks back from view.

James takes a deep breath and turns towards me. 'You'll meet her eventually. She's not been herself since Mick died.'

As we make our way towards the house, I feel the weight of my unanswered questions about my mother pressing against me with each step.

A gruff voice bellows, 'What do you think you're doing here? Get out!'

James and I startle.

'Speaking of neighbours,' says James as he holds up his hand.

I turn to see a scruffy middle-aged man standing with a pair of large dogs, who are barking viciously as they tug on their leashes. He glares first at James, then me, brandishing an enraged fist in the air. But the man's face slowly turns from angry to suspicious.

'Ah it's you again, always bringing trouble, O'Connor... Are you bringing more waifs and strays? We thought we'd seen the end of that malarkey when Mick passed. He was at least responsible for them, and they minded their own business.'

James lowers himself to crouch in front of the dogs, rubbing their bellies with both hands. In an instant, they switch from snarling beasts to docile bundles of fur, eagerly awaiting the scratches that James provides. 'I understand, Dom,' he says. 'But this isn't what you think.'

Dom makes a dismissive noise. 'And what do you know? That place is now a doss house. Parties with loud music, alcohol, drugs and all kinds of immorality. I confronted them last night. I said that next time I would show up with a shotgun.'

I inquire, 'Is it the people in the woods?' This must be who Stephen had been referring to with such contempt in his voice when talking about the eco-warriors, suggesting they were the cause of all the destruction and disorder at the house.

Dom shakes his head, still looking at me with a little suspicion. 'No, those folks are fine; harmless hippies if you ask me. It's some of the local gangs from neighbouring towns, always searching for vacant properties to use for their bad business and dirty work.'

James stands there, arms folded, intently listening to what Dom has to say. 'Well now, you'll be pleased to hear—'

But Dom continues talking without paying attention, his voice rising in pitch. 'I never sleep with both eyes closed, and I always have my pitchfork handy. There're all sorts of creatures roaming the area. I can hear them stirring, like pests. I will not wait any longer for this alleged benefactor. My petition to the council is on its way – that place needs to be razed to the ground, demolished before it brings the whole village down with it. I want this to stop, right now, O'Connor. You hear?'

He has an earthy, musky smell of smoke and general dampness.

As I open my mouth to introduce myself, I notice the man's right eye begin to twitch.

'Hi, I'm Daisy Clarke. Nice to meet you,' I say.

'Clarke?' he queries, his gaze narrowing as he turns it towards James.

'Rose Clarke's daughter; we found her in London – just in time. Rose has since passed, but Daisy is here now, Dom. We've just gone through the paperwork at Dad's office. Things are on the up.'

Dom's gaze sweeps over me as he mutters a prayer, blessing himself with a solemn nod. 'I'm so sorry for your loss – may her spirit find solace in God's embrace.' His head bows as he reaches up to make the sign of the cross.

I give my thanks to him, and I suppress an urge to press for more information on my mother; another person who remembers her, another possible clue towards understanding her better.

He steps forward, slowly scanning my features with his deep-brown eyes. 'Rose and Moya were really mistreated for no reason. They never did anything wrong, but people didn't take the time to get to know them, so they just assumed the worst because they were travellers – easy for people to tar everyone with the same brush if you don't know better. But that's it, small town, small minds as they say...'

'Traveller? What do you mean?' I ask.

Dom raises an eyebrow. 'What do you mean what do I mean?' He gives me a questioning look. 'You don't know what a traveller is? You didn't know that your mother was a traveller?' he says, seeming more befuddled than me.

'Daisy, your mother and Moya both lived on caravans here, on Mick's land for... well, as long as I remember, and their people before them. You come from a long line of travellers that passed through these fields, worked this land and set up home in Innisfree.'

I nod slowly, trying to process all the information being thrown at me. I glance at James, still a bit confused. 'I know of travellers, but I'm not completely familiar with what it means.'

'Travellers are a community of people who move from place to place living in caravans,' he explains patiently. 'They don't stay in one area for too long and often travel the whole country.' He pauses for a moment before continuing. 'It can be a hard life, with many laws and restrictions that they must abide by. But some choose to leave the travelling life behind and settle down in one area.'

I take it all in, my head spinning with questions. 'So why

was it just my mum and Moya here? Where was the rest of Mum's family?' I ask softly.

Dom takes a deep breath before answering. 'Your mother was running away from something, or someone – we're not sure what exactly – but she found refuge here until she was ready to move on.' He nods towards James. 'Your father helped out – Mick explained the situation, and he gave up some of his time to help with reading and writing letters, filling out forms and the like.'

I guess that's how Jonathan tried to give back, to atone, to make things right again. It sounds like it may have worked.

'Things aren't always easy for travellers,' Dom continues sombrely, 'they face discrimination from locals because they're different – prejudice is alive and well in small towns like this.' He pauses again, looking down at the ground before continuing more quietly. 'And there will always be those who take advantage of the vulnerable – which is why we need to protect them.' He gives me a knowing look before turning away and nudging James with his elbow. 'By my life, spitting image!'

A smile twitches on my lips. I'm coming to love being recognised as my mother's daughter – somehow it feels like she's still here in some way, still connected.

We chat easily as James explains to Dom that we'll be working on the house over the next few weeks so that should put a stop to anyone thinking it's vacant and attracting unwelcome visitors.

'Glad to hear it – and I'm here to lend a hand with whatever you need. I might not be as fast up and down a ladder as times gone by, but I do know a thing or two about fixing up old houses; I've done my fair share of patching things up over the years.' Dom pats me on the arm and says, 'You're part of this now, Daisy, part of something bigger.' He lets out a deep chuckle and rubs his chin. His toothless grin widens as he says, 'The apple never falls too far from the tree.' His hand, calloused from years of hard work, grasps mine. 'You look just like Mick. In fact, I'd say you're even prettier.' He laughs out loud and smacks his thigh.

Did he say Mick? I furrow my brow; he must have muddled his words. He must have meant Mum. Not wanting to embarrass Dom by pointing out his mistake, I glance over at James, hoping for some kind of validation that nothing is amiss.

But James just gives me a small smile and scuffs his shoe against the ground before saying simply, 'I agree. That very thought had crossed my mind.'

We watch Dom disappear from our sight, and my mind is filled with questions. Before I can ask them, James takes off in front of me, at pace. I quickly try to catch up with him, so I can get to the bottom of what Dom said.

'What was the meaning of that?' I cry out into the wind, but my words fall on deaf ears.

He doesn't answer, and his steps pick up speed as he marches away from me.

'James!' I yell after him. 'Is he saying my mum is a traveller and Mick is my father? Is that it?'

He stops and turns to face me, his hands raised in surrender. 'I don't know!' he says slowly, scrutinising me for any signs of emotion before continuing. 'You may never know.'

My body stiffens, and I clench my teeth together to keep any other words from coming out. He's right, of course. I may never get to the truth, and it isn't James' responsibility to tell me about my history. It's not fair to expect anything from anyone here.

We walk in silence, surrounded by unspoken questions. I'd been hoping for something more concrete, but deep down inside, I knew there was more to this story, that somehow I'm just scratching the surface. But I can't rely on others to piece it all together for me. To find out the rest of it, I have to do the work myself.

James touches my shoulder lightly and speaks in a reassuring tone. 'Daisy, I can't give you all the answers you want, but I can bring you to The Lake House, if you're ready?' he offers.

I look up at him, my heart beating fast with anticipation. I slowly nod and meet his gaze, feeling a tingle run down my spine as his eyes hold mine.

'Yes,' I whisper. 'I'm ready.'

He smiles gently and removes his hand from my shoulder. 'Then let's go.'

CHAPTER 26

THE LAKE HOUSE

'Welcome to The Lake House,' James says softly as we approach the house.

I can't help but marvel at how much bigger it is than I'd imagined. It stands three stories tall, with white walls and old-style roofing. A large terrace overlooks an expansive garden with overgrown bushes and trees, patches of grass and mossy stones on cobbled pathways throughout. To the left is a stable attached to an abandoned barn, and off to the right are several more outbuildings. The whole place is far from perfect – there's some peeling paint here, a broken window there – but it has a certain charm that feels inviting and comforting all the same.

'It's been home to the Kennedy family for generations.' He holds the door open for me, gesturing inside with his arm.

I step into a well-lit full of antiques: wooden furniture that looks like it's seen better days; yellowed paperbacks crowding shelves; milk jugs set out like decorations on ornate tables; faded tapestries hanging from walls; and even an old gramophone tucked away in a corner. It's like stepping into another world entirely – one that speaks to me in ways I never knew existed before this moment.

James guides me through the living room, past a staircase to the second floor, and towards a hallway leading to other rooms in the house. We stand before the tall double doors, feeling a mixture of trepidation and curiosity. The doors are thrown open to reveal a spacious dining room, but it's far from spotless. Bottles, cans and cigarette butts litter the filthy space like they were haphazardly strewn about. This must be where the 'parties' took place. I feel sick looking around this scene of debauchery, realizing that all of the warnings may have been true. He guides me downstairs into what was once a wine cellar but now seems devoted entirely to books – so many books they are spilling into every space available – and leads me around them to the French doors at the end of the room that open to the outside porch with its view of the sheer blue lake that spreads out in front of us. This is more than just a pretty view; it's a world unto itself, one that stuns me with its natural beauty.

I recall the postcard my mum cherished: this view of the mountains, lake and sun. The same postcard from The Boatshed, held fast in a frame by Mick. I hold it up now next to the sky, trying to match the perspective as closely as possible. It's an astonishing coincidence that all three of us have this image in common – my mum having it as a memento, Mick framing it and now me standing at this exact spot. I'm overwhelmed by this strange connection between us. Even though I may never understand why we're bound together, just being aware of it is enough to give me some peace. I can feel something growing inside me, something that I'm not easily able to explain away.

I join James down by the hand-made wooden pier. The air is filled with the scent of damp earth, overgrown gardens and the faint perfume of wildflowers, carried by the gentle breeze that whispers through the tall, swaying grass. I take a deep breath, letting the peace of the place envelop me.

James, seemingly attuned to my thoughts, remarks with a half-smile, 'This place is special, that's for sure, and it's in a perfect spot by the lake. But it's been neglected for a while, and it doesn't deserve that. We can have her shining again.'

I return a nervous smile, trying to match his evident enthusiasm.

After a moment, we head back inside and I find a great, lovingly decorated living area with exposed wooden beams and walls adorned with faded paintings. The room's grand stone fireplace, likely once the beating heart of the household, now sits silent and lifeless. Though dust has settled, it can't diminish the house's character and charm.

'It's lovely,' I say as I run my hand over the back of a dusty chair.

'It needs a bit of work,' James says with a laugh. 'But it can be a home again.'

He leads me from room to room, pointing out areas that need work – from the kitchen with its broken taps to the bathrooms with their peeling wallpaper – as we go. It's a big job, but I'm encouraged by James' enthusiasm. I have complete faith in him if he says it's something we can handle.

Sunlight streams through an open window, illuminating the dust motes dancing in its rays. As I stroll along the mantelpiece, I pause to inspect every photo frame. And that's when I see him. Mick Kennedy. I pick up the most detailed photograph, the one that appears to be most recent, of Mick wearing his trademark cowboy hat and bushy beard. He's standing alongside Dom with rods for fishing in their hands and waders on their feet by the lake.

I examine him closely, trying to find some sort of connection or similarity between us, even a vague sense of familiarity. But it's hard. I'm probably willing it to be there, projecting. I'd love to feel a lightning bolt, for there to be an unmistakable bond that I can't deny. But I don't let myself get ahead of myself – I know this could just be my wishful thinking. Part of me hopes he was a good man who loved my mother, but that could just be my desperate attempt to make sense of my story. Maybe he was just a pleasant single man who knew my mum at one point in time, like Big Sean did.

I study another, this time an older one with Marianne McDonagh, commemorating the market fair's opening ceremony. He's laughing as he wears a warm, Guinness-induced moustache. In the next photograph he's strumming away on his guitar, with a bunch of little kids standing around him outside on the grass, all giggling and clapping along. I wander through the large, wooden-framed house and take in all the memories. Pictures of Mick singing, hiking and surrounded by friends hang on the walls. Even in death, it's obvious that he was loved. I gaze out at the lake and say a silent thank you for bringing me here.

And then I spy the edge of a polaroid tucked away behind a silver frame and gently lift it out.

'That's my mother!' I exclaim as I point to a beautiful young woman in the image. I hold it up to show James. She's standing by the lake, Mick's arms wrapped around her from behind, her long red hair blowing in the wind. They look happy. Very happy. And close. Very close.

I peer at the photo. His fingers around her hips, his chin on her shoulder. She has a coy smile, her eyes dreamy and... in love. It's unmistakable – my mother was in love. Deeply and passionately in love. With Mick. And by the looks of it, he felt the same way. And it sends a tremor of shock through me as I think of what this could mean.

The warmth of the moment turns cold as I consider what life would have been like if my mother had stayed in Innisfree. Would things have been different? Would we be together now? Maybe if she had just stayed, she'd still be here, sharing all her stories about Innisfree and teaching me its history... Dom's words echo in my head. Why did she hide her traveller heritage and upbringing from me? Why did she never tell me?

'Wow,' James says, taking the photo from me to get a closer look. 'She's beautiful.'

His words snap me out of my thoughts.

We stand in silence for a few moments before James says, 'I wish they were both here with us, to help fill in the blanks.'

Suddenly, we both startle at the sound of something scurrying above us. I grab onto James' arm and squeeze it tightly, my fingers digging in.

'Who's up there?' I whisper, feeling a mixture of shock and embarrassment, both at the surprising invasion and at the sudden closeness with James.

He places a finger to his lips and gently rests his warm hand on my shoulder, his strong gaze locking with mine and, somehow, he conveys a tender yet unwavering promise to protect me no matter what. He signals for me to stay put, but I shake my head in protest.

'No, I'm coming too. It could be dangerous,' I reply.

He acquiesces with a shrug, and we move forward slowly, my fingers wrapped around his wrist as we tread cautiously up the stairs. My heart is pounding in my chest and a thousand butterflies swarm around inside my stomach. Is it burglars? Drug dealers? Squatters making a home in the empty house? I shake my head, trying to clear away any lingering fear or apprehension, and focus on what's ahead of us. Cautiously, we climb the creaky wooden staircase, past the chipped banister and onto the musty landing.

James calls out into the emptiness, 'Hello? We mean no harm – whoever you are...' His voice echoes softly against the walls but remains unanswered; until suddenly we hear something stirring in the bathroom – followed by a loud thump that shakes me to my core.

'Be quiet!' yells a voice.

'No, you be quiet!' retorts another.

'I'm already being quiet – you're the one that needs to shut up.'

The voices are youthful and boyish.

James glances my way and smiles, exhaling deeply. 'It's all right, lads. James O'Connor here – nobody is in any danger.'

We open one of the doors, finding two boys bickering on the edge of the bathtub. They're no more than sixteen or seventeen years old, their hands and clothing covered in dirt.

'Who are you two then?' James asks cautiously. 'And what are you doing here?'

The boys share a nervous glance before one of them, the younger one, who has copper curls and a smattering of freckles across his cheeks, stammers, 'We... I mean, we're just hanging around. We didn't want to cause any trouble.'

Sensing something amiss, I decide to probe further. 'Why are you hiding out up here? It's hardly safe.'

The older boy, with a darker complexion, scratches his head and answers, 'We've been suspended from school. Our stepdad... you don't want to be around him when he's angry. So, we come here. Mick always let us. We weren't stealing or anything. Mick said we could always come when we wanted.'

The boy stands up and points outside towards the tree house in the backyard. 'We built that tree house with him last summer... we were just coming in to borrow some blankets... that's all.' His voice quivers slightly, revealing a mixture of emotions: embarrassment, fear and perhaps even guilt. 'We didn't mean any harm,' he says quickly.

'Yeah, we're totally harmless,' adds the other boy.

'Oh, is that so?' James crosses his arms in front of his chest and pretends to be stern. I can see the amusement in his eyes. 'And what's your name?' he asks the taller boy.

'Liam,' he replies.

'And you?' I ask, turning to the little freckly one.

'Finn,' he says, looking at the ground, not making eye contact with anyone.

'Are you brothers?' I ask.

'Yes, I'm a year older,' Liam says proudly. 'But we're in the same class at school – just because I had low attendance. Don't let him tell you he's the smart one, because he's not.'

'I'm way too smart for you,' Finn says, sticking his middle finger up at his brother and grinning.

'You wish,' Liam replies, punching him playfully on the arm.

'Hey, stop it, you'll knock each other out,' I say, secretly glad to see them horsing around.

'Yes, I'll knock you out, Liam... watch me!' jokes Finn, but then he turns serious. 'We didn't expect anyone to be here. We didn't take anything, we swear,' he says, nudging Liam, who nods in agreement.

'So where do you boys live?' I ask.

They both point down the road to a small cottage in the distance.

'That's our house,' Liam says. 'But when we got suspended from school for fighting, our stepdad lost his head. He doesn't want us just hanging around – we make too much noise he says, so—'

'We thought it was best to find somewhere else to stay. That's why we came here. We hang out in the tree house, most-ly,' Finn says, finishing Liam's sentence.

A wave of empathy washes over me. It's difficult to ignore the boys' vulnerability, and I feel a familiar urge to protect them.

'I see.' James nods. 'Does your mother know you're here?'

'She knows.' Liam looks anxious.

'Is Stephen McDonagh your stepdad?' asks James.

Together, they make a face and groan, 'Yep.'

James gives me a look before nodding. 'I see,' he quietly utters.

'Did you manage to find any blankets?' I say softly to the boys.

They both nod. James and I exchange a knowing glance as if silently making an agreement.

'Excellent, well, anything else you need, you're welcome to,' I tell them.

The younger one starts speaking, a glimmer of hope in his eyes. 'We're good at fishing and woodwork and building fires too. If... if you let us stay around, we could, you know, help out?'

It dawns on me that this isn't just an empty property or a pile of bricks and mortar – to these two it's a shelter. It's a sanctuary. It's a lifeline.

And that's a feeling I know all too well.

'We're working on fixing up this house, you know. If your mum says it's okay, you can help, if you like.'

Wide grins break across their faces as they scramble to their feet, eager to prove their worth. As I watch them, I'm struck by how quickly life can change; how strangers become friends and enemies turn into allies within a blink of an eye.

'Right, I'll make a call to your mum, make sure she's all right with you being here and helping out,' says James.

'And all going to plan, we'll see you both here first thing in the morning to start work. We're a team now,' I tell them.

Liam reaches out a flat hand and Finn puts his hand over it. I follow suit and eventually James places his on top. We've formed a tiny tower of hands. Which is about as official as you can get.

CHAPTER 27

THE CARAVAN

While James and the boys go off to tell their mother where they are, I debate my next move. I realise that this is my best chance to pay Moya a visit. But it's risky. She has no idea who I am, and she certainly isn't expecting me. While it would be far better for James or Dom to introduce us, that could take up even more time, and I know that if I don't take a chance now, the opportunity could be lost forever. All the possible scenarios run through my mind – would she be pleased to see me or angry that I rocked up to her door unannounced? My heart races as I muster all the courage I have, hoping I'm ready for whatever reaction she might give me.

I walk up to her old-fashioned caravan, nestled in a secluded hollow, among the lush and wild greenery. The private spot seems perfect for someone looking for a quiet retreat away from the hustle and bustle of the everyday grind. The sun's soft golden rays dapple on the caravan's roof – a faded, weatherworn structure that echoes of simple times and rustic living. I can't help but let a small smile grace my lips as I imagine my mother and Moya sharing a hot cup of tea within its confines, catching up on old memories and stories.

The tiny chimney puffs out a curl of smoke. I knock on the door, disturbing the perfect silence. Nothing but the birds seem to answer, with little twitters of laughter. A shiver runs through me – perhaps it's the cold, or the anticipation of whatever conversation might unfold within. I start to run an impatient hand through my hair, but before I even have the chance to give the door a second knock, I hear it: the faint murmur of a radio playing inside the caravan. This and the smoking chimney tell me Moya must be home. Is she ignoring me? Would she if she knew I was here for my mother?

'Hello? Moya? It's... it's Daisy Clarke. I'm Rose's daughter?' I call out, trying to keep my voice steady despite the million questions swirling in my mind. 'I... I wanted to ask you about my mother.'

But there's no answer.

My heart sinks – I'm left baffled and discouraged by Moya's lack of response. Can she hear me? Is there a reason she doesn't want to see me? I thought she and my mother were friends.

Desperation seeps into my soul, and I can feel the determination that drove me there slipping through my fingers.

'Moya?' I half-shout, half-whisper, my voice not sure what to do and how far to push. I don't want to bother her, much less harass her, but I want to meet her. To try to see her face to face, even for just a moment... 'If you don't want to talk, I can come back later. I'll be at the house every day, fixing it up.'

Nothing.

I can't help but feel the weight of Moya's rejection prickling my skin. Is she hiding something? Or is she just a hermit who's lost all taste or tolerance for the outside world? And what does this all mean for my search for the truth about my mother?

The wind rustles the grass and tries to bolster my spirits, but deep down in the chambers of my heart, I can't help but wonder what I've done to deserve such a cold shoulder from a woman so dear to my mother, even if it was such a long time ago. She may not even know that she's dead.

My frustration mounts. I can't believe Moya won't answer the door. I came here because she was my mother's friend, to learn more about their past together. I thought she could help me unravel the truth.

I pace back and forth outside the van, my mind filled with questions that confuse and disorientate me. My gaze flickers to the door separating us, and the empty pleas inviting me to leave. Now, the dilemma presents itself. Should I keep trying, keep knocking on that frustratingly stubborn door, hoping she'll eventually open up? I could ask Dom for help – he's closer to Moya, and she would trust him, listen to what he has to say. But would that be enough to get her to open the door?

An idea forms, and I quickly grab my notepad, scribbling down my thoughts. I can slip a note under the door and let Moya know that I come in peace. Once she reads it, perhaps she'll let me in. Taking my chance, I scribble a note explaining myself and add my phone number on a scrap of paper, praying that Moya will respond. Decision made, I slide the paper under Moya's door, softly knocking as I do, hoping to catch her curiosity.

With the note delivered, I leave her doorstep, my heart racing with a mix of anticipation and fear. I glance back one last time, and my breath catches in my throat as the door shifts ever so slightly. The knot in my chest loosens, replaced with a glimmer of hope that blooms into a gentle warmth. There's a chance for the truth yet.

The thread that connects all of us – the stories that bind us together – they're fragile, breaking easily. But I've learned they can be woven back together with the right intention at the right time. For now, that's what I'll do. I'll keep pushing through, trying to connect with Moya until I've found the answers my mother left behind.

Though the heartbeat of anxiety remains, it's tempered by a growing sense of optimism, like tiny embers from a dying fire. I may not have the answers yet, but I'm going to keep searching. Forward I go, further into the unknown.

CHAPTER 28

THE TEAM

The smell of freshly cut grass fills the air as I watch Dom meticulously supervise all repairs to the charming lakeside country house. He has all the tradespeople well organised. In the distance, I hear the boys laugh as they paint and repair what's been left neglected for years. Kayla, with her trusty clipboard in hand, walks around, ensuring everything is in order. The sun radiates down, creating a picturesque glittering sheen on the lake beyond.

As I stand gazing at James, who enthusiastically tends to the garden or climbs the ladder onto the roof when needed while wearing a beaming smile, I feel the gentle warmth of the sun on my skin as it shines through a window. It's in these moments that Innisfree feels familiar, a place where I truly belong and worth every moment of graft that we're putting in every day. I yawn, my stiff limbs protesting my recent activities, as I stretch my arms towards the ceiling.

I wander downstairs, ready to tackle the next task on my checklist, kindly typed up, colour-coded and prioritised by Kayla – the project-managing dictator... I mean, director.

The past fortnight has been a whirlwind of crazy developments. Dom knows more about plaster than I know about life: he can mix it, apply it to the walls and smooth it out with ease, completely resurfacing the whole interior. I laugh now as I remember how my heart sank as I stepped into this dining room on day one; there was mess all over the floor, the walls were in such disrepair, chunks missing and patches of wallpaper peeling from them. They looked as if they'd crumble at any moment. I had no idea how we were going to make this place look habitable again. But then Dom arrived, with a wealth of knowledge, and suddenly I felt a spark of hope. He stumbled in wearing his work overalls, toolbelt slung across his chest, his two dogs at his heel, and instantly we could sense him taking charge. Any doubts I had disappeared as he spoke, explaining precisely what he'd do to tackle this seemingly insurmountable task.

Liam and Finn have become like part of our family at The Lake House. They watch everything Dom does, take the dogs for walks, grab supplies from town, haul water from the well, light campfires with twigs to grill up the fresh mackerel from the lake for lunch. Their mother appears to be pleased that they're outdoors and that things are staying busy. We haven't heard anything from Stephen McDonagh lately, which is probably for the best. They're such wonderful boys with neverending energy, playing outside for hours each day, chasing each other around the garden, their laughter ringing through the air. Their youthful playfulness is contagious, and I can never help but smile as I watch them run around, carefree and unburdened by the weight of the world. As it should be at that age.

James continues to fascinate me. Each day after his hours at the office are up, his true spirit emerges like a butterfly from its cocoon. He roars up to the house in his battered jeep, wearing a T-shirt and jeans, now stained with dirt and grease from his labour – his baseball cap shading his face from the sun. His new vocation is to build door frames, pull weeds, plant seeds and fix leaks.

It's incredible how quickly everyone has grown attached to each other; forming an unlikely bond in such a short space of time. We're all just trying our best to make our little piece of the world better – one small act at a time.

As I stepped into The Lake House that first day, I was over-whelmed by the memories and belongings of many decades past. It's my mission to make sure every inch of the property is cleared out, leaving no stone unturned. I started with the living room, sorting through all the furniture and other items, finding myself occasionally pausing to take in some of the stories that must've been hidden between them.

Kayla came up with a system for me – anything that could be used again had to be sorted into three categories: Save, Recycle or Donate. With Jacinta and Fintan's help after their shops close, we work diligently late into the night to ensure everything gets put in its rightful place. Once the living room had been sorted through, it was time to move on to bigger projects – like the bedrooms and kitchen. The task of clearing out these areas seemed daunting at first, but as more and more volunteers joined us – led by Dom – we've managed to make good progress. And around me as I've emptied old chests, walls have been painted, tiles laid down and cupboards installed – transforming each area bit by bit until there's little left to do but admire our hard work.

Finally, it came time to tackle the study – a dark corner situ-ated at one end of the house which hadn't been touched in years. We cleared out old files and papers in record time before moving on to bookshelves full of forgotten books and trinkets, which would eventually find their way onto charity-shop shelves or be donated directly to those who needed them most. We also found Mick's old guitar, which he'd used when he was younger; it brought a tear to everyone's eye as they remembered his love for music. We decided that it should be given to Grace McDonagh, who was forging her music career and bringing such joy to so many at The Tap House. When we told her the news, she was overwhelmed and couldn't believe we still had it after all these years. She thanked us all and proudly carried the guitar away with her.

With all the rooms cleared out, it was time to turn our attention outdoors; James had come up with a plan to clear out the garden and repurpose some of the materials found there. We set off in search of items that could be reused, collecting old wood, bricks, stones and metal to create new structures within the grounds. Everyone (especially Finn and Liam) grew excited as they began to envision what this space could become – a place for people young and old to relax in or even host events.

The work took a little longer than expected, but eventually we settled on a design we were happy with – an outdoor cinema with some seating areas and a wooden deck for people to enjoy barbecues or picnics on sunny days. This way, we figured it gave the best chance for sale to people that may want to set up a B&B or grow their own or give back to the community in some way. Of course, we can't control the sale, but we all felt pleased with what we'd created and were confident it could be the deciding factor for someone out there. We worked tirelessly all day, and into the night, until finally our hard work paid off – The Lake House now had something truly special that would last for many years to come.

It feels an eternity since I first stepped foot into The Lake House; yet I also feel as if I've been part of something everlasting – a project which will help others find peace in themselves and their surroundings, no matter how old they are. I consider my newly formed family, and I know without a doubt that each person here has made an impact which will reach far beyond these walls.

As I look around the kitchen, and dining and living rooms, I can see such a dramatic difference: how the new paint glistens and the wooden floorboards shine. In just a couple of weeks, the house has transformed before my eyes. The place breathes a little easier now that the rooms are opened, as if they've awakened from a long, deep slumber. The Lake House officially looks like a home worthy of living in once again – something I couldn't have imagined at first. It's come back to life; rooms are filled with laughter, conversations and an occasional bout of spirited debate.

As we work together towards a common goal, I can't help but feel that something special is being created here – more than just a beautifully restored house by a lake; a sense of hope. I take a deep breath, letting the peace of the place envelop me.

Dom, seemingly attuned to my thoughts, remarks with a half-smile, 'This place is special, that's for sure – perfect spot by the lake.' He leads me over to the pier and inspects the gaps in the wood, the rusty nails sticking out. 'It's not safe just yet,' he says, 'but it won't take much.' He hands me a hammer and screws, and I busily start to work while he looks around for more tools.

We spend the rest of the day fixing up the pier and shoreline; mending broken boards, painting over rusty rails, adding planks here and there. As we work, I take in all that this place has to offer – lush greenery, birds singing in nearby trees, rabbits darting across our path. The peace of The Lake House is palpable; worries slip away with each passing moment.

At sundown, we sit on a bench overlooking the lake. Dom lights a cigarette as we watch the stars appear one by one in the night sky. Neither of us speaks for what feels like hours, but it's comfortable – like an old friend, you don't need to talk all the time to stay connected.

Finally, Dom breaks the silence. 'You know, Daisy... you may want to make this your permanent home,' he says with a small smile before standing up and wandering back inside.

I'm left alone on the bench watching him go. Reality check is that London's calling. Ash is waiting, the deadline is looming and funds are low.

But his words linger, as if he knows something I don't.

CHAPTER 29

THE ART

Each night, as the star-strewn sky lulls me into a peaceful slumber, I find myself half-asleep on my makeshift bed of blankets and pillows on the porch. I'm still staying at the guest house, but once everyone else has left for the day, I love to steal these gorgeous hours to myself to work on the *Forest Fables* artwork. And whether it's the solitude or the silence or the amazing star-scape, I find myself sketching, painting and drawing the day's discoveries with Fintan's art set. My hand reaches for it unconsciously in the dim light, the charcoal pencil gliding across the paper as if it has a mind of its own. Scenes from the day – mouldered stone walls crested with briars, stone circles covered in lichen, majestic stands of forest with paths disappearing into their depths – feel as if they're sketched onto the drawing pad by an unseen hand.

My creativity is flourishing, and new ideas race through my mind, as if life and art are merged; as if they are one with nature itself – dual spirits blended with each stroke of paint or dab of clay or smidgeon of charcoal on canvas. A paw print in the sand; the tread marks of red deer hooves in the wet earth; the detail of a fern frond; the big, adoring eyes of Dom's dogs as he scratches them under their chins; the formation of birds in flight; the amazing sunsets and sunrises over dew-drenched fields; skies that mirror such changing moods on the glittering lake; the wild beauty, grandeur and majesty of Ireland. In that half-awake state, part-dreaming and part-sketching, I see things that make my head spin. So much so that I can hardly work fast enough.

Despite the excitement, the weight of sadness settles in my chest. Everything that's unfolding, that's sweeping me up in this beautiful fairy tale, is only temporary... my time here in Innisfree is limited. Sometime in the next few weeks, I'll be saying goodbye to this house, its people and everything that's lifted my spirit. Soon, I'll return to London where the hustle and bustle awaits. The idyllic landscape, the sparkling waters of the lake and the laughter that echoes through this house will slowly drift away like the tendrils of a fading dream. And I'll be back at my desk, in a gated estate somewhere, without birdsong or fresh air or a chance of catching an eyeful of the sun painting orange and pink hues on the sky, feeling close enough to reach out and touch.

Ash's texts bombard my inbox multiple times a day reminding me of the need to start looking at potential properties in London. The sale of The Lake House will allow us to invest in the fast-paced real estate market. 'Start climbing the property ladder.' 'Secure a good deal.' His words are a constant reminder that it's time to focus on our next step. I try to keep my spirits up by thinking about the excitement of moving in with Ash, of finally having a place of our own, being able to share our day-to-day lives together and grow closer. But no matter how hard I cling to the thought of living a busy city life again, as I sit here surrounded by the lapping lake, chirping crickets and rustling leaves, I can't deny the way I'm feeling.

I've only been here three weeks and yet I feel more attached than anywhere else I've ever lived. How can that be?

I hear footsteps nearing me and look up to see James, a warm smile on his face as he holds two steaming mugs of tea.

'Gus McDonagh just called – your bags have been delivered by taxi to the guest house,' he says, handing me my tea before sitting down next to me. 'That means your paperwork has arrived safe and sound. The Lake House is ready to go on the market.'

I take a deep breath and smile. 'Well, looks like it was goof-proof after all.'

James raises an eyebrow. '*Goof-proof*?'

'Yes, just something my boyfriend says. Never mind.'

'Ah, he'll be glad,' James remarks. 'The deposit will come in handy in London, especially at those prices.'

'Exactly! This is great news: we did what we set out to do. Job done!' I say, my voice a little too forced, a pitch too high.

James nods and excuses himself, and I wave him goodnight.

I should be dancing for joy. I should be jumping up and down with excitement. I should be heading out to The Tap House to celebrate. Yet I feel stuck to this spot; my feet remain firmly on the ground. We'd all worked so hard on this project – repainting the walls, sanding the floors, fixing every broken window – and in the end, we gave a brand-new life to The Lake House.

But here's the thing. And there's always a thing...

Soon, it'll mean giving all this away, handing it over, letting go and saying goodbye.

Soon, someone else will get to live their happily-ever-after here.

My heart sinks as I realise what this means. All of this, this quest for answers and sense of purpose, will have to come to an end. I'll have to let go of this search for my past and the people who played a role in it. I'll have to say goodbye to this newfound family, and leave behind their stories and memories. It's a bittersweet realisation, one that leaves a hollow feeling in my chest.

But this is what I need to happen. This quest for answers and purpose has been my everything for so long. Too long. Maybe the closure of this chapter will allow me to move on to the next, to create my own story back in London with Ash and all the exciting plans we've made. There's definitely lots to be excited about.

Definitely.

I take a long look around The Lake House, trying to commit every detail to memory, and I know that I'll cherish this place, this time for years to come.

And who knows, maybe someday I'll find my way back here; maybe someday I'll have the chance to make new memories.

Maybe.

CHAPTER 30

THE TICKING CLOCK

The crisp evening breeze brushes against my cheeks as I unlatch the newly painted gate leading to The Lake House. I step onto the now lovingly tended gravel path and the scene before me is straight out of a folk ballad: a beautiful rural lakeside Irish house, standing as proudly as it did decades, even centuries, ago. Just four weeks ago, this place was ready to be torn down – but look at it now, restored to its full potential. I can't believe the transformation that's taken place in such a short amount of time – it proves that miracles can happen when good people work together. I'll be sure to pass that on to Lenka.

Almost a month has passed since first arriving in Innisfree. It feels like only yesterday and a lifetime ago all at once. The last phase has been reached; I've gone to and from Jonathan's office all week in order to wrap up the paperwork. All the administrative processes have now kicked into gear. It's upped the ante in terms of final clearance and getting things moving with The Lake House. For the rest of this week, I'm tasked with clearing out the remaining contents and scrubbing away years of dust and grime. Finn and Liam are always willing to lend a hand, no task too difficult or menial. They never complain nor whine; in fact they seem happiest when the workload is heaviest, loving to paddleboard in the evening on the lake after a full day's graft.

As The Lake House nears completion, I've grown ever more desperate for answers about my mother's past over these last few weeks – a woman with a secret so great she spent most of her life hiding it. Since seeing that photo of Mick and my mum so in love, I know he's somehow tangled in this mystery; I can feel it in my bones alongside the fact he left her this estate. Surely that speaks of their enduring bond, especially after so many years apart?

I need to find out before I leave Innisfree, and I believe Moya Collins holds the key to unlocking my mother's cryptic life.

I haven't seen her since my first day at the house when James called out to her in the distance and I went to see her in her caravan and she wouldn't answer the door. Let alone speak to me. James suggested she could be afraid I was going to evict her. I realise he might be right – maybe she thinks I'm here to take away her home. Tears sting my eyes as I remember how it felt to be kicked out, moved on, pushed away – I would *never* do that to someone else. I know only too well the fear and uncertainty that comes with losing your home, your sense of security, in an instant. Somehow, I need to make it clear to her that's not why I'm here. She needs to understand there's nothing for her to fear. So I'm going to try again.

With determination lighting the fire in my soul, I walk through the brisk Irish mist towards Moya's caravan. Its weathered exterior carries the burden of a thousand storms, with paint peeling in places like old secrets refusing to stay hidden. I rap my knuckles on the door, but silence meets my ears. My second knock yields a louder echo, but still nothing stirs inside.

I stand in the fading light on a patch of grass, the dew beneath my feet creating a damp, cool sensation. I reach out and place my palm against the slightly damp wood, feeling the faint warmth radiating from within. My voice cracks as I earnestly plead, 'Moya, if you can hear me, I understand why you're scared. But please know that this land is your home now and for as long as you want it. James has already agreed to put a clause in the paperwork that ensures it stays that way, even if the estate is sold. Please let me talk to you before I go back to London.'

The clock is ticking on my time here. Will she ever let me in?

The stillness of the night is suddenly pierced by an owl's call from somewhere nearby, its hoot reverberating through the chill air. I wait a moment and then realise that she isn't going to open up. I start walking back to the house, turning around in the hope that she might change her mind.

As if slowly waking from a long slumber, the curtain near the window twitches, revealing Moya watching me as I walk away.

CHAPTER 31

THE SICKNESS

'You still don't look too good.'

I sit on the edge of Kayla's bed, and she peers at me with a sour expression before sticking out her tongue. 'I feel better-ish. My nose won't stop running, my body aches, and I have this terrible headache. I feel like I want to puke, but I don't... it feels worst in the morning; maybe it's before the painkillers kick in, like I've been run over by a bus. Repeatedly run over.'

I think my beautiful friend may have been right all along – perhaps she is allergic to housework. Or, more likely, has succumbed to the long hours we've all been putting in.

When I returned to the guest house at lunchtime to check in on her, she was fast asleep and snoring her head off, so I thought it best to leave her be.

'How was today?' I ask. 'Anything I can get you? It's nearly dinner time. You've slept most of the day.'

She groans and snuggles further into her sheets, yanking them up around her neck. 'I'm good thanks. Grace has been great, checking in on me every five minutes. I think she's grateful for the guitar you gave her.'

I give her a pitying smile. 'I'm sorry you're feeling so bad.' I grab one of the pillows that's propped against the wall and place it under her head.

The soft rapping on the door causes Kayla to pause in the middle of a sneezing fit. She wipes her nose with the back of her sleeve and calls out, 'Who is it?'

As the door opens, a rush of cold air brings in Grace, whose bleached hair is slightly dishevelled. Her skin is the colour of porcelain, and her green eyes seem to sparkle against the paleness. A wide, friendly smile spreads across her face as she ducks her head in, her arms filled with a tray of steaming hot soup, fresh sandwiches and a bowl of colourful fruit.

She sets the tray down on the side table and starts to arrange the contents, as Kayla weakly asks, 'What yummy treats do you have this time, Grace?'

With a reassuring smile, she says, 'I'm here to bring you some healing food. I hope it helps.'

When Grace puts the food in front of Kayla, she gives her a thankful smile before she starts to tuck in. 'Grace has been an angel, looking after me and providing entertainment,' she says. She performs an elaborate bow and tips her head. 'And it's been my pleasure, Kayla. You've entertained me with stories of London's nightlife – the clubs, fashion shows, theatre – it all sounds so wonderful.' She claps her hands together, almost childlike. 'I could listen to you talk all day long.'

Kayla and I exchange a knowing look. 'Well, if you ever want to come visit us in London, you're always welcome!' I say.

Grace's face comes alive with a smile as she stares out the window at the sun setting over Innisfree. She shakes her head and scrunches her nose. 'My brother Ciaran is in Chicago – he was only supposed to go for a summer but fell in love with the lifestyle there and never came home! Broke my parents' hearts.' Her voice catches, and I feel a pang of sympathy for her, but before I can say anything, she grins and winks, her eyes twinkling. 'It's fine – Innisfree is my home.' She places one hand over her heart. 'And there's no place like home.' She turns to me, eyes full of curiosity. 'So, how'd it go today? Anything interesting happen?'

I take a deep breath and tell her about adding the final touches to the house, and how amazing it's been to see it all come together. 'Now I just have to get used to the idea of leaving you all behind!' I say, trying to sound upbeat.

'But at least that means that you can sell it and have something to put towards your new place in London with Ash,' Kayla says.

Grace taps her fingers together. 'Oh my days, how exciting is that? Living your best life with your boyfriend in your own place... I can't wait to live with my boyfriend. To share every moment together, to cook and chill and do whatever we want, whenever we want... Mum and Dad are strict about it, so I'll have to wait. They think that people will talk...'

'I'm sure they just want what's best for you,' I say. 'But in the end, it's your life and you have to make your own decisions.'

'Oh, I know,' Grace says with a grin. 'But sometimes that's easier said than done... Small towns are great on the one hand, but on the other, it can be hard. If we were in London, with all those people, nobody really knows everyone else's business. It's easy to reinvent yourself, be who you want, leave your hang-ups and history behind...'

I take a moment to pause and reflect on how fortunate I am; I have a great job, awesome friends and soon I can have a beautiful house in London. I'm so lucky to call London home. The city throbs with life, filled with merging cultures and lifestyles. As the day melts into night, the city transforms into a different kind of buzz. The London Eye lights up the sky, and the streets are full of people out for a night on the town. Trendy bars and chic restaurants line the streets, from the bright lights of Soho to the opulence of Mayfair. Everywhere you look, something new awaits, a constant reminder of what makes life so exciting.

Grace is right... There's no place like home; it's what I know, what I've always known. Innisfree has been a fantastic experience, but it's not long-term.

Ash and I are long-term.

Our plans are long-term.

Kayla starts to cough, bringing me back to the present.

'Do you want me to call a doctor or go to the pharmacy?' I ask.

She shakes her head. 'No, it's just the flu. My fault; I've been pushing myself too hard lately. This is my body's way of telling me to slow down, and I can't think of a better place to recuperate than here.' She flashes Grace a smile.

Grace grins back. 'I'll let you rest now. Anything you need, just holler – I'm not going anywhere.'

My phone rings in my hand. My stomach drops as Lenka's name flashes on the screen. I wasn't expecting a call; I still have a few weeks until my deadline... Hesitantly, I lift my gaze to Kayla, grabbing my sketchbook and excusing myself for some privacy further down the hallway. Lenka doesn't do good news.

CHAPTER 32

THE DEADLINE

I stand enclosed within the cosy hallway of the guest house, my gaze transfixed on the sepia-toned photos lining the walls, a recollection of the people who've passed through this haven.

'Hey, Daisy, quick update for you,' Lenka says with urgency in her voice. 'We're bringing the deadline forward to beat a competitor release. Also, the illustrations are now an open call. We want to cast a wider net, make sure we get the very best... No offence intended, of course. We don't want to leave any stone unturned!'

Panic and shock set in as the pressure climbs to the mountaintops. The crushing weight of less time and fiercer competition bears down on my shoulders.

But Lenka reassures me, 'You can do it, Daisy. This is a make-or-break moment – every illustrator in the country is whipping up their best work for this right now, so don't hold anything back. Give it everything you've got.'

Gathering every ounce of courage, I thank her for the update and hang up the call, my thoughts a whirlwind. Today is Tuesday. She wants them Friday. That's two weeks earlier than planned.

Granted, I've been working tirelessly on the illustrations at night, but my days have been entirely devoted to the house. And I loved how she just slipped in that it's now an open call. My heart skips a beat as panic sets in – it's not just my commission anymore. I'm fighting for my life against every other hungry illustrator now. Lenka's just gone and Hunger Games'd my life.

I glance at my sketchbook, my latest illustration staring back at me, and I can't help but focus on its imperfections. The pressure of delivering earlier than expected feels suffocating. I'm so afraid everyone will realise I'm not as great as they think I am. Insecurity overwhelms me. Yet, I have no choice but to face my fear.

I let out a deep sigh and drag myself to the kitchen table, trying my best to shake off the feeling of impending doom. There's never enough time, never enough energy and never enough inspiration to make something perfect. Not for Lenka, not for Matilda Wilder, not even for myself. This task is too big for me; it requires patience and talent that I'm not sure I have. My heart races as I think about it all – pleasing everyone, attracting new readers, staying relevant – and how easily everything could fall apart if I fail.

With one hand pressed to my temple and the other gripping tightly onto the edge of the table, I realise I've got myself into something much bigger than myself *again*.

As I flick through my sketchbook, I think back to my first meeting with Lenka. She'd been so impressed with my portfolio, and that's what granted me this opportunity in the first place. I try to cling to the memory of the confidence I felt that day, but it's difficult. Why is it so hard to believe in our own abilities, even when others see them?

I pore over the *Forest Fable* illustrations I've done since arriving in Innisfree. I do love them and I'm proud of them. For the first time in so long, I felt the joy of pure flow, of creative spark coursing from my heart to my hand onto the page. However, I know talent is only one part of the picture – determination and hard work are just as vital. So I take a deep breath and start listing out all the remaining illustrations, prioritising those I need to focus on first and allocating enough time for revisions. The task ahead is intimidating, but if I'm organised and focused, I can do it. If we can turn The Lake House around in such a short space of time, I'm sure I can pull this off with the same belief.

I feel a tightness in my chest as I contemplate the launch of a similar book from another publisher and how crucial it is that we release before them. Everywhere I turn I feel the burning eyes of an army of up-and-coming illustrators, all hungry for this chance to outshine me. My sense of urgency intensifies to a fever pitch. It's an all-or-nothing situation: make the bold move or risk forever being left behind. A renewed sense of purpose drives me forward. I may never feel completely prepared or completely content with my artwork, but I can no longer afford to be hesitant and put things off. I need to let go of minor imperfections. It's time to keep creating.

I stand up and arch my back, letting out a sigh of relief. I have less than three days to finish this project. But I've been working on it for weeks, and I realise I should be proud of what I've done so far. So I promise myself to put in my best effort, regardless of the outcome. I'll do the best I can with the time I have, but I'm determined not to sacrifice my life and goals for someone who doesn't respect me or my efforts again. I'll live my life on my own terms.

CHAPTER 33

THE PARTY

I stand in the foyer of the once-crumbling lake house, breathing in the scent of freshly painted walls and newly polished floors. My gaze roams around in admiration of the high ceilings, intricate crown moulding and the warm glow cast by vintage chandeliers. I can't help but feel a swell of pride as I reflect on the weeks of renovation work our team poured into the house and now it's finished. Right on schedule. Ta-da!

We'd been complete strangers when we first stepped foot into the abandoned building, each with our own talents and personalities. But soon enough, we grew close, genuine buddies, clocking in countless hours of work and lots of laughter, fuelled by cups of tea. Bringing a shared dream together, turning this relic into something wonderful. As I run my fingers along the smooth balustrade of the polished staircase, I feel a gentle touch on my shoulder. I look up to find James, the lawyer turned tour guide turned historian turned odd-jobs man with quiet confidence and skilful hands that saved me here countless times.

He hands me a plastic envelope of documents. 'Insurance has been approved,' he says. 'One of the last things you'll have to sign.'

I take the packet and sit down on the bottom stair. As I slowly scan each page, James brings over two cups of coffee and slides onto the step beside me. He smiles knowingly as I sign off on the final page.

A hint of sadness hangs in his eyes as he gazes around the house. 'It's bittersweet, isn't it?' he says softly. 'It turned out better than any of us could have imagined, but all good things must come to an end, eh?'

Without conscious thought, I take his hand and give it an encouraging squeeze. 'We should celebrate our final night here at the house, while we're all together,' I suggest. 'Something that'll leave us with good memories.'

A sly smile creases James' lips. 'I may have just the thing. Be here for 8 p.m.'

'Thanks, James – you've been such a great friend. If there's ever anything I can do for you, let me know.' He raises an eyebrow at me. 'Like if you need any help? Like you broke your leg, or your account got hacked and you had no money, or if you got food poisoning...?'

'Sounds like a great offer. Thanks.' He grins back at me, and I feel my heart flutter.

I laugh and throw my hands up in the air. 'You know what I mean. I'm here for you, just like how you've been here for me.'

I think about all James has taught me since I got here. He's helped me realise that it's okay to not have everything figured out right away; that life will give us what we need when we least expect it and that being brave enough to take risks will lead us to places we never dreamed were possible. Even against the odds.

'James,' I begin hesitantly. 'So what's next for you now? What's your plan?'

'Well, I've had a little bit of news myself on the career front.' He raises an eyebrow, almost coy.

'Go on – tell me more!' I gently nudge him in the ribs.

'It's a human rights position in Brussels that I've wanted for a while, but the timing wasn't right – I couldn't just leave Dad to manage the office on his own. But, strangely enough, it was him who suggested I apply! Not sure if he's trying to get rid of me or if he's thinking of scaling back a bit. Odds are I won't get it, but I'm in with a slim chance,' he says with a sigh.

'A slim chance is still a chance,' I reply optimistically. 'We've faced tough odds before and come out on top!'

'You're right – if anyone can do it against the odds, it's us, Daisy.'

I swallow. My cheeks flame, and all of a sudden, I just don't know what to do with myself.

Oh dear.

Oh no.

Oh please.

Please don't make me think that this is anything even close to real and confuse me and make me screw up my entire life just when I've finally got it together.

I hold his piercing gaze. If I were single, wow, would this be a moment.

I'd tell him how much he meant to me, wrap my arms around him and press myself against him, inhale his scent, run my fingers through his hair. I'm close enough to feel the warmth emanating from his body. My breath hitches; it's difficult to contain the desire that courses through my veins when he's so close, like now. The way his touch electrifies my skin, the way we complement each other – it's impossible to ignore our chemistry.

My eyes flicker down to his lips, and I watch as he bites them softly with anticipation. It takes everything in me to resist kissing him right now, right here, to finally give in to what I know has been stirring from the moment I saw him in The Fox. And I can tell by the way he's looking at me that it might be the same for him.

We're both caught in this moment and hyper-aware of the tension between us. I know I have to do something before it becomes too intense for me to handle. Before I make an irreversible mistake.

I can't. I won't. I couldn't... It's not fair to Ash. It's not fair to anyone.

I jump up from my seat and walk away with my back turned towards him, pretending to busy myself with anything else besides him.

As Kayla and I step into the Lake House dining room, a wave of warmth and light embraces us both. She turns to me, gobsmacked. This is the first time since Kayla has been ill that she's seen the place in its full glory.

I can see the awe in her eyes as she takes in the beautifully decorated space, her hand holding on to mine tightly. I can't help but smile, knowing that this is all because of our hard work.

'Wow,' Kayla breathes, her voice filled with wonder. 'It's so beautiful.'

'It really is,' I reply, squeezing her hand affectionately. 'And it's all thanks to everyone here.'

The scent of home-cooked food lingers in the air, and flickering candles add a soft glow to the long table set with delicate vases filled with wildflowers and crisp linens. Friends, both familiar and new, surround the table, joyfully chattering as James presents an Irish feast: honey-and-mustard-glazed ham, buttery mash potatoes, stew, fresh carrots and peas from his garden – each dish garnished with love and care.

We take our seats, and I can feel the excitement in the air. Everyone is chatting and laughing, sharing stories about their time at the Lake House. The food is passed around, each dish more delicious than the last. I can see Kayla taking small bites of everything, putting on a brave face despite still feeling under par.

As we enjoy the lavish meal, my eyes can't help but drift to the man across from me, the one who made all this happen. Amidst the hearty conversation and playful banter, his presence feels like the gravity that keeps us all grounded. If I'm being fully honest with myself, I've been feeling an intense pull towards James since our first encounter, and my friendship with him is something that's grown deeper than I ever expected. His company has been a bright spot in my life here in Innisfree, and I've loved all the moments we've shared together. It's like he sees the real me, the person behind the doubts and fears. He makes me feel like I'm enough, just as I am. And I see the same in him. I've been realising that my feelings for him are more than just platonic, and my reluctance to leave the Lake House has just as much to do with James as the property itself.

As I watch the laughter and friendship zigzag across the table, my heart fills with joy, while the unknown territory of my feelings for James brews a subtle cocktail of confusion and anxiety and, of course, guilt over Ash. Believe me, I didn't set out to feel this way. It's what I do with these feelings that matters. I daren't even speak to Kayla about this. I was hoping that the feelings would go away, but instead they're only becoming more intense and harder to ignore.

Suddenly, a hush falls over the room as James stands up, a glass of wine in his hand. He clears his throat and raises his glass, looking around the table with a smile.

'I just wanted to say a few words,' he begins, his voice carrying through the room. 'You all have made this project so much more than just a job. You've all become friends, and I couldn't be more grateful for that. This isn't just a beautiful space; it's a space filled with memories and laughter and love.'

There's a murmur of agreement from the group, and I can see tears in Kayla's eyes as she listens to James' heartfelt words.

This place has become more than just a project for all of us – it's become a home.

'To the Lake House,' James says, raising his glass high. 'May it always be a place of love, friendship and happiness. And to Mick, who made it all possible.'

The whole group raises their glasses, echoing James' words with resounding cheer. I take a sip of my wine, feeling a sense of contentment wash over me. This is where I belong, amongst friends and loved ones, building a future filled with laughter and joy. I look over at Kayla, who's smiling through her tears, and I know that this is exactly where we're meant to be. I just don't know how realistic it is to even think this way.

Actually, I do. Completely unrealistic. Nobody should capsize their life after a few weeks away from home. I'm sure they even teach that in schools.

After dinner, we move out to a massive campfire that Finn and Liam have lit. Grace and her friends pull out their instruments – guitars, fiddles and even a borrowed accordion. Grace strums away and happily takes requests as Fintan belts out much-loved favourites, and Dom and Jacinta dance together, holding their hands high in an old set dance. Kayla whoops and claps, wrapped in a blanket, giving herself a night off from high kicks and what can only be described as 'interpretive jigging'. The music and wine weave a magical web around us, filling the night with a sense of camaraderie and comfort I've never experienced before. Despite the simple beauty of the moment, however, I can't help but be overwhelmed by a sense of impending sadness. As we share stories and laugh in unison, I find myself desperate for time to slow down so I can stay here forever.

James and I sit side by side, sharing a blanket to ward off the chill of the night air, mesmerised by the orange glow and dancing sparks before us. The warmth of the blaze adds a deeper hue to the silvery moonlight, and for a moment I'm sure I can feel my heart swell with the sheer beauty of it all.

James turns to me and smiles. 'You did it,' he says softly.

There's a beat before I reply, my throat tight with emotion. '*We* did it,' I finally whisper.

A glance between us hints at the unspoken bond that's been growing ever since I set foot here in Innisfree. Aching with bittersweet sadness, I know our time is up.

The stars twinkle in the night sky, like a million eyes watching us from above.

'You're something special,' he whispers, his blue eyes piercing into mine with undeniable longing. 'I wish we didn't have to say goodbye. I wish you weren't heading back to London.'

My breath hitches as I feel emotions swell up and threaten to overflow. Reaching out, I place my hand in his, feeling the strength of his calloused fingers intertwined with mine. I can't help myself. It was as natural and as sudden as a reflex. For a moment, time stands still. I know I won't be able to forget this night or the way it makes me feel.

As the moon slowly inches across the sky, James' thumb grazes gently against my knuckles and I feel an overwhelming warmth flow through me. It's everything I want and yet... I can't. This isn't right. It isn't fair. It's not to be.

I slip my hand from his grasp. 'I should go,' I say softly. Even as I say this I'm fighting against what my heart is telling me. But he knows it too. He bows his head, a slow, sad nod of acceptance.

With one last glance at the campfire, my hands deep in my pockets and my eyes trained downwards, I make my way back to the house. The moon rises above the treetops, casting a pale light over the meadow. The grass shimmers with dewdrops that glisten like diamonds in the moonlight. The air is alive with the sweet fragrances of wildflowers, and I take a deep breath, letting them fill my nostrils. I close my eyes and listen to the music; crickets chirping and frogs croaking, the campfire sing-song and the easy laughter of my Innisfree family wrapping around me like a blanket, wishing to carve this perfect stolen moment into my memory forever.

CHAPTER 34

THE SWIM

As I stand here, thinking about all that Innisfree has given me, all that I'll have to leave behind, the brilliant stars above remind me that there's one thing I haven't yet done – a midnight swim in the lake. I quickly pack my rucksack, knowing this is my final chance before Friday, before my time here is up.

I feel the cold sand under my feet as I walk barefoot along the shoreline, which leads me towards the still waters of the lake. Lost in thought, I almost don't take notice of what's ahead: a small stone cross on the beach. I stop short in my tracks. This must be where Mick perished – and where my future was forever altered.

I'm haunted by the idea that he could have come to such a tragic end when he'd been so full of life. For the past few weeks, all I've heard about Mick are tales of his life, joy and excitement. I wish I could have met him. I also wish my mother had spoken of him, told me what had connected them and what had ended their relationship... but that's lost forever now. Kneeling on the damp sand, I find it hard to reconcile what I see with what happened here. No matter how much I stare at this small memorial, it still feels impossible to grasp. I think of the days when Mick and my mother were still alive. Did they throw stones into the lake and watch the ripples travel to the other side? Did their eyes light up when huddled around the camp-fire, telling stories and singing songs?

I smile when I remember Marianne's story of stumbling across Mick bathing in the lake completely nude, and I know this is the place where I need to take a leap of faith. It's a wild thought, one that excites and scares me all at once. I want to rid myself of the heartache, the pressure on my chest and the burden that has been pushing me down. With no further hesita-tion, I begin to take off my clothes. As each item falls away, I feel as if it signifies something I'm leaving in the past. Standing there without a stitch of clothing on, I decide this must be what rebirth feels like – laying your soul bare and being open to all the choices the universe gives.

The lake is chilled, as is the night air that surrounds me. I take one step in and taste fear in my mouth like a tepid tide, but little whispers flutter in my chest, telling me that I can do this. I take another step, and another.

The cold water reaches my waist, forcing me to take a deep breath and let the chill completely consume me. The sudden sensation makes my body tremble, but I push forward into the lake's depths.

As soon as I submerge myself underwater, the sound around me fades away, plunging me into a deep silence. I'm immersed in liquid darkness, all alone in the stillness of the night, held securely by the cool, dark water.

But I don't feel scared. If anything, swimming out further, deeper, seems to be an act of liberation. I love the sensation of my arms and legs slicing through the silken water without any effort at all.

With each stroke forward, I've let go of something until it doesn't matter anymore; until there's nothing left for me to cling on to except this moment right here. In this silence, my fears are washed away with the water, and in their place is a renewed trust in myself that fills me up with gentle warmth and peace.

I slowly swim back towards shore and breathe in everything around me. As my feet touch the sandy bottom again, I feel connected with something much bigger than myself – a force that's been guiding me here all along.

I make my way out of the lake, dripping with water and draped in nothing but moonlight.

'Hey! Are you trying to catch your death?'

I'm startled by the voice, and I look up to see a woman with long dark hair running towards me, her face flushed with panic.

'Do you have any idea how dangerous it is to swim at night by yourself?' she warns, shaking a wooden stick in my direction.

'I'm sorry,' I say, quickly grabbing my clothes and hugging them to my body. 'I didn't mean to cause any trouble.'

Moya steps closer to me, and her beauty becomes more apparent as she does so. In the moonlight, she seems like some sort of mythical creature.

'There's a storm warning,' she says, pointing towards the increasingly ominous sky. 'It's time to finish here and move on.'

She's right, I think, looking up. Come Friday, I'll be finished here and back in the real world, ready to move on. The clouds have deepened in colour, and a gentle breeze has started up; just like when we first arrived in Innisfree. I gather my belongings and place them in my rucksack.

'I'm sorry for coming to disturb you, Moya. I'll leave now so you can get some peace – no need to worry about seeing me again.'

Moya's dark eyes lock on to mine. 'Come on,' she says, motioning for me to follow her. 'I'll take you back to mine.'

CHAPTER 35

THE PUZZLE

I find myself sitting at the tiny table in Moya's caravan. The inside is lit by a string of pink lights, and the air is laden with the lingering scent of jasmine incense, the atmosphere a unique blend of serenity and mystical charm. The caravan is a tapestry of colours and patterns. The corners are filled with stacks of books, worn and well-loved, like the pouches of herbs hanging from the ceiling.

Across from me, Moya's wise, dark eyes seem to hold the answers I seek. With careful hesitation, I venture to introduce myself and the matter of my quest.

'Moya, it's a pleasure to meet you. My name is Daisy Clarke, and I've come to Innisfree seeking information about my mum, Rose. She passed away many years ago, and I inherited this house that I knew nothing about.' I delve into my rucksack and pull out Mick's postcard in the wooden frame. 'The only thing linking my mum to Mick and The Lake House is this postcard,' I say, handing her the worn piece of history. 'My mum had the same one in London that she cherished.'

Moya, her eyes full of curiosity, reaches out to examine the box frame more closely. She runs her fingers over the carved exterior of the object but doesn't speak.

'James said Mick made this?' I inquire.

'Yup, he was always tinkering away on something. He had a knack for making things that weren't just plain ol' boxes,' she replies with a smile.

Raising an eyebrow, I ask what she means by that.

She taps the frame and says, 'This isn't just a picture frame; it's a secret box. We used to call them monkey puzzle boxes growing up; they were where we'd stash our money or jewellery – anything you wanted kept safe.'

I'm instantly intrigued and can feel my curiosity pique. Moya smiles knowingly, as if she can tell what I'm thinking and hands me the box to inspect more closely.

Time seems to slow as I fiddle with the frame, searching for any sign of a secret panel or hidden lever. As my fingers trace over the intricate patterns and notches of the object, I struggle to find any answer. I peer more closely, examining each groove for some sort of opening mechanism. My fingers linger on the edge of the frame as I wonder if I should risk using a hammer to try to smash it open. But I daren't destroy it – it's a treasure chest, a puzzle, a piece of Mick's heart, waiting to be discovered.

A spark of inspiration comes over me, and I press on a decorative knot with both thumbs. Suddenly, a small, well-concealed drawer springs open, revealing a weathered envelope marked 'To Rose'.

I take a deep breath as Moya and I cautiously look at the treasure. The weight of the decision to read the letter in the absence of its intended recipient sits heavy on our shoulders. We exchange a solemn glance.

'Do you want to read it on her behalf?' Moya asks me.

I delicately peel the ageing paper to reveal the faint ink of what lies beneath. And immediately I'm taken aback. The way the capitals are written and how the cursive flows is so familiar.

I now see why James was so taken aback by me signing my name that day; my penmanship is almost indistinguishable from Mick's.

Breathing deeply, I scan the words, and I feel the world shift under my feet.

Dear Rose, if you're reading this, I'm gone... but you've returned and you've remembered our special place, where I've thought of you every hour of every day of my life since I met you all those years ago. My love for you remains eternal.

I hope you cherish the house by the lake and find solace in our memories there as I have. I want you to know that you have had my heart all along and you always will.

Until we meet again, forever yours, Mick x

I rest the letter on my lap, feeling a heavy tug in my gut, a tight knot of sadness for the man behind the words who poured out his heart, only for it to remain hidden and unanswered.

A mix of emotions washes over me – sorrow, longing and the faintest flicker of hope. The words on the page paint a vivid image of the love Mick held for my mother. Held for her his whole life.

Moya's breath falters, and I look up to see her eyes brimming with tears that threaten to spill over. The weight of the loss and the unfulfilled love story between Mick and Rose hangs between us, filling every nook and cranny of the caravan.

I look again to the handwriting – the curves and loops with subtle flourishes, the uncanny similarity to mine. It all makes sense now – the inheritance, the undeniable familiarity that draws me towards him, to this place. My heart quakes as the truth unfurls, like a bolt of lightning striking my chest, so bright and so glaringly obvious that there's no way of not seeing it.

'Moya?'

Tears pool in her wide, sad eyes, and she looks up at me, trembling, anticipating my next question even as I steel myself to ask it.

'Is Mick my father?'

Her mouth moves as she offers a slow nod, but no sound emerges. She seems to struggle for the right words for a long moment before finally whispering, 'But he never knew.' She averts her gaze and looks towards the floor.

I slump back in my seat, feeling a mix of confusion, disbelief and frustration. My heart feels heavy with sorrow, unable to fathom how my mother could have abandoned such a perfect life. The life she had with Mick, my actual father, in this picturesque Irish village. And why she never told me about him.

Moya rubs her temples. 'Mick loved her. He loved her more than anything.'

'Then why didn't they stay together?'

'Rose was a dreamer, always chasing the next big adventure. She was never content to stay in one place for long. And Mick... he was a homebody; he loved his life here. He couldn't bear the thought of leaving, even for a short while.'

Moya pauses. 'It's complicated,' she says with a sigh. 'Mick was from a respectable family and your mother was... well, she wasn't from his world. Rose was a free spirit; she didn't believe in conventional things like marriage and family. She wanted to explore the world and have adventures. Mick's family were very traditional – they wanted him to settle down. We travellers have a different outlook, a different way of life. It was never going to work out between them, not in the long run.' She shakes her head as if to rid herself of regret, of deep sadness.

I sit in silence, digesting everything Moya is telling me, my mind racing. So much has happened in the last few weeks, and I'm struggling to process it all.

'So, they just gave up?' I ask eventually. It's hard to hear that my parents hadn't loved each other enough to fight for their relationship.

'Oh no, they didn't give up. They fought, tooth and nail, but sometimes you have to accept that something isn't meant to be. And, in the end, Rose did what she thought was best for you.'

'Which was?'

'Leaving here, making a fresh start, so you weren't born under a cloud of judgement.'

'Why didn't she ever come back?' I ask, my voice barely a whisper.

Moya looks at me for a long time before answering, as if she's trying to decide whether to tell me something. Finally, she speaks. 'It wasn't easy for her. She loved Mick with all her heart, but she didn't want to drag him away from here, from the place he loved, the only home he'd ever known. Of course, she was trying to do the best for everyone: you, Mick and herself. And it turned out well enough – you grew up loved and educated and healthy. That's all she wanted. Isn't that enough?'

I consider her question and then turn it back to her. 'Do you think she made the right decision?' I ask after a long moment.

'Yes, I think she did. Mick never understood; it nearly killed him. He loved her very much. But he'd never have stood in her way; it wasn't his place to tell her what to do or how to live. He wanted what was best for her, even if that meant running from here, from him and all she loved. It was best she never told him she was pregnant – it would have broken his heart twice over.'

I nod, understanding a little more. 'What did you mean that I would have been "born under a cloud of judgement"?'

'Well, they weren't married and they were from two different worlds. She came to me in the middle of the night. She was terrified. I gave her the money for the bus fare to Dublin and promised to protect her from any questions.'

'And Mick?' I ask, my throat tightening.

'I sealed my lips... until this very day. It was hard to hide the truth from him; he was desperate to find her, but I'd made an oath,' Moya says quietly. 'He took it very hard. He was told she was spotted in a London pub, and he went over to see for himself, but she wasn't there. Nowhere to be found. After she left, he was never the same. Never went with another – and he had plenty of admirers...'

I sit in silence for a long time, digesting everything Moya has told me. My head is buzzing.

'Try not to judge her too harshly. Try not to judge any of us too harshly. We all should have done things differently when it still could have meant something... God forgive us.'

Understanding what Mum, Mick and Moya went through makes my heart ache – my mother had desperately wanted to keep me and Mick safe, while Mick just as desperately wanted to reunite with her. And all the while, poor Moya found herself caught in the middle, a loyal friend until the very end. If Kayla asked something similar from me, I'd do it without a second thought.

I look outside and watch as the dark clouds grow thicker, and despite Mick and my mother's story being a tragic Irish ballad, destined for tears and heartache, I feel a sense of peace wash over me. They were in love. And there's happiness in knowing that my mother had known love. That I'd come from a place of love.

My entire life, I've wondered where I truly belonged, and the knowledge that The Lake House is my family's home makes me swell with pride. While it breaks my heart that Mum never returned, I understand that some stories never get a proper ending. But in this moment, sitting in her caravan and surrounded by my family's history, I feel a sense of closure.

'When are you going back to London?' Moya asks.

'End of this week.'

'That's soon. You're not staying for the auction?'

I shake my head. 'I've got a lot on, and it's best if I stop avoiding reality and just get back to normal.'

'Is that right?' she asks, her voice gentle.

'Yes... I mean, I've got a whole life in London – boyfriend, job, flat. It's where I grew up, me and Mum. All our memories are there.' I shake my head, then look into Moya's clear dark eyes once more and sigh. 'I'm not sure what I want anymore, to be honest. Except that I don't want to make the wrong decision and end up regretting it.'

'Only one thing for it.' She reaches under the table and pulls out a small wooden box. Inside, there's a tarot card deck, cloaked in dark-red velvet. 'Shall we?' she asks with a knowing smile.

I look at her, not sure what to say. I've never had my cards read before.

She takes my silence as a yes and begins to shuffle the deck expertly. 'Pick three cards,' she instructs me.

I do as she says, feeling slightly ridiculous. If Ash or Lenka could see me now, sat in a traveller's caravan, sheltering from a storm on the West Coast of Nowhere, trying to decide what to do with my life via the tarot, they'd never let me live it down.

Moya deals out the three cards I've selected in a line. She studies them for a moment before looking up at me. 'The Tower.'

The card shows a castle being struck by lightning. A man and woman are falling from the parapets.

'It's not good, is it?' I ask, feeling slightly apprehensive.

'It's not always what it seems,' she replies. 'Much like everything. The Tower can represent a time of change, upheaval. This is your past. It suggests that you've been through some kind of upheaval in your life, something that's shaken you to your core.'

I think back to my mother's death and then my stint in foster care. So far, spot on.

She closes her eyes tightly and is silent for what seems like a long time, as if she's listening to something, or someone, I can't see or hear. 'Yes, I see...' she finally speaks, her eyes remain closed. 'Daisy, you've been through great trials, but you've come out the other side stronger for it. You're a survivor.'

I feel touched by her words. I've never thought of myself as a survivor, but maybe she's right? After all, I'm still here, despite everything that's happened to me.

'This is your present. The here and now.' She moves on, turning over the next card.

I lean in to examine the card more closely but can't help noticing that this one is quite different from the last one. It looks a lot less ominous. A man and woman are featured, both nearly nude, facing each other – hands outstretched. My cheeks flush a deep red as my thoughts inevitably stray to James; not Ash, James.

Moya eyes me solemnly, her expression serious. 'The Lovers. This suggests that you're at a crossroads in your life, uncertain which path to take.'

Again, she falls silent and I wonder if she's going to say anything else.

She raises her chin to the ceiling, breathing deeply through her nose. 'Daisy, you have a choice to make. A very important choice. One that will determine the course of your future.'

I swallow hard, my heart pounding in my chest. I'm not sure I want to hear any more.

Moya opens her eyes and looks at me, her gaze intense. 'You can either stay on the path you're currently on, or you can make a change. A big change. But whatever you decide, know that there will be consequences. There will be loss but also gain. If you stay on your current path, you'll be safe, but you'll also be unhappy. You'll always wonder what could have been.'

'And if I make a change?' I instinctively find myself asking.

'If you make a change, you'll be risking everything. But

you'll also be opening yourself up to new possibilities, new experiences, new happiness. But, like I said, there will also be loss.'

'What kind of loss?' I ask, even though I'm not sure I want to know the answer.

'The loss of your old life, your old self. You'll have to start again from scratch. But if you're willing to take that risk, I think it will be worth it in the end.'

Moya falls silent, but I know there's one card left and I'm terrified about what it will tell me.

She looks at me as if reading my mind. 'The decision is yours, Daisy. Do you want to know what the last card reads? You must decide for yourself and accept the consequences, whatever they may be.'

Do I want to know? Do I dare ask? I think about Moya's question carefully, appreciating now how much risk there is in delving too deep. But this whole trip has been about uncovering the unknown, and it's led me here to my mother's friend, my father, James, the house, the village. I've discovered more about myself than I ever thought possible.

With a deep breath, I pick up the last card; the end of a tale that spanned lifetimes... It's the Devil. A man and woman chained to a demon while flames lick at their feet.

'This is your future, Daisy,' Moya says softly. 'This is where one path leads; this is what awaits you. A life of unhappiness, pain and suffering.' She runs a finger around the card. 'You'll notice that these two want for nothing; they're surrounded by riches, finery – to the external eye, they have everything they could ever want. But what they don't have is freedom – they're trapped here, in this place, because of the choices they made.'

'What choices?' My voice is barely a whisper.

'The choice to take the easy way out, the choice to give into temptation, the choice to ignore their better judgement. These are the choices that led them here, to this place.'

She looks at me, and I know she's waiting for me to say something, but I'm too shocked to speak.

'Daisy, you have a choice to make,' Moya says again. 'No one but you can make it.'

I feel a shiver run down my spine. I stare at the card for a long time, my mind racing. 'But this card doesn't tell me which path to choose... how will I know if I'm making the right decision?'

Moya smiles at me and takes my hand. 'You won't know if it's the right decision until you've made it. But sometimes, we must take a leap of faith and trust that everything will work out in the highest good. For everyone.'

I sigh. 'I just don't trust myself. It's too far a leap. Too risky.'

Moya nods and sweeps up the cards in front of her. 'Of course, they're only cards,' she says as she gently stacks them together. 'Believe what you like. That's another choice that's yours alone.'

I know our time is up. I stand, and Moya does the same.

'It's eased off a bit, the storm. Go now while you have a chance,' she says. 'The longer you wait, the harder it will be.'

I give her a hug and zip up my coat. 'Thanks for having me here, Moya,' I say as she leads me to the door.

'You're welcome, Daisy. Thank you for letting me stay on. Oh, and tell your friend to take some ginger tea in the mornings for her stomach and put on this bracelet.' She hands me a gemstone bracelet with pink and white beads. 'Rose quartz and moonstone – they help with nausea.'

'Like travel sickness?' I ask.

'And morning sickness,' Moya explains, winking at me.

I furrow my brow. 'But she's not...'

Moya taps her finger on her nose.

Right, well, I don't believe that. I can't. Out of all the things I heard tonight, Kayla being pregnant is by far the least believable to me. And that's saying something.

As the light of the caravan casts a glow across the path, I see a fox standing still and facing me. Its eyes appear to be questioning if I'm ready to face what lies ahead. I take a deep breath and try to muster up my courage. All I can do is put one foot in front of the other and try to move in the right direction. I cast my gaze one last time upon the fox before it vanishes into the shadows of the trees, a refuge of seclusion and security, far away from harm and danger, wishing that I could do the same.

CHAPTER 36

THE LAST DAY

James stands against the guest house's facade, his weathered leather boots crossed in front of him. I arrive with my rucksack slung over my shoulder and stride up to him.

'Did you get your work sent in on time?' he asks.

'I did! Thank you. Sent it first thing this morning, bright and early.' Friday is finally here, and the past few days have flown by as I worked on the finishing touches of my illustrations. Despite any other opinion, I'm super-pleased with them; they're the best effort I can offer. I'm proud of them. I'm proud of myself.

I hold my hands up in the air. 'If Lenka likes it great, if she doesn't, then I'll figure something else out.'

He nudges me playfully with his elbow. 'That's the spirit. So, what time is your flight?' His voice is gentle, like sunlight trickling through the trees.

I sigh. 'Later this evening, so we've got some time to make the most of our last few hours in Innisfree,' I say, trying to sound more casual than I really feel.

'Pity you can't stay on a few days longer. It would be nice for you to be at the auction in person,' he says.

'I wish I could, but I've already booked my ticket – everything's ready to go.'

'I understand,' he replies. 'Rest assured, most people will be tuning in online from all over the world, so you won't be the only ones following remotely. And, as ever, I'll be here on the other end of the phone during the whole thing, so any issues at all, just give me a call.'

'It's been great being here with you all – feels like home now.'

We share a look, but with our business completed, the time has come for me to move on. Together we walk to the O'Connor & Sons offices. We've come a long way in the weeks since I arrived in the village, and I can't help but feel indebted to him for all his support and friendship. But I refrain from telling James the full story of why Kayla and I must be back in London as soon as possible.

She's still poorly, but when I mentioned Moya's prophecy, she shot me a sceptical look.

'Well, she gave me this bracelet for you – apparently it helps with nausea and motion sickness, so maybe worth a try?'

Kayla's drawn to shiny objects like a moth to a flame so she instantly loved the gemstones. She asked me to thank Moya for her but to spare her any more superstitious diagnoses.

Thinking back on it now, it was silly of me to put any stock into the tarot readings; I rub my face, feeling more and more like I'm losing my mind.

I need my head checked. I need to focus on the present.

I need to catch up with Ash. Spend quality time together, in person, instead of just exchanging quick emails and brief texts; virtual communication isn't the same, and things between us have become strangely distant over the time I've been here. He's clearly in a mood with me for being away so long, although we discussed it beforehand. Meanwhile, his lack of interest in anything besides the auction and the eventual sale is beginning to bother me. We're at an impasse, and neither of us appear to be winning.

James and I reach the office, and we step through the door together. I'm hit with the familiar musty scent of old paper and leather-bound books, and Jonathan O'Connor greets me, his silver hair complementing the lines on his weathered face, a testament to the years he's devoted to this establishment.

'Ah, there you are,' he says with an unusual lightness and informality. 'A good day for you today, Ms Clarke! Everything looks in order!'

My lips curl into a small smile; I appreciate the familiarity and warmth.

James leaves us to it, and Jonathan swiftly ushers me into his office, where walls adorned with generations of O'Connor family portraits watch over us. He gently lowers himself into his worn leather chair behind the massive desk, its mahogany surface showcasing endless paperwork and abandoned cups of cold tea.

We chat through the legalities and next steps. Amidst the signing and dating of all the documents required, he hesitates for a moment before letting out a long sigh. 'Ah, and I suppose it's time I broke the news to you. After all these years and generations, O'Connor & Sons has come to an end.'

I blink in surprise, feeling a sense of loss for a thing I hadn't even realised held such a dear place in my heart. 'Oh?'

'You see, despite all my efforts to uphold our family tradition, it seems life has other plans,' Jonathan continues, a bittersweet smile gracing his lips. 'It's time for me to retire, and James has been given an opportunity he couldn't pass up, a prestigious role at the Human Rights Advisory Council. New horizons for him in Brussels.'

When I hear the news that James has been hired, I'm ecstatic for him. He's worked so hard and has overcome all the odds to land this job. But with his success comes a strange feeling of loss that I can't shake. Innisfree won't be the same without him, and the thought of my life without him brings on a wave of inexplicable sadness. Inexplicable that I should care so much about this, considering I'm leaving in a few hours. James and I will never cross paths again – so what difference does it make?

'Brussels... Wow, that's amazing.' I force a smile and manage a congratulatory remark, though it feels as if my heart is slipping somewhere far away with every word.

As we continue discussing James' departure, mixed feelings surface within me. On one hand, I'm filled with pride and happiness for James, progressing his career far beyond the confines of this small village and embracing his true passion. On the other, a familiar sadness envelops my heart, realising that our paths have already started moving in different directions, that my life will grow a little duller without him by my side.

Out of the corner of my eye, I catch James' likeness in an old photograph adorning the office wall. The beaming young man has black hair tousled from a day of adventure outside, and an infectious grin plastered on his face. I've seen that same grin over our time together in Innisfree – playing with Liam and Finn, flirting with Jacinta, sharing a joke with Dom and Fintan, joining in with Kayla's teasing of me. I turn away, realising that with James gone, everything I've come to love about Innisfree will simply be reduced to another page in its past.

Jonathan then stretches his hand out, and I can see he has a bottle of whiskey in it. He hands it to me and says, 'This is just a little token to remind you of us all when you arrive – something to raise a glass with when the sale goes through. It was Mick's favourite, so it might be a nice way to remember him.'

I take the whiskey from him and thank him sincerely.

'It's me who wants to thank you, Daisy,' he says softly, fumbling with his bow tie in a way I've never seen before. Jonathan O'Connor doesn't get tongue-tied.

I'm taken aback, laughing in confusion. 'Thank me? For what?'

'For bringing the light back into his eyes. I feared it was gone for good. But it's back. And I dare say brighter than before.'

My eyes fill with tears, and I give him a hug in return. He nods and looks away again, but this time I notice that his eyes are shining with emotion too.

We stand there for a few moments, both lost in our own thoughts. The sound of Jonathan's phone ringing breaks the trance, and I motion to the door, knowing it's my time to go.

As I pack the remainder of my things, all I can think of is James. I wonder what he's doing right now, what he's thinking about and if our paths could ever cross again. I can't get the conversation with Jonathan out of my head.

'For bringing the light back into his eyes.' It's hard to hear that James had lost that light before. I couldn't imagine what he'd gone through, just knew how deeply it had affected him.

'But it's back. And I dare say brighter than before.' I quickly catch myself, take a deep inhale and flop onto my bed. I miss James already, even though he's only been gone for a few hours. It's strange how someone can become such an integral part of your life in such a short amount of time. But I need to snap myself out of this nonsense because in a few hours' time, I'm going to land right back into my life with Ash. When the house sale goes through, we can begin to move forward.

I lean against the doorway and unfold the brochure with the listing of The Lake House – the auction details, reserve price, times, dates and all the terms and conditions. I run my fingers over James' neatly penned notes in the margins...

Suddenly, I hear the doorbell downstairs. It must be our cab. Grace answers the door, and I recognise the voice immediately and my heart skips a beat. I smooth my hair back, lick down my brows and compose myself to walk down the stairs.

I see James, standing in the doorway, a sheepish smile on his face.

'I was hoping I hadn't missed you,' he says quietly, his eyes not meeting mine.

'James,' I start, unsure where to begin. 'Congrats on the job! Brussels! You're really going!'

His eyes suddenly find mine, and his face softens. 'I only found out officially this morning. You have your own stuff going on, so I thought it best just to keep things... simple.'

I force a smile and swallow my emotions, saying, 'Well, congrats!'

He mumbles in response, and I get the sense he's avoiding physical closeness. Does he suspect like I do what could happen if I brush his skin, smell his cologne or feel the heat of his body next to mine?

I take a step back, needing some time to compose myself. 'Why are you leaving?' I ask. 'You love it here. You have friends and family and your own little piece of the planet.'

He heaves a deep sigh before finally confessing, 'I've always wanted to travel more, experience something new. If nothing ever changes, nothing ever changes. And I've decided that I'm ready for a change. Ready to change.'

'James,' I say, swallowing hard, 'I'm really going to miss you.'

My words surprise both of us. We stand in an awkward silence for what feels like ages before James finally speaks, though he looks away as he does so.

'I'm going to miss you too,' he says quietly before walking away without another word.

CHAPTER 37

THE RETURN

One laptop. Two glasses of whiskey. Three minutes till show-time.

Ash and I sit on the sofa in my London flat, watching the auction screen with bated breath.

The catalogue of the new build lies open before us, filled with plans for a carefree life together in a gated community. Our dreams just a decent bid away.

'Let's go!' Ash beams, lacing my fingers in his. 'It's happening exactly according to plan.'

I nod, a myriad of emotions coursing through me as the clock ticks down.

The auctioneer's voice breaks the silence – 'And we're off! Ladies and gentlemen, welcome to the online property auction.'

Bidding starts low, and every digital click of a mouse builds the tension before us. The auctioneer reminds us that this is an opportunity to purchase a piece of iconic property in one of Ireland's most desirable locations at a very attractive price. Ash squeezes my leg and pours us both a second whiskey, the first one not even touching the sides. We both know that our future happiness lies on this screen.

The auction begins with bids from around the world – Sydney, Chicago, Dubai, but none have matched the reserve. For a moment, everything seems to stop and there's silence. Then suddenly, a flurry of activity: bids fly back and forth in the tens of thousands. How far will they go? The numbers turn green as the reserve is met, signalling one minute left until the highest bid is determined. I take a quick sip of whiskey before shutting my eyes tight – I don't want to watch. The bell clangs out sharply: SOLD!

The overseas bidder's price appears on the screen and we suddenly become motionless. The reserve exceeded beyond my wildest dreams. The bid is accepted. The Lake House is sold.

The Lake House is SOLD!

Ash jumps out of his seat, laughing and punching the air. 'We did it! It's a brand-new start, sweetheart!'

But instead of joining him in his enthusiasm, I find myself studying the photos of The Lake House. It's gone. Just like that. Is this really what I wanted? Did I do the right thing by leaving The Lake House behind – the Kennedy family home; my legitimate family's home? If only there had been a way to keep it while heading off in this new direction.

'You okay?' Ash inquires with tenderness, softening his joyous face.

'I'm fine,' I reply, plastering a grin across my lips. 'Just feeling peculiar about it... everything happened so quickly... it was all over in no time.'

'Yes, thank goodness – we deserved a bit of speed after all the pointless flat hunting we did! Anyway, we made it! It's done!'

Ash heads to the fridge to open a bottle of champagne. 'Hey, Daisy, what's that line from *Jerry Maguire*?'

'You complete me.' He can be endearing in his own way. And I know he's excited about the future we now have together, that this is a new start for us, and that bolsters me.

'What?' He comes back to the room with a chilled bottle and two glasses.

'You complete me,' I say again.

He shakes his head and laughs. 'No, it's SHOW ME THE MONEY!'

I feel my stomach drop as I hear Ash's words. Is he kidding? My mind scrambles to think of something to say, but before I can utter a single syllable, my phone chimes. It's Jonathan O'Connor.

'That'll be the confirmation call from Ireland,' I tell him, pausing before I answer.

Ash flashes a thumbs up at me and fills a glass with champagne as he sends out an update to his family and friends.

I leave the room and step into the kitchen to take the call. 'Hey, Jonathan. Everything good?'

His voice wavers, tension emphasising each word. 'The auction is over, but... there's a catch. The buyer wants to remove the non-eviction clause.'

My heart skips a beat. This was non-negotiable. 'Absolutely not. The Lake House comes with the tenancy clause so Moya can stay, no matter what.

And then suddenly I'm saying, 'Just reject the offer.'

'Daisy? Are you okay?' Jonathan asks.

'Yes. Reject the offer. I'm taking The Lake House off the market.'

'What? You're sure you just want to throw in the towel – take it off the market altogether? How about you list it with a local agent – that way, you'll have more time to think it through?' he says.

I can tell by his voice that he's taken aback by my decision.

'Thank you, Jonathan,' I say, fighting to keep my voice steady. 'But I've decided I'm not going to put it up for auction again, at least not yet.'

His voice lowers. 'Why the change of heart?'

The words spill out before I can stop them. 'It's too soon. I've just come to terms with my past, and something inside me is telling me there might be more to uncover, and even to treasure. I need to hold on to that house for a little while longer, just to collect my thoughts and see if life has anything else in store for me.'

Jonathan clears his throat. When he speaks, his tone sits somewhere between shock and curiosity. 'There may be some disappointed investors, but I understand. If you feel there's more to uncover, it's important you take the time you need.' His next words carry a hint of affection. 'You are sure about this, Daisy? Even with your new knowledge, you might never find the answers you're looking for. There are no guarantees – for anyone.'

'I know, Jonathan,' I reply, my voice holding an unfamiliar determination, excitement coursing through me. 'But for now, it's what I want. I need to trust my intuition.'

Silence settles between us for a moment. It's an odd kind of camaraderie, understanding someone's choices without necessarily agreeing with them.

'I respect your decision, Daisy,' he says. 'I'll take care of it for you right away.'

I can feel my heart pounding in my chest as I end the call with Jonathan. The weight of my decision hangs in the air. I'm proud of standing up for Moya, but I can't help but feel guilty about how this affects Ash. I've upended all our plans, our future together now uncertain. Yet, deep down, there's a part of me that wonders if this delay is a blessing in disguise. Are we really ready for this leap?

I walk over to the window and take a deep breath. The crisp autumn air fills my lungs as I stare across the tiny communal garden, the soft hues of countless falling leaves painting wholesome, warm colours across the chilly scene. The trees' leaves are rustling in the gentle breeze, creating a soothing soundtrack to my internal conflict. They remind me of the day Ash and I first met. It was this time of year. I stood, wrapped up in a scarf and bobble hat, waiting for him to show up with the keys so I could view this flat. I barely noticed him until he struck up a conversation, and then the words seemed to flow so easily, his optimism, the energy, the chemistry. The memory makes me smile, and yet I can't help but wonder if the magic's gone. Or if there'll only ever be magic when Ash is getting what he wants. And what if we want different things? Watching that proposal on the beach on my first day in Ireland made me question if I'm being selfish for expecting joy in my own life. We've both had to make some concessions in order to get where we are now, but when does compromise become sacrifice? How much is too much to lose?

I realise how much our future had become intertwined with the sale of The Lake House. Yet, perhaps it's that very interconnectedness that caused these doubts to grow, to fester. With real courage and determination, I prepare myself to move forward. I need to communicate with Ash and tell him how I feel. This isn't just about the house anymore; it's about our future, whatever shape or form it may take, whether we're together or not.

'I need to talk to you, Ash,' I say as I return from the kitchen to the sofa, my eyes meeting his. I explain what was said in the call and why I don't want to sell the house for now.

He furrows his brow and looks down at his feet, saying nothing. After a moment of silence, he nods slowly before sitting down heavily with a deep sigh. 'I thought we had a plan,' he murmurs, looking up at me. 'Now it's all gone up in smoke.' His voice is filled with hurt and confusion.

I reach out my hand to take his, but there's no warmth in our touch anymore, only distance, but I don't want to hurt him or cause any pain. 'I understand how you feel, Ash,' I say softly. 'But think about it. We seemed to be moving so fast. Maybe this is a sign that we're not meant to move forward together. It's time we take a hard look at what we really want, as individuals.'

'So, you're asking me to change what I want?' he says.

'And you're asking me not to,' I reply.

I take a deep breath and look into his eyes. He looks so desperate, it breaks my heart.

'Ash, I'm sorry,' I say softly. 'But I don't think this is something we can fix with words or even more time together. Our differences have been gently pulling us apart for months now. We aren't meant to be together.'

He shakes his head in disbelief. His hands grip mine tightly as he pleads with me to reconsider. His voice cracks with emotion as he speaks, his words coming out in a desperate plea for me to stay with him, for us to keep moving forward together.

'I know you can make somebody the happiest girl in the world, it's just that I don't think it's me, and deep down I think you know it too...'

He looks up at me and speaks after an eternity of silence. 'I understand what you're saying,' he says. 'But... I don't get it. And that's where you're right, because I don't get you, Daisy. I don't get you anymore; I don't get how you want anything else than what we could have right here.'

Despite the pain in his voice, I can feel the love he has for me – and his fear of the unknown. But deep down I know that this is the right thing to do.

'So, what are we going to do now?' he asks me.

Taking a deep breath, I make my decision clear. 'I'm going to follow my gut and not sell the house. As for us...' I shake my head slowly and say in a soft voice, 'I think this is goodbye.' I take one last look at him before gently pulling my hands from his grasp.

Ash looks at me, his face betraying the hurt and confusion he's feeling, but he doesn't say anything. He simply nods and walks out of the flat, away from me and everything we thought we wanted, slamming the door behind him.

It's over. It's done.

I know this feeling. I can taste it. I felt it as I followed my mother's hearse down the street. Just a handful of us, her few close friends and my social workers.

Grief.

Grief for the childhood I never had with my father.

Grief for a life unlived, unliveable, a life unrealised... the life I may have had growing up in The Lake House... if things had been different. Different times, different circumstances, different possibilities.

Grief for all the ways I've not been true to myself and what that may have cost others as well as me.

I walk into the bathroom and turn on the shower, letting the hot water cascade over me. As I stand there, water streaming down my body, I think about what Moya said, that it's all up to me and always will be my choice alone to make. I just need to find the courage to choose.

Well, this is me. Choosing courage.

CHAPTER 38

THE FLAT

The rain falls steadily onto the cobblestone streets, shrouding the city in a cold, dark mist. I glance out the window of my tiny London flat, focused on the simple task of cooking dinner for Kayla and myself. She's come to stay with me since Ash stormed out a few nights ago, leaving me raw with the pain of our break-up, even though it was my decision and, in my heart of hearts, I know it was the right one.

My heart swells with gratitude for Kayla, my lifeline. It's not that different from our days in the children's home where we spent our evenings huddling from the cold and dreaming of the future. Yet, here we are, two fully grown women; still staring into the horizon, uncertain of what lies ahead.

As I remove the steaming pot from the stove, I shoot a nervous glance in Kayla's direction. She sits on the corner of my worn-out sofa, looking drained, haunted shadows beneath her eyes.

'It smells so good, Daisy,' she murmurs, wrapping a threadbare blanket tighter against her huddled frame. Her vibrant features are marred by the shadows of the rollercoaster days that have unfolded – my break-up, her return to her chaotic house-share and a hectic work schedule for us both.

'You okay over there?' I ask, ladling the warm stew onto two simple white plates.

'Yeah,' she replies softly, 'just a little tired.'

I set the plates on the table and call her to dinner. 'What do you fancy? I've got everything – water, juice, wine, beer, vodka.'

As she rises to join me, she pauses, choking back a gagging sensation. Her cheeks are flushed, and she fans herself with the edge of her shawl. 'I need to find that bracelet Moya gave me. I packed it coming over, but the nausea is back.'

We sit at the quaint round table in my small dining area, with the dim overhead light accentuating shadows across her face. I can tell Kayla is exhausted and stressed, but I want to give her some space without pressuring her too much. She knows I'm here for her when she's ready to talk.

If I were a gambler, I would put all my money on Moya's prediction: my eternally tired, puffy-faced and teary Kayla is pregnant. I just need her to admit it – first to herself, and then to me.

'Anything I can get you?' I ask with growing concern.

She reassures me with a weak smile. 'I think it's just something I ate. It'll be fine,' she says.

Her phone buzzes, and she smiles as she picks it up.

'A video message from Fintan and Jacinta. So cute.' Her pale face reflects the worn-out feeling I recognise in myself. 'I wish we were back in Innisfree,' she says quietly, her head resting in her hands.

I know exactly what she means. A wave of nostalgia washes over me with the thought of our simple lives over there.

Kayla opens the video message. The sight of Fintan and Jacinta fills my heart with warmth and affection – they're like family to us now.

'Hi, Kayla! Mooney's here,' Jacinta says cheerfully.

Fintan chimes in behind her. 'We just wanted to send you a big hello and hope you're well.'

'My little online shop is booming! Lots of orders coming in from everywhere – I'm selling my wares all over the place. It's marvellous!' Jacinta continues with enthusiasm. 'All thanks to you. I'm loving it, so keep sending me those hashtags and all the other bits and bobs we need.'

Fintan chips in again as he clumsily attempts to sip on his coffee while talking into the camera simultaneously. 'And don't forget our weekly catch-up on Thursday night at 8 p.m.! I have some more musings for you on our friend Nami Zen.' He laughs heartily before wishing her well and signing off.

We watch the entire video with smiles on our faces – they make us feel connected even though we aren't all physically together anymore.

Through dinner, I notice Kayla's expression growing paler. Finally, unable to hold back any longer, she rushes to the bathroom to throw up. I want to take her to the hospital, but she tells me again that she's fine. That it will pass. But for the next hour, Kayla seems even more pale and sunken. With a wild, fearful look in her eyes, she stays by the toilet, collapsed to her knees, retching. I sit beside her, pressing a cool washcloth to her forehead.

'Kayla, this isn't getting better. I think you need to see a doctor.'

She pushes my hand away, saying with tears in her eyes, 'I don't need one, Daisy. I'm pregnant.'

I take a deep breath and feel the relief wash over me. At least we're dealing with it. Dealing with however she's feeling about it – I don't want to sway her either way. She's unwell, but it's nothing life-threatening or dangerous.

'I'm going to have the baby,' she says with determination, her eyes lighting up for the first time in weeks. 'I know it'll be hard, being a single parent, but I'm ready for this, even if it means raising the baby alone.'

I get the fear. She's carrying the child of a man who's not around, who can't be found, so I hug her tightly and promise her she'll never truly be alone. This little one is going to be showered with so much love... Kayla is going to be a mother! And a brilliant one at that. She knows the pain of not having a supportive family around, so this child will be everything to her – and to me too. This is really the best, most wonderful, most life-changing news!

We spend the rest of the evening laughing and crying, the future spreading out ahead of us like a beautiful, untamed landscape. We sip ginger tea as we discuss baby names, nursery themes and parenting books, and I ask Kayla when she knew she was ready to face parenting alone. Her answer comes in the form of a story so poignant that it moves us both to tears. She tells me of a dream she had, where she was cradling her baby in her arms, feeling something more profound and fulfilling than anything she's known before. This dream solidified her conviction that she could face the challenge.

In the days that follow, Kayla moves out of her house-share and into my flat with me so she's got support and comfort. We spend hours poring over pregnancy websites and blogs, taking notes and sharing what we've learned. Together, we visit doctors and scan shelves of prenatal vitamins. We face each challenge, figuring it all out together. It's clear that we're navigating this new adventure as a team.

At night-time, I often look over at Kayla reading the stack of parenting books that continue to grow by her side of the bed. On the outside, she appears ready, soaking in all the advice and guidance she can. But I can't help but notice the shadows of doubt flicker across her face every so often. As I turn off the light and lie in the darkness, my heart swells with love and respect for my best friend. She's a warrior preparing for battle. I witness her strength and dedication as she so bravely faces this significant life change, and I vow to walk beside her. Her steadfast determination inspires me.

We press onwards, hand in hand, embracing the thrilling unknown that awaits us. Happiness intertwines with fear, laughter mingles with tears, but we march on, fuelled by courage and powered by love. And in this unpredictability and chaos, I know that the bond we share will carry us through, no matter where life takes us.

CHAPTER 39

THE MEETING

Stay cool, I tell myself as I step into the bustling atmosphere of the super-smart restaurant in London's West End. The mirrored walls make the whole place seem glittering and boundless, adding to the enigmatic aura that entangles the room. The air is filled with the clink of expensive silverware against delicate china, a soft musical hum complementing tasteful murmurs of clever conversations. Chandeliers of sparkling diamonds hang solemnly from the ceiling, casting a warm glow upon Lenka and I as we slide smoothly into a corner booth of buttery soft leather and tufted velvet.

We sit in silence for a moment. I cross my fingers under the table, as if the simple action might suffice to offer some comfort, any solace at all. Even though Lenka invited me to meet her here, she's too erratic for me to feel at ease. Anything could happen.

Lenka clears her throat, taking my attention from my fingers to her glowing face. She's suddenly wearing that knowing smile of someone about to reveal a secret.

'So, let me tell you something,' she begins, her cheeks flushed with excitement. 'Your illustrations were total Marmite

– completely divided the team. And that's exactly what we wanted! A unanimous no is bad, but a unanimous yes means mediocrity. Nothing truly extraordinary is loved by everyone, so the fact your work splits us right down the middle is ideal! In the end, we went to Matilda Wilder herself to decide.'

My illustrations have a bold and expressive style, so I get why they may not be for everyone, but unlike last time when Lenka and I met, I know these are good. I know they're my best work – I'm proud of them, and I'm going to stick by them, whichever way the needle falls.

I bite my lip, waiting for the verdict. My heart pounds so hard it threatens to escape my chest like a frantic, captive bird. Matilda Wilder is the author of *Forest Fables*, her words the very lifeblood that gives character to the pages I so carefully crafted. To have her approval, or, better yet, her appreciation, would mean everything.

Lenka leans forward, her eyes twinkling with joy. 'She picked yours, Daisy. Congrats.'

In that moment, time seems to freeze, crystallising into a memory that can't be tarnished. In a completely surreal, absurdly improbable, un-Lenka-style move, she pulls me into an embrace... Lenka is hugging me. As I feel her arms around me, my entire body fills with both fear and elation, but I accept the congratulations, clinking our glasses in celebration, and I marvel at how wonderful this moment feels.

Matilda Wilder, the greatest living children's author of our time, has chosen my illustrations. It's a dream come true.

Suddenly, a carefully wrapped package slides across the table towards me, the anticipation in Lenka's eyes almost as tangible as the weight of the small present. My fingers tremble as I pull away tissue paper, revealing a signed first edition from Matilda herself. Through my tears, I read the simple yet profound words inked on the page: 'Thank you, Daisy.'

I'm so grateful for this achievement, but I also know that it was Innisfree, and the creative passion and self-belief I felt there, that really gave me this success. Without that spark of inspiration, I wouldn't be here today.

A soft breeze tickles the air as I step out of the restaurant, feeling as if my entire world has shifted. The busy London streets are alive with swirling colours and vibrant energy, and I walk with true purpose, carrying the treasured Matilda Wilder book tucked under my arm. Goosebumps crawl up my arms as the reality of the contract and the book's significance wash over me.

As I make my way home, I feel a tug towards The Fox. It's a stark contrast to the posh restaurant I just left, but I know it's the perfect place to truly celebrate. I want to share this with Big Sean.

The doors to The Fox open with a creak. The air is thick with the familiar scent of hops and the raucous chorus of laughter and music that accompanies any good Irish pub day or night. Big Sean and I exchange a heartfelt hug before settling into the cosy, worn leather seats. We're soon sharing a pot of tea together, reminiscing about old times and catching up on everything that's happened since I left for Innisfree.

Big Sean gazes into his cup for a moment and then turns his misty eyes to me. 'Daisy,' he begins, his thick Irish brogue softened by emotion, 'I'm so glad you've found happiness again, but I have to ask – did you ever find out why your mum never returned?'

Silence descends as I consider the question. It's a mystery that's haunting me still, but after everything, perhaps I'll never know the full answer. My heart aches with the knowledge that there's still a void where my mother's reasons should be as I explain all this to Big Sean.

'Some closure is better than nothing, Daisy,' he tells me. 'You can lay your mother's past to rest now. And your father's.'

It's true. But I still feel so restless.

Just then a thought occurs to me, offering a glimmer of hope. There's still a way to find out the truth.

When I'm back home, I glance around the flat, taking it all in. The realisation that I can go back to Innisfree, that I can keep the house and make a home there, fills me with immense happiness. The thought of Kayla staying in my flat here, enjoying the peace and quiet that I know she needs, brings a warm smile to my face.

Still, a voice in the back of my mind whispers to me, reminding me of the uncertainty waiting for me in Innisfree. James... I don't know how things will be without him there. But as I think more about it, I realise that there's still so much left to discover. Big Sean is right: some closure is better than none, but still, I'm desperate for answers. I try to imagine what could have pushed my mother to leave Innisfree – the idyllic setting, the kind faces, Mick's love – but I come up empty.

I take a deep breath, trying to steady myself. I've always believed that everyone has a story to tell and that I deserve to know mine. My roots lie in this village, but my mother's flit to London has left a piece of me missing. A piece I won't be able to find until I know the full story. I can't simply give up, not when I've discovered the identity of my father and the love he shared with my mother.

My heart races as I open my laptop and search for my flight to Ireland. One way.

CHAPTER 40

THE OFFER

I'm welcomed back by the sweet scent of the Irish countryside as I arrive, home, to Innisfree. Nostalgia rushes over me, coupled with a strong determination to find the answers I crave. The wind whips through my hair, and I draw my coat tighter in response to its chill. Taking in the vibrant shades of green that make up this beautiful place, I'm overwhelmed by a deep sense of belonging and connection to my past. And now also to my present and future. Armed with Matilda's first-edition book, dear friends and true courage, I am ready. No more suppressing or hiding away from my past; it's time to embrace it and grow.

My feet crunch on the pebbles of The Lake House path as I fill my lungs with fresh air and summon the courage to seize every opportunity that life has to offer. When I reach the edge of the sparkling lake, I carefully slip off my clothing, piece by piece, until I'm standing in nothing but goosebumps. I close my eyes and take a deep breath before plunging into the cool depths. Just as my father before me.

After my swim, I glance at my phone. There's a new notification from Jonathan. I call him and he tells me the anonymous overseas bidder has reached out about the property, upping their original offer if we remove the clause regarding tenants. He asks me how I want to proceed, though I suspect he already knows my answer.

My response is simple – I'm declining their offer. The Lake House is no longer available, now and forever.

It's good to be home.

I prepare for the night ahead, my first as the proud new owner of The Lake House. It's been a while since I've had this feeling – the feeling of coming home to a place that's truly mine. First night in my family home. First night going to sleep without the burden of a sale or deadline or money worries hanging over me. What a luxury to start dreaming before I even shut my eyes.

I check my phone one last time. A message from Rory, Lenka's personal assistant.

Subject: Team Wilder Always!

A sneak preview of the 5-star review going in the Sunday Journal *tomorrow. You did it! Enjoy Innisfree.*

Rx

When Matilda Wilder's new edition of her beloved fables was announced, the reaction was instant. Everyone wanted to get their hands on the beautiful new version, complete with illustrations by Daisy Clarke. People eagerly anticipated the release, and when it arrived for review, I wasn't disappointed.

The illustrations in this new edition of Matilda Wilder's tales are breathtakingly gorgeous. Daisy Clarke has managed to capture both the whimsy and wonder of Matilda's stories while also adding a unique perspective that feels fresh and modern. Her style is full of colour and energy, creating vivid images that transport readers into each tale. Nature scenes crackle with life and emotion, while characters brim with personality and charisma.

In addition to her creative flair, Daisy Clarke's work also conveys a deep sensitivity that allows readers to unlock old memories while discovering new ones. In every frame she creates, there is an undercurrent of emotion – a feeling of nostalgia for days gone by or a longing for something different but still relatable. With each turn of the page, readers find themselves becoming more deeply invested in every character and scene she brings to life.

The result is a triumph for both artist and author alike as Daisy Clarke's vibrant artwork combines with Matilda Wilder's timeless tales to create something truly special – an enchanting collection that will be treasured by readers for many years to come.

Sweet dreams all. We done good.

CHAPTER 41

THE FAIR

The famous market fair buzzes with excited energy, as hearty laughter and friendly chatter fill the air. Strings of fairy lights wink across the early-evening sky, casting a warm glow over the market-goers. I've wandered through the bustling maze all day, and when the evening turns cooler, I make my way to the packed Tap House, seeking both warmth and company.

As soon as I walk through the door, I'm swept away by the vibrant atmosphere. Grace is on stage, playing Mick's guitar like a master musician. Glancing around, I spot my dear friends, Jacinta and Fintan, who are sitting with Marianne and Gus, all surrounded by an electric energy. They signal me to join them, and they each take turns hugging and shaking hands with me. But there's one face I'm looking for tonight.

'What brought you back so soon?' asks Marianne. 'We don't have you booked for any nights at the guest house.' She looks at Gus, who shakes his head in confusion. 'And it's even busier tonight because of the fair... there's not a bed left in town.'

'It's okay, thank you!' I say cheerfully. 'I'm not here on holiday this time – I'm moving here permanently! I'm going to be staying at The Lake House.'

Jacinta and Fintan let out cheers and clap their hands together.

'Oh, that's wonderful news! And it makes perfect sense – you've been madly fixing up that house so why not move in yourself and enjoy it?' Jacinta says as she jumps to her feet to give me a huge hug.

Over her shoulder, I can't help but scan the room for any sign of James. Rumour has it he leaves for Brussels this week, and I've been plagued by the gnawing fear of missed chances. I've told myself not to expect anything, that James has his own road to travel, and I shouldn't hold him back. But still, my heart can't help but race at the thought of our eyes meeting one last time.

I navigate the lively crowd, feeling the rhythm of the music vibrate through my chest, pulsing in time with my fervent beating heart. Laughter, stories and music flow around me like a river, yet I swim against the current, single-minded and determined.

It's when I reach the bar, where the light is a touch dimmer and the chaos of the room fades to a low murmur, that I spot him. His black hair tamed but still artfully tousled, and his eyes an ocean blue I could drown in. In fact, I already have in the past.

Our eyes meet, and it's as if the room stills, our connection slicing through the din like a beam of sunlight after a storm. He's still here, and as his gaze holds mine for a fleeting moment, I know that I'm not the only one holding on to hope.

He offers a tentative smile, and my heart stutters, caught like a moth in amber. With a glass of red in hand, I approach him, the warmth radiating between us growing as I close the distance.

'I thought we'd seen the last of you,' James says.

I smile softly. 'As it turns out, you can't get rid of me that easily.'

He glances over my shoulder. 'All alone?'

I nod. 'Yep. Kayla's staying at my place in London for a bit.'

We lock eyes before I finish the update. But I need to.

'And Ash and I are no longer together.'

'I'm sorry to hear that,' he replies.

I quirk an eyebrow at his response. 'You are?'

He laughs. 'Okay, honestly and selfishly, not too sorry.'

Our conversation begins with tentative stutters, punctuated by awkward pauses, but soon we find ourselves drawn like magnets into each other's stories. Our laughter intertwines as we trade anecdotes and dreams, and it becomes clear that we're more than just two souls happening to cross paths at a crowded bar – we've uncovered a breath of fresh air in a world that can feel stifling.

But before long the gnawing doubt in my mind returns. He's leaving, and the more time we spend together, the more it hurts to consider bidding him farewell.

As I sit here at the bar, the hum of other voices scattering the air around us, I'm torn by the realisation that this is it. My heart races knowing we have just this one short week together, before he sets off to Brussels to pursue his dreams. But I'm determined to make the most of it. James, this charming, kind, clever man has become everything I didn't know I needed.

As we talk late into the night, our conversation evolves into something more intimate. Sharing pieces of ourselves that feel too vulnerable to utter out loud in any other setting. We fall deeper into each other until our connection feels like an extension of ourselves – like a missing puzzle piece finally slotted in place. And even though he's leaving, my heart feels fuller than it ever did before and I realise that – if only for one night – love has come and changed everything.

I glance at him, his eyes sparkling as we share in this fleeting moment, and I can't help but think of my parents' story. They taught me that love is a precious gift, and life never hands us a guarantee. Tonight, it's up to me to seize this moment and make the most of the hours we have.

But as I sit here, the clock ticking away on our limited time, my heartache sneaks in. Losing him is unimaginable. As if sensing my struggle, he reaches for my hand and tugs me gently from my stool, his touch alleviating my fears, however fleetingly. I sway, drawn towards him with an invisible thread that binds us, our bodies already unwilling to part.

He shuffles towards me, our chests touching. His arms loop around my waist, his eyes still locked on mine. James smiles tenderly before coming closer, hovering his lips above mine as though he's unsure whether to take the next step.

His warm embrace grounds me again, and all I want is to savour this love, even if it only lasts until tomorrow morning. So, when he finally kisses me, I can't help but give in. Its taste is bittersweet; our souls meshing in a whirlwind of emotion and uncertainty. We both know that things will change beyond repair. But in this moment, with our fingertips laced together beneath the bar lights, I forget about tomorrow's pain and dive into the bliss of his embrace. As my mum once said, 'Better to have loved and lost than never loved at all.'

Time stops as our lips move in perfect harmony and an unknown sensation stirs inside me.

CHAPTER 42

THE STREET

By midnight, The Tap House is alive with the sound of traditional Irish music. It's the final night of the market fair and the whole village seems to be here. The atmosphere is electric and everyone is having a great time dancing, laughing and drinking. A smiling, bearded man in a flat cap has taken to the stage, playing his fiddle passionately, and the crowd roar with excitement and clap along. The woman next to me, who I've just met, starts to sway from side to side, and I can't help but join in. It's infectious.

I dance with James until my body is soaked in sweat from a night of good music and better Guinness. When two o'clock hits, the musicians leave the stage and the bell tolls for last call. I bid my friends farewell, feeling elated and fulfilled, knowing tonight was a good one.

I look at my watch. 'It's late; I'll be heading home now,' I say to James.

'To The Lake House? Let me walk you there,' he replies.

'It's fine! I was going to get a taxi. I can manage.'

He shakes his head. 'A taxi will be hard to come by. We can take a shortcut through the fields; it'll take no time at all.'

'Are you sure? I know you're packing and getting ready for your big move,' I insist.

He grins in response. 'Don't worry about me. It's important you get home safe, especially at this hour. Got to be careful on the mean streets of Innisfree,' he jokes.

'All right then, thanks,' I tell him with a grateful smile. Not because I feel unsafe in Innisfree, but because I'm not ready to say goodbye just yet.

So, together, we meander down the main street, making our way through the closing-time crowds spilling out of the pubs into the street. Everyone is laughing, singing, embracing each other. Today has felt like a festival in every sense, celebrating everything that makes up their culture: music, entertainment and, most of all, the people. And I feel like I'm part of it all; as if I belong. It's a feeling I'd almost forgotten, a hope I'd nearly stopped wishing for.

As we walk through the throngs, I feel the warmth of James' arm wrapped snugly around my waist. This gratifying haven, the gentle scent of fresh country air holds me captive. After a night of great fun, all I want is to ball up this joy and save it, like a firefly in a jar.

We keep walking through the revelling crowds, our steps light and quick as we make our way through the village streets. For a moment, the melody of the night falls silent, and suddenly there he is: Stephen McDonagh, swaying drunkenly at the edge of the square. He lurches towards us, his red and bloated face twisted with malice.

'Hey, James, who's your new girlfriend? She's a lot better than the last one!' he calls.

James' cheeks flush. 'Good one,' he calls back. 'Now go home, Stephen McDonagh, and sleep it off.' James leans in to my ear. 'He loses the run of himself when he hits the bottle.'

Stephen nods to me. 'Hey, Daisy? Do you've any friends who look like you?' And then he turns back to his friends in the street, laughing and eating chips, before he stumbles over and wraps his arm around my neck.

'Stephen, that's enough – leave us in peace. We don't want any trouble from anyone.' says James, suddenly looking serious.

'Now, now, James, there's no need to be jealous. Daisy is a girl after my own heart,' Stephen says as he stumbles away from me and James pulls me closer, protectively. 'I'm just being friendly.' His hand reaches out to grab my arm.

'Then go be friendly somewhere else,' says James, pushing him away. 'Cop yourself on, Stephen – you're acting like an idiot.'

'It's late; we're all ready to go home now. Goodnight, Stephen,' I say without turning around.

'Suit yourself, James. If you want to take a thief home, that's your lookout! Like mother, like daughter! Hide all your valuables around that one,' Stephen shouts. 'Daisy Clarke, eh? Back to lord over us all from The Lake House!' He spits the words, enunciating every syllable in his attempt to maintain composure. 'D'ya hear about Rose Clarke? They say she's a filthy thief!'

I raise an eyebrow, disbelief pooling in the depths of my eyes. Why is he calling my mother a thief?

James' grip tightens around me. 'He's just a drunk idiot. Come on – let's go.'

I try to rein in the hot rush of emotion, but the words spill from my lips, 'You've no right to talk about my mother.'

But this only spurs him on, his sneer growing wider, feeding on our despair. 'Oh, I hit a nerve, did I?'

James' jaw clenches, and he narrows his eyes at Stephen as his voice deepens. 'You've had your fun. Now step off, yeah?'

James takes my hand and we walk away from the jeering crowds and into the night. I wonder what Stephen meant by his comment – but James is right, he's a drunk idiot and there's no sense wasting our precious time on him. But I can't shake the feeling that there's more to it than that. When I was first at the guest house, Stephen went silent when I asked about my mother, yet now, he has plenty to say.

'Keep your crown jewels in the safe when you bring Rose Clarke's daughter home!' Stephen calls out after us again.

I turn to James. 'What did he mean by that? What crown jewels?'

But before James can answer, Stephen is standing on a bench, using it as a stage. 'You know, a thief broke into my house last night. He started searching for money so I woke up and searched with him.'

His friends break down laughing, jeering him to continue.

'Did you hear the one about the thief in the cemetery... t'was a grave mistake.'

Again, more laughter.

Stephen's getting louder and more animated with the attention.

'Did I tell you I was mugged last night on my way home... Pointing a knife at me... he said, "Your money or your life!" I told him I was from Innisfree... so I have no money and no life... We hugged and cried together. It was a beautiful moment.'

I look up at James, but he just shakes his head, before turning on his heel and walking back towards Stephen.

'James!' I shout after him, but he doesn't stop. He just keeps walking until he comes face to face with Stephen and then lands a punch on him that spins him around until he's lying on the ground with blood streaming from his nose.

Stephen's friends move in to hold James back, but he shrugs them off.

The air crackles with the electrifying tension of a storm about to break. My heart races, pounding against the walls of my chest as James steps forward, giving Stephen a menacing scowl. 'I'm warning you, Stephen. You've crossed a line.'

Stephen laughs, slurring his words as he replies, 'Come on

now! Can't handle the truth, can ya? Her mother was a liar and a thief... everyone knows it... but she comes back here thinking she's welcome with open arms. We don't want that kind around here.'

'Go home, Stephen. I don't ever want to hear such vicious lies coming out of your mouth again, do you hear me?' shouts James as Stephen lies on the ground in a heap.

His friends are too stunned to move, and I just stand there holding my hand over my mouth in shock.

James walks back to me and takes my hand. What's just happened?

CHAPTER 43

THE NIGHT

The night sky sprinkles a constellation of stars above The Lake House, their light reflecting softly off the surface of the lake. Unlocking the door, I step into the dimly lit house and flick on the lights, accompanied by James, who cradles his swollen hand. His injured knuckles are testimony to his recent altercation. Jonathan won't be happy when he hears of it in the morning; he'll not appreciate James brawling in the street right under the office that bears the family name. And it's all because of me.

I hurry to the freezer, fetching ice, my thoughts racing.

'Why does Stephen have such an issue with me?' I ask, suppressing my frustration as I gingerly wrap the ice in a towel and hand it to James.

He shrugs, his eyes conveying a sense of vulnerability unfamiliar to me. 'A few old families around here think they can decide what's best for everyone,' he says, a slight edge in his voice. 'Maybe they had their sights set on buying this place themselves. Maybe Stephen fancies you and we've just seen the clumsiest mating dance in history.' He laughs and shrugs. 'I gave up trying to work people out a long time ago.'

I can't help but feel a stinging pang of guilt. As much as I wanted to learn all I could about my own past, I couldn't fathom the thought of being entangled in other people's affairs or upsetting them to this extent.

Dressing James' hand with gentle care, my mood shifts from frustration to gratitude. Despite everything that's transpired, our connection has only deepened, and this tender moment in the quiet calm of The Lake House is an echo of the hope that remains.

'I'll sleep downstairs, on the couch,' James announces, breaking the silence. 'So you feel safer. The market fair can be raucous at night, as you've seen. Better safe than sorry.'

'Thanks, I do feel safer now.'

He smiles and leans in to kiss me one last time, his lips brushing mine with understated passion. 'Goodnight, Daisy,' he murmurs as he retreats to the living room. His gaze catches mine, and for a moment I can feel an energy passing between us, a silent question of what might be if he stayed in my bedroom instead. I force myself to take a breath and look away; I don't want to rush this fragile thing that we're building together.

Retiring to my bedroom, my thoughts continue to drift towards our uncertain future. In the quiet darkness, I sit down heavily on the bed, my body still trembling. How did things get so out of control? I wonder, my hands twisting in my lap. It all seemed like such a storm, with Stephen's drunken accusation and James' fierce defence of my family's honour.

As I sit there, lost in my thoughts, I remember the feeling of James' lips on mine, the way his arms encircled me as if I were the most precious thing in the world. I can't help but smile through my tears, warmed by the knowledge that he cares for me that deeply. The thought of James sleeping on the couch downstairs ignites a yearning within me that I can't seem to shake. I want to be with him, in his comforting embrace, but I don't want to move too fast, not after all the emotional mayhem of earlier.

But the thought of spending this night apart is too much to bear. My heart aches as the battle between my desires and fears rages on. As the clock ticks, each second feels like an eternity. The suffocating silence of my room weighs heavy on my shoulders and magnifies my loneliness.

Frustrated and overwhelmed, I take a deep breath and step out of my mind for a moment. Sorting through my emotions, I consider my options. If I stay in bed, I'll carry the anguish of tonight's drama, potentially losing the chance of kindling the bond I've begun to form with James. On the other hand, if I give in to my heart's calling and reach out to him, I might be risking our newly sown connection.

I recall every little detail of our time together, and my heart stutters with the happy moments we've shared. It's been a wild ride, and at every turn, James has filled my life with a new shade of wonder. How can I let this energy between us slip away when we have no idea what lies around the corner?

Gathering the courage to face my fears, I decide. Though I don't know what awaits us in the future, the here and now feels like all that matters.

Shuffling quietly to the door, I find my way downstairs to the couch, where he sleeps peacefully. I hesitate for a moment, watching his chest rise and fall with each steady breath. Even in his slumber, James emits an aura of calm warmth that draws me closer.

Ever so gently, I slip in beside him, my body fitting perfectly against his. Slowly, he awakens, and I feel his breathing change as he realises I'm there. Our lips meet in tender kisses, and we explore our connection – cautiously and lovingly. Eventually, we make love, cherishing one another and our unique bond.

As I lie in his arms, basking in the afterglow, I feel a strange peace wash over me. It's as if healing is possible, even after the roller coaster of emotions. And as the night gives way to morning, the weight of the turmoil from earlier dissolves. In this moment, the future is uncertain, but our hearts beat as one, and for now, that's more than I ever dared to dream.

CHAPTER 44

THE VISIT

This morning, the air is still and crisp, and the sun just barely peeking over the horizon paints the sky a fiery orange. James left in the early hours, leaving a very sweet note to explain he had to return to work but would be back soon. The letter was finished with a kiss. I held it up close to my lips and gave it a quick peck just like a giddy teenager. My bare feet crunch softly against the ground as I make my way to Moya's caravan, my breath creating puffs of mist in front of me. I knock on her door, the sound of my knuckles echoes in the stillness of the early morning.

She takes one look at my tear-streaked face and her expression softens. Sighing, she opens the door wider and gestures for me to come in. The lines around her eyes deepen as she speaks. 'The theft?' Her voice is gentle, but she looks concerned.

I nod, unable to meet her gaze, my bottom lip quivering as I try to hold back sobs. Closing the door to the caravan behind me, I take in the quiet stillness of the space. The morning light filtering in through the windows is soft and comforting, and Moya's presence helps soothe my trembling heart.

We sit down together, and a silence grows between us,

punctuated only by the distant chirp of birds in the trees beyond. Moya looks at me with an understanding gaze, and her steady calm allows me to feel safe enough to unload everything that's happened. I tell her about Stephen, the horrid things he said, how James punched him...

Moya takes my hands in hers, her touch sending a jolt of energy through me. 'James punched him? Oh my goodness,' she murmurs, shaking her head. She squeezes my hands. 'It sounds like James did the right thing by defending you. No one should ever have to endure such verbal abuse.' She pauses for a moment before continuing, 'But now you need to think about what comes next. People can be cruel when they feel threatened. I know it's hard to do so right now, but you must think about what's best for you and for James in the long run. Sometimes all you can do is protect your peace. Stay low-key, until things settle down a bit.'

'But why would he say that? My mother would never steal, never! Even when we had nothing, she'd never...'

Moya sighs, and I can see the conflict in her eyes. 'It doesn't matter now. Let it go. It's in the past. People believe what suits them, Daisy.'

'No, Moya, please. I need to know,' I say, exasperation creeping into my voice.

Moya pauses for a beat, her brow furrowed in thought. 'It's bad luck to tell the secrets of the dead, don't you know?' She appears agitated as she shakes her head at me. 'Your mother did everything she could to protect you from this wickedness. I'm trying my best to do the same, keep Rose's wishes alive – but, Daisy, you never stop pushing, do you? I'm just an old woman, and I don't have the strength to fight you any longer. Have it your way. Here's the truth, and let this be the end of it, you hear me?'

I keep my mouth shut and sit back in my seat.

'Rose had a shift as a cleaner at The Tap House. There was

lodgings upstairs and a jewellery box disappeared from a guest's bedroom. It was full of very expensive pieces, and they said your mother was the only one who'd a key to the room that day. When a traveller finds themselves in a situation like that, you can imagine the rumours that start doing the rounds... and then, of course, the police were called. She was very afraid that she'd be arrested and end up in prison and all with a baby growing inside her.'

'But it wasn't her! I know it wasn't!' I protest.

'I believe you. And I believed her,' says Moya with a sad smile. 'But sometimes no one listens to you, even if you're innocent. Pregnant, unmarried, alone and labelled a thief by the town, the situation left her no choice. You'd always be tainted by that, no matter what. And so, she did all she could do: run. Run and never look back.' She puts a hand on mine.

I let Moya's words sink in. My mind reels with the implications of what she's just told me. I feel my heart break for my mother, who had to endure such suffering and shame all on her own. Tears prick my eyes and I look down at my hands, struggling to find the courage to ask the next question.

'If you knew she didn't do it, why didn't you help her to clear her name?'

Moya looks up to the ceiling and breathes deeply. 'Times were different then. Not that that's an excuse. I knew she didn't do it; all of us who knew her felt just as you feel right now – that's just not her character, not in her. We went to Tom, Rose's father, and told him what had happened, about the false accusation. Said it wasn't a battle she could win. He told her she'd made her bed, so she'd have to lie in it and he washed his hands of her.'

I can imagine it all too well: their poor attempt at salvaging this sinking ship of a situation, the demoralisation and helplessness I can hear in Moya's voice.

She sighs heavily. 'He said he couldn't take any risk; he

wasn't a young man anymore – too weak to fight, too old to move on. He wanted no trouble. "We need to take care of this situation, and quickly," he said. "Rose, you can't stay here." So, he told her to get out or... or else.' She looked away as she said this last part.

'And you said before she never told him she was pregnant?'

Moya shakes her head.

'But wouldn't that have made a difference?' I ask.

'Oh yes, it would have – but not in a good way,' says Moya. 'It's like I said: Tom would have been furious; he'd have felt that Rose had been taken advantage of – and he'd have had Mick punished for it. He'd never have accepted a child out of wedlock, let alone one that wasn't from our folk. He would have had Mick beaten to a pulp if he found out he'd got her pregnant. That's why Rose needed to stay quiet.'

I feel my stomach sink – no one had come to my mother's rescue when she'd needed it most. No one had been on her side or fought for her innocence when the allegation arose. Her own father had abandoned his only daughter. No wonder she'd never returned.

Moya looks up at me slowly and wipes a stray tear from her cheek with trembling fingers. 'She left that very night,' is all she says before bringing her gaze back down to the tabletop once more.

We sit in silence for a few moments – each of us lost in our thoughts – before Moya finally breaks it by saying softly, 'Your mum made sure you'd have a fresh start.'

I nod silently before thanking Moya for sharing Rose's story with me. I bid her farewell and step out into the bright sunshine.

As I walk away from the caravan, my heart feels heavy with sadness but also with a deep understanding of my mother's actions. My mum had had no choice – she'd had to give up her home and Mick, for me and for herself. When Mick arrived in

London, she'd steered him away for his own safety. If Tom ever found out they had a child together, Mick would be put in serious danger. To protect us all, she'd chosen to do the one thing that would keep everyone safe – disappear from Innisfree for the rest of her days. She'd taken on this burden alone, running away so that we could start again somewhere new. Even though the circumstances were less than ideal, she found a way to turn it around for us – finding strength in the face of adversity; fighting against the odds – the irony being, for all she did to protect everyone, it was her who perished first. There's no way my mother stole anything in her whole life. This fight isn't over.

CHAPTER 45

THE CHOICE

We pass the following days in a state of wonder. As I soak in the warmth of James' embrace, the reality of our situation sinks in. It's a beautiful contradiction. Wrapped up in each other's arms, it feels like we've created a sanctuary within the walls of The Lake House. But outside these walls, our world is teetering on the edge of a delicate balance, a precarious peace that could easily shatter under the weight of small-town grudges.

Though Moya's warning still lingers in the back of my mind, I can't deny the happiness that's bloomed within me since James and I have started sharing our lives. Surrounded by the love and support of friends like Jacinta, Fintan, Dom and the boys, I can't help but think that this is where we're supposed to be.

As we sit by the water, the sun casting both light and shadow on the lake's surface, it seems silly to worry. How could there be darkness amidst so much beauty? I lean my head on James' shoulder, searching his face for an answer. Lately, we've agreed to simply not speak of the malevolent cloud hanging over us, creating a stubborn bubble of denial.

'What are your thoughts on leaving?' I question. I don't

want to be a hindrance to James' success. I can't demand nor require him to give up any ambitions or amazing opportunities just because of me. Even if that means we need to do something long distance, I'm sure it'll work out. If there's anything I've learned from this experience, it's that where there's a will, there's always a way.

He gazes at me, a look filled with sentiment. 'Well, I've been considering the idea of not going.'

'Oh?' I bite the inside of my cheek and force my gaze to remain steady as I ask, trying not to betray any flicker of hope.

'Well, initially I thought that something else, something more satisfying, was waiting for me elsewhere... but now I don't think so. And that's all down to you.'

'Really, James? You mean that?'

'Oh yes. What I'm looking for isn't so far away anymore. Is that okay to say? Not too overpowering?'

I turn to study him, but he pulls back, and I put my hand on his chest to make sure he doesn't go any further.

'No, don't move away,' I whisper.

His pulse quickens underneath my fingertips, his heart pounding against my palm like a drum in the night. He looks deep into my eyes and reaches for my face, lightly running his hands along my cheeks and cupping them gently.

Our lips meet, and the world around us fades away.

There's a future for us. And it's already begun.

CHAPTER 46

THE BLAZE

The fact that James is staying and our future is wide open feels too good to be true. We celebrate with a bottle of wine, then head to bed excitedly, eventually surrendering ourselves to sleep after deep, hungry kisses.

An alarm blares in the quiet night, and I jolt awake. Everything feels warmer than usual, and a faint orange glow from outside casts shadows around the room. I sniff cautiously; the sharp, familiar smell of smoke fills my nostrils. There's an ominous crackling coming from something close by.

Panicking, I shake James awake.

His confused eyes struggle to focus on me. 'What is it? Is everything okay?'

'No! We need to leave now,' I say urgently, my voice trembling with fear. 'Can't you smell the smoke? We have to get out of here!'

His eyes fly open, a mix of sleep and disbelief clouding them, then he jumps up as the severity of what's happening dawns on us. James acts quickly, throwing on his clothes at lightning speed, and I rush to do the same, my limbs shaking with terror.

Our house is on fire – the heat and crackle of the flames licking the walls. I feel it in my lungs, on my skin. Everywhere we look around us is an inferno, an unstoppable force devouring every inch in its path.

'We need to get out now!' he yells over the roaring blaze, fiery sparks soaring around us. We both run for the door, our hands clasped together as if we're clinging to a lifeline. The heat from the fire slams against us as we escape down the stairs. Sparks fly and embers dance in the air like a deadly light show. Our vision is blurred by sooty tears as we stumble through the front door and out into the night.

Exhausted, James and I collapse onto the grass. We're unharmed. Dense clouds of smoke billow over our heads, and in their tendrils, we see what was a beautiful home engulfed by a rage of orange and yellow flames. The flames lick up each beam and post hungrily, devouring anything in their path. We breathe in deep gulps of clean air, watching as our beloved Lake House slowly burns as the fire sirens wail in our direction.

James pulls me close, pressing his face into my hair and whispering softly, 'It'll be okay,' as if he's convincing himself as much as me.

A droplet of water hits my arm, then another lands on my chin. Then another and another until sheets of rain come thick and fast, as the heavens open up with a thunderous roar, drenching The Lake House with heavy rainfall.

Maybe there'll be something left to salvage.

CHAPTER 47

THE CAR

I wrap the blanket tighter around me as I sit on the dewy grass, the smell of burned wood and smoke hanging heavy in the air. The firefighters continue to work on dousing the last of the flames. Dom arrives and sits beside me, the dogs nestled at our feet, their eyes wide with worry. The juxtaposition between our current situation and our past happiness from the renovations makes my head spin. It's a shocking sight to behold. The fire had started in the barn and quickly spread to the rest of the house due to the wind. The fire brigade's efforts were too late for the barn, which has been reduced to ash and rubble. The house was salvageable. Salvageable being a very subjective term.

'Thank God you're all right, Daisy,' says Jonathan, who runs towards us. 'I came as fast as I could.' He spreads his arms and I run into them, tears streaming down my face.

'I'm sorry to have to tell you this,' Sergeant Brennan says solemnly as she walks towards us, 'but we've taken a statement from two boys, Liam and Finn Quinn. It sounds like a small vehicle was seen leaving the scene early this morning.'

'Oh no,' I say, my voice trembling. 'Were the boys around?

In the barn? Are they hurt?' I clutch at James. 'Dear God, please tell me they're okay.'

Sergeant Brennan nods. 'They're fine,' she says. 'The boys had been camping by the lake. They were woken up by the dogs barking and stuck their heads out of the tent to see what was going on, and that's when they saw the car driving away. They didn't know a fire had been started.'

Despite the destruction, I sigh with huge relief. They're safe – that's all that really matters. But who would do such a thing? The idea that someone would go to such extremes is incomprehensible. Who would deliberately set fire to the house? It just doesn't make any sense.

'Off the record, it's possible that it was the eco-warriors. You know, the ones who live in the woods – tricky folks to catch a glimpse of, and you can never be too sure when they'll rear their heads. And just when you think nothing is going to happen... Boom! They certainly know how to grab your attention when you're least expecting it.' She gestured towards the smoking house with her head.

'We have no reason to believe it was them – we've never had any issues with them, and they've never posed any threat to us before...'

Sergeant Brennan lifts her eyebrow and states, 'It's your call,' as she skims the tip of the pen over her nose. 'In that case, any other potential suspects in the area who may want to harm you?' she asks.

James and I exchange a glance; his eyes are laced with concern and confusion, a mirror of my feelings. I stammer, struggling to catch my breath. 'I can't think of anyone who would do something as drastic as this...'

It's clear that Stephen McDonagh isn't fond of me, but I find it hard to believe he would go as far as this – especially after being reprimanded by James. Also, would he really put his two stepsons at risk? He's certainly a potential suspect, but something doesn't add up about him being the perpetrator. So for now, I'm going to keep his name out of the conversation in order not to lead the investigation off course. We'll allow the police to do their job, and we'll focus on ours.'

James nods, his face a mixture of disbelief and heartbreak. 'Neither can I,' he admits, his voice cracking.

We look back at the smouldering remains of the house, the beautiful space we worked so hard on transforming into a home taken from us in a matter of hours.

I have to find out who did this.

I feel my heart pounding in my chest as I try to make sense of the situation. The flames are almost gone now, but thick, black smoke is still billowing into the sky.

'I'm so sorry this has turned out the way it has, Daisy,' Jonathan says, his head bowed. 'If there's anything I can do, please let me know.'

Dom attempts to put on a brave face. 'We'll do all that we can to help, Daisy,' he promises. 'And whoever did this, we'll make sure they're brought to justice. I've never seen the like in Innisfree.'

James clears his throat, his face still pale from shock. 'Thank you for your help tonight, officer. We'll talk to our friends and family, see if anyone has any information to pass on.'

I chime in with a final question, hoping for more clues on the perpetrator. 'One last thing, officer. What kind of car did the boys say it was?'

'They couldn't give us an exact make or model, just that it was small, and it drove away so quickly that they likened it to a *cartoon* car,' Sergeant Brennan says hesitantly, as if trying to temper our expectations. 'Kids, eh?'

'It's not much to go on,' Dom sighs, his shoulders slumping.

'And with the boys being the only eyewitnesses and it being dark, them half-asleep, the car speeding off... it's hardly something we can move forward with,' she says, shaking her head.

'Did they mention any specific cartoon?' I ask.

Sergeant Brennan looks at me with her eyes wide open and starts laughing as if my query is the most bizarre thing she's ever heard related to an arson investigation.

She leafs back through her notebook. 'Ah, yes.' She nods. 'Here it is – they said it was like Luigi from *Cars*.' She gives an apologetic shrug.

'Could I have your pen and a piece of paper?' I ask.

Sergeant Brennan nods solemnly, and I quickly start sketching out the character the boys mentioned. Whilst I'm not too up to date on car models, when it comes to popular characters in children's movies, there's nobody who knows their stuff better than me. I just hope that my drawing has enough detail that someone else can make out the design.

The sun is rising as we bounce along a gravel road to the O'Connor family home. We've escaped The Lake House with our lives, and that's all that matters. For now.

After what feels like an eternity, the car skids to a halt in front of a small cottage between the trees. Jonathan jumps out and gallantly offers us both his arm as we step out of the car. Inside, we clean up, warm up and rest up to get our strength back. Then we'll turn our attention to who did this.

I wake up after midday and pad down the hallway to find James and his father in the kitchen. Jonathan offers me an array of bread and buns, and James puts on the kettle. But I can't eat or drink anything. I can't think about anything else other than who would try to burn down The Lake House. 'Any updates?' I ask.

Jonathan nods solemnly.

'My contact at the fire station informed me it was arson – a home-made paraffin fire-starter was used to start the blaze that spread all over the barn and then on to the house.'

I show James the sketch I made. He takes the drawing and studies it carefully, furrowing his eyebrows in concentration. 'I think this is a Fiat 500,' he says, turning the paper in his hands. 'Quite rare around these parts, don't you think, Dad?'

Jonathan glances at the sketch. 'Yes, it looks like the little run-around the McDonaghs have parked in their driveway. They're the only ones around here with an old Fiat that I know of.'

James and I glance at each other, gears simultaneously clicking in our heads.

Although all signs point to Stephen McDonagh, I still can't entirely believe it. But if the car he was driving matches up with evidence from the scene, then that should be enough to close the case.

'The McDonaghs?' Jonathan asks. 'Why on earth would they be speeding away from The Lake House in the middle of the night?'

'Certainly, unusual behaviour,' James agrees. 'Dad, can you bring us there now? The sooner we check this out the better.'

CHAPTER 48

THE QUESTION

Gus appears on the scene before we reach the gate, hollering and flailing his arms.

'You here to intimidate my poor brother again?' he fires off at James. 'I was all night with him at Doctor O'Toole's the other night, thanks to you! His stitches burst and we had to get him patched up... I'm calling the police on you if you touch him again – assault charges.'

Jonathan shoots James a look.

James sighs and rubs his temples. 'Gus, please calm down,' he says calmly. 'I am sorry about that... but Stephen was well out of order – I didn't punch him for no reason.'

'Oh yeah? What was your reason then?' asks Gus, getting right up in James' face.

'He was... heavily intoxicated. I'm sure he wouldn't want me to repeat it,' replies James quietly.

Gus's face softens a little at that and he steps back. 'He's a good lad – just gets a bit rowdy when he's had a few drinks,' Gus says, more to himself than anyone else.

'I understand,' says Jonathan. 'But we're here on a separate matter. Would it be all right if we came in and spoke to you, Gus, off the street?'

Gus takes a moment before replying. 'I suppose so...' He opens the door and gestures for us to follow him inside.

Marianne gasps and grabs her chest in surprise when she sees us in the hallway. 'Oh my gosh! You just gave me such a fright!' she exclaims, still wearing her robe and slippers as she speaks.

'I'm sorry,' I say quickly. 'We didn't mean to startle you.'

'It's okay,' she replies, her voice shaking a little. 'I'm just a bit jumpy at the moment.'

'She's been a bit on edge since... well, since Stephen came in again this morning looking like he'd done rounds with Tyson Fury,' says Gus. 'He's been on a bit of a bender the last few weeks, truth be told.'

Marianne huffs and stomps off into the kitchen.

Gus leads us in, gesturing for us to take a seat. 'So, what can we do for you?' he asks, folding his arms and leaning against the sink. Stephen is seated, looking puffy and hung-over. He simply groans when he sees us. Grace is texting on her phone, a half-eaten cooked breakfast in front of her. James and Jonathan sit down, while I remain standing by the counter.

'What is it now? More earache?' mutters Stephen, who's looking sullen.

'No,' says James. 'Stephen, I'm sorry for the punch. I should have dealt with the situation better.'

'Ha!' he snorts. 'You think a simple sorry is going to make up for what you did?'

'Stephen!' scolds Gus. 'That's enough now. We don't want trouble. We're running a family guest house here – it's not good for our guests to see people traipsing in and out of here at all hours.' He puts a hand on his brother's shoulder. 'So please, can we just put all this behind us?'

Stephen nods and glares at the floor. 'I'm sorry too.' He

looks up at me. 'I'm especially sorry to you, Daisy. What I said. I didn't mean it... drink, you know.'

I give a slight nod to acknowledge his apology. But I'm done thinking about his antics the other night; it actually gave me the answers I needed from Moya. Right now, I'm here solely to learn more about The Lake House fire, and nothing else is going to distract me from that task.

'Right, so...' continues Gus, turning his attention back to us. 'What can we do for you?'

'We need to ask you all some questions,' says James.

'Questions? What about?' Marianne's brow furrows in confusion and she looks to Jonathan.

'About the fire last night at The Lake House,' replies Jonathan.

Marianne's face turns white as she leaps up, then puts a hand out to steady herself on the counter. 'A fire? What? I had no idea... Was anybody hurt? Oh my word... Daisy, I'm so sorry! I know how much you put into that place. What happened?'

'That's what we're trying to establish,' says Jonathan. 'With your help of course.'

'Of course! Any way we can. Do you need somewhere to stay?'

Jonathan shakes his head. 'Thank you, Marianne, that's very kind. But we're trying to get to the bottom of what happened in terms of how the fire started... You see, the police have reason to believe that it was started intentionally.'

Gus, Stephen and Grace all gasp. A barrage of questions follows.

'But who would do that?'

'Why would someone set fire to The Lake House?'

'Are they sure?'

Stephen slams a hand down in front of Grace. 'No big mystery, is it, Grace? It'll be the usual suspects. Your misfit friends from the forest.'

Grace lunges forward. 'Stephen, would you just shut up! You have no idea what you're talking about!'

Gus stands, rubbing his chin. 'Any clues as to who may have done it?' he asks.

'Well,' says James, 'as it happens, a Fiat 500, like your little run-around, was spotted in the vicinity of The Lake House, around the time of the fire.'

'What? No! That's not true!' says Marianne, shaking her head.

'I'm afraid it is,' replies Jonathan. 'The police are taking the matter very seriously. It would of course be helpful to eliminate you from the inquiries so we can proceed with the investigation.'

Marianne looks to Stephen, who just shrugs and looks away.

'I was at home all night!' Marianne exclaims.

'We have multiple witnesses who saw a Fiat 500 drive away from the crime scene. Now we can do this here or down at the station – the choice is yours...' Jonathan speaks to her with the technical parlance of his profession, lending a sense of gravitas as if he were a top-ranking officer himself. Or else he's watched a lot of Line of Duty. Either way, it's working.

'Multiple witnesses?' she asks, looking around the room, as if seeking help from her family, but they all just stare back at her. 'I don't know what you're talking about,' she says, her voice trembling. 'Unless...' She looks to Stephen.

He baulks, nearly choking on his tea. 'Oh, I get it – you think because James here hit me that I went over to The Lake House and set fire to the place?' Stephen remarks, his voice booming.

'It's a possibility we have to consider,' replies Jonathan.

Stephen rises and squares up to Jonathan, his fists clenched by his side. 'You have no right to come in here and accuse us of something we know nothing about! Just because James hit me doesn't mean I went out and burned down a house!'

'Stephen would never do something like that.' Gus says, standing between them. 'You have to believe me. We didn't even know anything about it until you just told us. He's far from perfect, but he's not an arsonist.'

'We'll have to hand this over to the police. We thought we'd try to figure out whether there had been any misunderstanding, something we could iron out before that...' Jonathan replies calmly.

'Stephen,' says Marianne as she turns to him and lowers her voice, grabbing his elbow. 'Your behaviour lately has been quite... unpredictable, shall we say... is there any way that, maybe in a blind fit of rage, you may have taken the car and drove out to The Lake House?'

Gus and Grace's eyes widen.

'Mum!' Grace says. 'What are you saying?'

'I'm just saying that if there are witnesses who saw the car out there, and we know it wasn't any of us... well, then the finger does point to Stephen. He has motive, means... the car keys are hanging there for anyone to take. And, well, he's not been himself. He may not have realised what he was doing.'

Stephen shakes his head and glares at her. 'Oh no you don't... don't you dare try to pin this on me! Whatever happened out there has *nothing* to do with me... I went to The Tap House, I came home, I fell asleep.' He looks at Grace.

'It's true. I was playing all night, and Stephen was holding up the bar. And then I watched him shadow-box his way home and fall asleep in the chair like he does every night of the week. He was too pissed to stand, never mind get into a car, drive it and set a place alight without killing himself. I told Dad he was in, and Dad steered him up to bed.'

'And after that, I sat up chatting with guests. Regulars – the Robinsons. They're upstairs now – I can call them down if you like?' says Gus.

'And I was with them too,' says Marianne quickly.

Gus blinks. 'What?'

'You know what I mean! I was here, with you all. Present and correct,' she hisses at him.

Grace's eye shift across the room. 'Mum? You weren't here last night...'

'Where were you, Marianne?' asks James.

'Right here, safe at home. I may not have been in the same room as everyone the whole time, but I was here. Of course I was. I mean where else would I be?' she replies quickly.

Gus just stares at her, his brow furrowed, then he looks around the room, as if he's trying to figure out what's really going on.

'I think you should leave now,' says Marianne, her voice trembling. 'We have nothing more to say to you.'

The room stills with anticipation.

'This is so hard... especially as I so loved my time staying here, our chats over tea,' I say, holding up my hands in a placating manner. 'We're not here to accuse anyone; we're just trying to get to the bottom of this. If you can think of any reason why someone might want to set fire to The Lake House...'

'It'll be the ragtag, free-spirited vagabonds living up by The Lake House in the woods,' says Marianne. 'At least one of them has fingers like a thief, matted, unkempt dreadlocks, not a word of English. Mick's house should have been put up for auction immediately – these vacant homes are a breeding ground for troublemakers.'

Grace's eye glare. 'Mum, how can you say that?' Her eyes flash with rage as she turns towards her mother. 'His name is Jose, not "vagabond with the long hair" not "misfit". It's Jose and we're in love.' Her words are like steel, the force of her conviction ringing through the air.

Marianne doubles over, like she's been hit in the stomach, reaching out to grasp at Grace's arm. 'You are breaking my heart

– I'm not changing my mind. I said what I said last night and I meant it,' she says, her voice straining.

'Were you with Jose last night, Grace?' asks James.

She nods. 'Yes, I'm with him every night – there are loads of us – you can check with them if you want – we sit around, sing, hang out – we don't cause anyone any harm.'

'Grace, tell us what happened,' I say. 'It's best we hear your story from you.'

She sighs and looks to the ceiling, dabbing tears in her eyes.

Gus comes over to her and puts his hand on hers. 'It's okay – say what you need to say. Just tell the truth.'

Marianne says nothing, but I can see something in the quick glance she throws Grace's way. Her mouth is a tight line, and her eyes are wide. Is she warning her or pleading with her? It's hard to say.

'Jose and I were together. We did nothing wrong, we're doing nothing wrong... but my mother can't accept it. Won't accept it.' She sighs and wipes her eyes with the back of her hand. 'Last night, I went out to the woods after I came back here to drop my guitar and tell Dad that Stephen was in. When I got there, Mum was waiting for me by the lake. She told me to come back home with her that instant or there'd be consequences.'

'What kind of consequences?' I ask.

'I didn't wait around to find out. We fought. I left.'

'Marianne, did you go to the woods last night?' Gus asks her, his tone firm.

She nods.

'In the Fiat?'

She nods again. 'But I came straight home. Just because I drove to the woods to protect my daughter doesn't mean I burned down anything. I had a right to be there.'

Oscar the cat stares up at me with big yellow eyes as he scratches the toe of my shoe. His claws click against the laces, and he makes a mewling noise. When I scoop him up, James, who's standing nearby, comes over. He gently raises Oscar's tail. The fur is dishevelled and clumped unevenly around it, and there's something caught in the fur.

'You've been doing some carpentry out there?' James asks Marianne, nodding towards the cat's tail.

Marianne's eyes widen and she stands up quickly, her chair scraping against the floor. 'I don't know what you're talking about!' she exclaims, her voice trembling.

'Wood shavings,' replies James calmly. He picks off the wooden slivers from Oscar's tail. 'The fire brigade told us the fire was caused by a paraffin fire-starter.'

'So?' asks Stephen.

'So, most are home-made, and are a basic mix of sawdust and wood chips,' James explains as he holds up the tiny piece of wood for all to see.

'I think we should take this to the station and get it analysed,' says Jonathan.

Gus rushes over to the bin, opening the lid. He rummages around for a moment before taking a deep breath and shaking his head, holding up a small, clear plastic bottle. 'Paraffin,' he announces. 'I was using it to clean the engine of the car.' He turns to his wife slowly, his face full of sorrow. 'Marianne? What on earth...?'

'Wait, just wait...' cries Marianne, her eyes wide in panic. 'I can explain...' She looks around the room before she slowly sits down again, her face ashen.

Gus takes a deep breath. 'Why would you do something like this?'

'I had to!' she cries, her face crumpling in despair. 'You don't understand what it's been like...' Marianne swallows, her face serious. 'Because it was all going wrong!' she says, her voice breaking. 'I was so sick of it all... We had the perfect plan! Ciaran would buy The Lake House, develop it and move into it, and we could hand the guest house business over to him – we could retire and he'd be set up for life. That way he'd move back from Chicago and we'd be a family again. He'd sort Stephen out – give him some tough love, not be an enabler like you – and... he could talk some sense into Grace... he'd be here, back at home, where he belongs!' She turns to Daisy, her voice rising to a shout, 'But then you came... And you ruined it all, turning down our bid! Letting Moya stay on! Turning your nose up to our offer. It was meant to be ours! You just couldn't leave it alone, could you?'

'Marianne... how could you?' asks Gus as he stares at her, disbelief in his eyes. 'I told you I would come up with something, that I'd find a way.'

'Well, I needed more than words. I had to do something,' she replies, her voice shrill. 'It was all falling apart... I couldn't let that happen!'

'So you decided to burn the house down?' asks Stephen, his voice incredulous.

'You could have killed someone!' Gus trembles and his voice quivers.

'I didn't mean for it to happen. I set the barn alight; it was just a small fire – a warning! I didn't know that it would take like that... but the wind... I didn't want to hurt anyone; I just wanted Daisy to sell the place,' she cries, tears streaming down her face.

'And frame me to get rid of me in the process? Send me behind bars?' Stephen exclaims with uncontrollable anger.

Gus wipes his hands across his face, shaking his head in disbelief. 'I don't believe this... I just can't believe it.'

'I'm sorry,' Marianne sobs, tears still flowing down her cheeks. 'Please, Gus, you must believe me. I did it for us and our family... but I didn't think it would turn into such a mess.' She covers her face with her hands and continues to cry inconsolably.

CHAPTER 49

THE END

'It's not the first time you've taken matters into your own hands though, is it, Marianne McDonagh?' says a voice at the door. 'Not the first time things have got out of control. Not the first time you've tried to frame someone so you can get your own way.'

Everyone turns to see Moya standing there with Sergeant Brennan.

Marianne gasps and shakes her head. 'What are you talking about, you mad ole witch?'

'I think you know exactly what I'm talking about,' replies Moya as she steps into the room. 'I've kept your lies too long. No more.'

'What are you talking about, Moya?' I ask.

'I'm talking about the fact that Marianne here framed your mother because she was jealous – she wanted Mick as her own. She wanted to move into The Lake House and live the life of lady muck as Mick Kennedy's wife. But he wasn't interested. He was already head over heels for Rose Clarke. A traveller, an outsider, an unworthy object for his affections, according to Marianne. So she decided she'd take matters into her own hands, stage a theft and pin it on Rose,' explains Moya, her voice cold. 'And it worked... in so far as it drove Rose away – never to return. But Mick still didn't want Marianne. The Lake House was still out of reach. Scores were still to be settled.'

My hand flies to my mouth. 'Is that true?' I look between Moya and Marianne.

'You're delusional – always were, always will be,' replies Marianne, her voice shaking.

'Don't give me that, Marianne!' snaps Moya. 'I know exactly what you did! You took Rose's key from her coat pocket, let yourself into the guest room and stole the jewellery box. You staged the whole thing – made it look like it was an inside job, that it could only be Rose. It was the reason she left. You scared her off then, just like you tried to scare Daisy off now... well, no more.'

'You're lying!' exclaims Marianne.

Moya shakes her head and speaks louder. 'No, I'm not! See, I witnessed it myself – I saw you let yourself into the room with the key.'

'Moya, you knew all along?' I stammer.

She softly bows her head and places both palms together. 'I'm truly sorry, Daisy. There isn't anything I can say or do to return what was taken away from you. Shame, fear and guilt have ruled my life and kept me silent when I should have spoken up – until now. I'm here to try and right those wrongs... if you'll let me?'

I nod, and Moya turns back towards Marianne.

'Yes, I was there, too afraid to speak a word, my own neck on the line, a decision that haunts me still. But here I am with a second chance to make things right and prevent history from repeating itself,' Moya says in a cold voice. 'God is the only one who can judge you now.'

'Marianne... is this true?' Gus demands, his eyes displaying incredulity as he stares at his wife. 'Is this true?'

She swallows hard, finally nodding. 'Yes, it's true,' she rasps, trembling from head to toe.

Sergeant Brennan steps forward, allowing Marianne to offer her wrists for handcuffs, tears streaming down her cheeks as she's taken away. But when she looks up, it's directly at me. 'I'm sorry, Daisy, I'm not proud of myself, but I'll say this: I did what I did to protect my home and my family. To survive.'

She scans the kitchen full of people before continuing. 'I'm sorry to all of you.'

For a moment, our gazes lock, and it feels as if the world tilts on its axis. I take a deep breath; Oscar wraps around my legs as I look around the room. Gus has his head in his hands. What will this mean for him? Losing his wife to prison? Grace looks pale and stricken – how will she cope with the shame of villagers gossiping about her? Stephen is trembling from shock and alcohol addiction: he'll keep drinking until he blacks out. And then fall into an early grave.

I don't want this to be the way it is. I'd rather not start another round of sorrow, deception and disgrace. I think of my favourite *Forest Fable* verse, the one that's stayed like a sticker on my heart since I first heard my mother read the words to me.

> *Let's leave behind what no longer fits*
> *And build something better, with exciting bits.*

Sergeant Brennan brushes off her uniform trousers and steps closer to Marianne saying, 'Right, time to go.'

I hold up my hand and say, 'Hold on – not yet.'

She looks at me suspiciously.

'No handcuffs. There's no need for any as I'm not taking this any further.'

'What about the charges?' she inquires. 'We're looking at second-degree arson under the Criminal Damage Act because of the fire alone... never mind all else: theft, defamation, suppression of evidence.' Sergeant Brennan looks to Marianne. 'You're facing serious punishment, Marianne – this is no minor offence here – you could have killed these two.' She looks at us.

As we stand in the McDonaghs' kitchen, shock, anger, disgust all mingle together to form an undefinable mixture that leaves me breathless. Yet, even as my heart aches, I can't help but think about the what ifs.

What if my mother and Mick were still here?

What if this nightmare had never unfolded?

What if everything could have been so different? *Better?*

Marianne, the person we once trusted and thought of as a close companion, set the fire that caused so much harm – and tried to put the blame on others she wanted out of her life. I thought of her as a friend, but do I really know the person behind the pleasant facade? Is she truly malicious or more a scared, desperate individual struggling to maintain control over matters that are out of her reach?

I glance at James and see he's feeling the same doubts as me. He reaches for my hand, offering his understanding and help. With his touch, my determination begins to build inside me.

What if I don't let myself be overcome by darkness – by the dark clouds of Marianne's behaviour?

What if I can shape my own destiny in Innisfree?

What if I don't give away my power to change this story and take this chance to give it a brand-new ending, this time a much better one?

I came to Innisfree in search of the truth and have found it. I always had faith that the truth would set me free.

I step forward to Marianne and give Sergeant Brennan the nod. I've made my decision.

'The truth is,' I confess, 'you took away my mother. You robbed me of my past.' I look to James. 'But I've grown tired of fighting against the tide. I'm ready for a new beginning, to get on with my life. Thank you for your assistance, Sergeant. I won't be pursuing this further.'

Sergeant Brennan shakes her head in disbelief. 'You can do what you want, but I think you're making a mistake.'

'I know what I'm doing, thank you,' I tell her.

She shrugs and walks out of the kitchen, muttering under her breath.

Now it's just us.

And it ends here.

I walk towards Marianne and I pry her hands from her face. I meet her gaze, this woman before me who changed the trajectory of my life. The road we've travelled has been fraught with deceit and secrecy, but it has also been paved with courage, empathy and with the desire for a better future. I think of Kayla, of the tiny new life growing inside her.

'Why are you doing this?' Marianne asks me.

'Same as you. To protect my home and my family. To survive.'

Marianne stares back at me, her expression fearful, unwilling to look away from our intertwined fingers. 'What happens now?' she whispers softly in uncertainty.

'We start again. But this time, we do it right.'

EPILOGUE

THE BEGINNING

'All good, kiddo?' Big Sean grins at me.

'Couldn't be better!' I reply, smiling back.

The Irish countryside is beautiful this time of year: the hills are lush and green, and the still lakes reflect their curves like a mirror. It's in this magical setting that I'm about to become James' wife, and the joy we both feel is almost too strong to contain. It's as if the air is charged with the promise of a fairy-tale ending, of new beginnings and endless possibilities.

I stand beneath the arched flowers, my arm looped with Big Sean's, ready to take our place in front of all the family and friends who've gathered for this momentous occasion. There's an overwhelming feeling of contentment as I gaze upon their happy faces here to witness our very special day, our wedding by the lake.

As the sun begins to set, its golden rays cast a dreamy hue over our outdoor wedding, right here at The Lake House. The tables are adorned with white linens, floral centrepieces of rust and amber blooms, and clusters of flickering candles. As I wave to my loved ones, my gaze falls upon my bridesmaid Kayla. My beaming best girl stands tall and proud. The vintage lilac dress that hugs her frame was a gift from Jacinta's, of course, comple-menting our lavender and baby's breath bouquets perfectly.

Fintan sits in a nearby chair, with Kayla's beautiful little Rosa nestled in his arms – her tiny fists balled up tight, her body snugly swaddled in dainty blankets. Rory and Lenka stand nearby, both beaming as they hold hands, an office romance that no one saw coming but makes perfect sense. And now having visited Innisfree, she understands exactly how I was inspired to illustrate our gorgeous *Forest Fables* new editions. We've won awards, we've broken records, we're a global sensation – but, most importantly, we've reached millions of new readers, each one falling in love with the idea that maybe there are worlds within worlds, and, given the chance, they can be beautiful again.

Just like now. Just like this.

A single tear escapes down my cheek as I contemplate the grandeur of life and all its beauty – the immense joys and sorrows, the countless journeys, the infinite moments of togeth-erness, the new beginnings.

Everyone is looking for new beginnings. Big Sean sold The Fox to move back home to Ireland. Stephen is in recovery, and the McDonaghs made the leap of faith to head to Chicago to be with Ciaran.

Grace and Jose are making a name for themselves with the guest house, offering traditional Irish music, tours and delicious home-made meals. And you can bring your pets, which Oscar is not overly pleased about.

Moya looks better than ever, her black hair gently blowing in the wind as she sings an exquisite ballad in her native Gaelic. She and Dom spend nights together walking the dogs around the lake, sharing laughs and, recently, holding hands. Her voice resonates harmoniously through the air, like a sign of triumph from all we've overcome together, strengthening our friendship and love.

Jacinta's online business empire is thriving, and she and Fintan have affectionately taken Kayla and Rosa under their wing since she decided to move here to Innisfree too. The Mooneys are Rosa's godparents. And have become 'honorary' parents to Kayla too. Fintan likes to say that 'bonds are better than blood'.

As I walk forward, I'm reminded of the many friendships I've come to cherish along the way. Love goes beyond a connection between two people; we're all simply pieces of a puzzle, held together by the fragile thread of love in its various forms.

The background music carries us away with its gentle melody as I walk towards my beloved. After this long journey, the step we're about to take feels both life-changing and like coming home all at once.

James looks dashing in his stylish suit, his ocean-blue eyes shimmering with love and determination. I approach him, dressed in a delicate lace gown, our hands outstretched to touch just the tips of each other's fingers. The air around us stirs, and a gentle breeze lifts my skirt as if it wants to join in this special moment. The verdant fields of grass and wildflowers whisper their blessings for us. This dreamlike moment almost seems too real to be true.

We persevered for our chance at joy. And it was worth it a million times over. Now, we stand with confidence and hope brimming in our hearts. When I gaze into James' eyes, I can see the tears that are reflected in mine. We finally made it and now we start a new life, side by side.

Our palms come together as James pulls me close; I'm overwhelmed by his adoration and devotion. It feels like ages since we set off on this unpredictable path that brought us to this moment – this beautiful, blissful moment where everything is possible.

As we stand here, the sun begins to set and the sky turns a beautiful blend of orange and pink. It feels like the universe itself is putting on a show to celebrate all we've got here. We exchange our vows, promising to love and cherish each other for the rest of our lives. As we kiss, the world around us fades away, leaving only the two of us and the warmth of each other's embrace.

The reception is a blur of dancing, laughter and love. We eat, drink and toast to our new life together, to have and to hold here in Innisfree. This has also been a journey to discover my mother, my father and the past. I'm now certain of who I am, where I'm from and how I can be true to myself in life. Each morning, evening and day that I spend in The Lake House 2.0 brings forth those same views that my parents cherished, the same soil they trod upon and the same glittering lake water that lapped against their skin. Knowing they lived here and loved here makes me feel closer to them than ever.

As I hold James' hand tight on our first night as husband and wife, I can't help but feel grateful for this chance together to build even more special memories under starry skies. Our life has come full circle – from strangers unsure of what tomorrow would bring to two people unafraid to take risks together – and no matter where life takes us next, we're here for it.

Here for it all. Together is a beautiful place to be.

A LETTER FROM COLLEEN

Dear reader,

I want to say a huge thank you for choosing to read *The Irish Lake House*. If you did enjoy it, and want to keep up to date with all my latest releases, just sign up at the following link. Your email address will never be shared and you can unsubscribe at any time.

www.bookouture.com/colleen-coleman

I hope you loved *The Irish Lake House* and if you did I would be very grateful if you could write a review. I'd love to hear what you think, and it makes such a difference helping new readers to discover one of my books for the first time.

I love hearing from my readers – you can get in touch through social media, or my website, links below!

This book is my heart poured out on paper, a journey through the West of Ireland, and an exploration of the ties that weave us together, regardless of where we are in the world.

The idea for this story was kindled during a chance encounter at the London Irish Centre. A beautiful stranger shared a snippet of their life, and it struck a chord in me. It's these personal tales, these intimate insights into someone else's world, that truly inspire me. I'm forever grateful for the brave souls who share their experiences, they often make for the most touching stories.

A heartfelt thank you goes out to all those who have walked beside me on this writing journey. To my eagle-eyed Bookouture editors, whose insight and wisdom have been invaluable. To my friends, who have been there with lasagne, encouragement and laughter when needed. And to my family, whose unwavering support and encouragement have kept me anchored, even when the seas of writing got rough!

I'd love to hear what you thought of the book. Join my email list, leave a review, and help this story reach more readers like you. Your feedback is priceless.

In a Book Club? For those who love a good discussion, you'll find some thought-provoking questions on my website. I hope they spark interesting conversations and deeper reflections on the themes we've explored.

In closing, I just want to express my deepest gratitude for you, dear reader. You've embarked on this literary adventure with me, and for that, I am eternally thankful. Keep turning pages, keep chasing joy, and remember to reach out as I love to hear from you!

With warmth and gratitude,

Colleen xx

colleencolemanauthor.com

 facebook.com/authorcolleencoleman

 instagram.com/authorcolleencoleman

 twitter.com/CollColemanAuth

BOOK CLUB DISCUSSION PROMPTS

1. **Identity and Belonging:** Daisy Clarke embarks on a journey to the west coast of Ireland, a place she's never been but holds significant meaning for her late mother, Rose. Can a physical place we've never been to still hold a part of our identity?

2. **Special Childhood Tale:** Reflect on a childhood book, film or character that holds a special place in your heart. Why is it special to you? How does it continue to influence or inspire you today?

3. **Dream Destinations:** Innisfree, with its rolling green hills and cobbled streets, is described as a magical place. If you could choose a dream destination from anywhere in the world, where would it be and why?

4. **Soul Mates:** In the story, Kayla and Daisy discuss the concept of soul mates. Do you believe in the idea of one true soul mate for every person, or do you think love is more complex than that? How does this belief shape your reading of Daisy and James's relationship?

5. **Daisy and Marianne:** Do you think Daisy did the right thing in how she dealt with Marianne? Was it cowardly or courageous? Explore the nuances of this situation and discuss how it reflects on Daisy's character development.

6. **Secrets and Revelation:** When Daisy discovers the shocking truth behind her inheritance and her true family, it changes everything for her. Have you ever discovered a family secret that changed your perspective or understanding of your family? How did it impact you?

7. **Hope and Future:** Despite the secrets unearthed about her mother's past, Daisy hopes for a future in the beautiful Irish village. Do you believe that one can build a future amidst the ruins of the past? Why or why not? Discuss how hope plays a role in Daisy's journey.

Printed in Great Britain
by Amazon